Soul Dancing
with the Brass Band

Book One

by
Vicki Renfro

Vicki Renfro

Edition 2

IngramSpark
A Division of Ingram Publishing

This book is dedicated to Ed and Hattie,
my husband and best friend
who were with me when I found my Guru.

Vicki Renfro

ACKNOWLEDGMENTS

I would like to thank all of my readers
who pointed out errors and made invaluable suggestions:
Kristina Hall
Susan Freilicher
Sally Renfro
Joanne Dubay
Denise Stoner
Angela Tapp
Corey Colombin
Mel Nuchols
and most of all my dear friend Hattie Owen

Thank you to The Ice House Coffee Shop,
which became The Muddy Buck during this writing,
for letting me spend endless hours writing at their location.

And thank you to Ed Bischoff for his endless support.

Soul Dancing with the Brass Band

PART ONE

CHAPTER ONE

AT THE Dark Moon, December 27, AD 37

I sit astride my battle mare, stroking her mane to keep her calm. I can feel the tension pulsate through her muscles as her skin twitches beneath me. Yet, she stands as quiet and motionless as a stone. The sun is dawning, and it is imperative that we don't give away our position at the forest's edge.

I have spent many sleepless nights trying to devise a scenario that will keep my eight companions and small army alive. I know two will survive this day because they remain in camp, many miles to the west. They are watching over the elderly and the children in order to ensure that our bloodline survives. Born to meditate, these two are in many ways the most important among us. They are "the dreamers," the ones with the power to tap into the energy field that surrounds us. I have given them orders to break camp and disappear with the remaining Druids if we are unable to hold the battle line against the Roman army. If our lives are lost, they will feel the energy shift and vanish into the mist.

Inhaling deeply, I take in the scent of the lavender that grows underfoot as I gaze down at the three Druids who stand beside me. They are the ones I hold most dear. All are very powerful, but only one is a true warrior, scarred and hardened by battle. The other two have refused to be left behind and will die in my stead if given the opportunity.

To my right, hidden high atop the trees, sits a small but formidable figure. I can see a fog bank building and I know he is bending the magic of nature to his own desires. He will advance or retreat, whichever is the gods' will today.

Two daunting forms, black robes billowing in the wind, stand on the bluff to my left. They desire to be seen. The mere sight of them strikes fear into the enemy's heart. Their names are whispered around Roman campfires, for these mystics are known to plant confusing and terrifying thoughts in the fertile minds of others.

I hear the clank of armor as the first group of Roman soldiers marches into the clearing. I look into the faces of those who have chosen to follow me, and I know our numbers are far too few to guarantee a victory today. I fear the shadow that will fall over mankind when the last of the light beings have perished and there is no living reminder of the magic within.

I close my eyes and begin to pray to my deities. "Please provide me with the strength to defend my homeland ..." but before I can open my eyes or finish my prayer, I hear the sickening sound of an arrow entering the body standing next to me. As my nostrils fill with the stench of blood, I scream to the gods, demanding it not be so. I hear my name on my beloved's last breath, "Hilsbeth ..." My mare bucks violently beneath me.

I jolted straight up in bed, waking from a bad dream and trying to gather my scattered thoughts. Sweat soaked my pillow and my heart beat at a dangerously fast pace.

"What the hell?" I said, seeking to get past my panic so I could remember the details before they once again retreated into the void from which they had come. I'd had this same dream regularly, in one form or another ever since I'd moved into my freshman dorm. During sleep, it created anxiety that shook my soul, but when I woke I was unable to hold on to the specifics long enough to make much sense of it.

Exasperated, I fell back on my pillows. "Get up, Trinity," I said, coaxing myself to get out of bed. Usually I'm inspired when I think of this fictional character from *The Matrix*, but this morning it was of small comfort in light of the apprehension I'd been feeling.

Halfheartedly, I dragged myself out of bed and down the hallway to the steamy dorm bathroom.

If I were one of the hot girls, maybe I'd have all of this figured out. But I'm not and I don't. I'm not bad looking, but I'm not beautiful. Everything about me is kinda average. I'm average height and average weight. My hair is average dishwater blond, which gets lighter in the summer from working outside on my folks' farm. I'm a little shy, very smart, and still a virgin.

The girls hardly noticed me as I entered the bathroom to take my shower. Everyone was much too busy talking about the big Spring Fling.

I found myself one sink down from a group of the most voluptuous girls on campus. I stared at their reflections in the mirror and wondered how they could be so perfect. Were they born that way or did all of those expensive products in their bags really make that much difference?

I must admit I was feeling more envious than usual that morning because I was also signed up to attend the Spring Fling. These girls had already picked up their invitations and knew which fraternity they were going to, but I still hadn't worked up the nerve to walk down to the Student Union for my packet.

I'd like to say I don't eavesdrop, but I do. Lord knows I could use some tips on the whole social scene thing. I moved into the freshman girls' dorm last August, and what an eye opener that was! I got my sex education while standing in the dining hall line, and what I heard there was similar to the earful I heard here in the shower room. The gossip was mostly about the wild behavior at the Spring Fling parties, and it got more unbelievable as it was told. But whether the stories were true or not, I promised myself I wouldn't chicken out. If I put myself out there I might actually find a friend.

I stood in a shower stall and let hot water run over my head until I calmed down. Returning to my room, I dressed in my "springiest" outfit—a short jean skirt with a pink sleeveless t-shirt—and pointed myself toward the Student Union to pick up my party invitation. The lines weren't long, but I hung back anyway. That shyness was rearing its ugly head again, and I really just wanted to go back to my room. Instead, I dug in and with a few deep breaths made my way to the shortest line. I lowered my head, thinking that would make me less obvious. It's always hard to be a party of one.

"Miss ... Miss—" I heard, and looked up to see I had reached the head of the line. "What's your name?" the guy asked.

I always hated this part. My parents named me Hillary. Bill Clinton was the first presidential candidate they had ever voted for, and as loyal Democrats they decided in a moment of insanity to name their first and only daughter *Hillary*. They hoped it would make me a strong woman like Mrs. Clinton, but it just made me feel old fashioned. Naming me Bertha or Mildred couldn't have been any worse.

"Hillary Rubner," I answered. Honestly, could a name get any worse?

"Here's your package," he said, and handed me two stapled pages. The top page was the name and address of the fraternity that had drawn my name, coupled with basic information about approved party behavior. The second page was a map with thick purple lines drawn from the spot where I stood and ending at the front door of my intended party. *I can do this!* I whispered to myself, and turned toward my Spring Fling destination.

As I put one foot in front of the other, it didn't take long for me to notice that I was walking off campus. I had expected to be walking with a large group of girls, but there was no one else going in my direction. I began to wonder if I were lost. Maybe this was some elaborate prank! I rechecked the map one more time and figured my only option was to walk a block or two further and then turn back toward home. As I scanned the area for any sign of human life, I noticed one girl about a hundred feet ahead of me. She was slightly overweight and wearing a rather formal green cocktail dress. I wasn't sure if she was over-dressed or I was under-dressed, but I did know that I was going to try to catch up to her in case we were going to the same party. The last thing I wanted was to arrive at the party alone.

Hollering didn't seem appropriate, so I kicked off my flip-flops, picked them up, and ran to catch up to her. She seemed startled when I touched her on the shoulder, as if I had appeared out of thin air. I imagined she was as baffled by the empty street as I was.

"Hi, my name is Hillary," I huffed, slightly out of breath. "I think we might be going to the same party." When I saw the relief on her face, I knew she was happy for the company.

"My name's Ruth," she said enthusiastically, extending her hand. "I'm so glad to meet you."

Her face was really quite pretty, with flawless skin, hair in artful disarray, and green eyes the same shade as her dress.

I found myself staring into those eyes for much longer than what would be considered normal. "I'm sorry, you seem so familiar," I said, while I shook my head to dislodge the feeling of déjà vu. When her face broke into a spontaneous smile, I was even more confused by my instantaneous feeling of genuine friendship.

Looking down at my map, I took a minute to recover my senses. "Looks like we are getting close," I said.

"If we're the only girls at this party, we'll be the center of attention," Ruth said happily.

I smiled back at her, but with great apprehension. The last thing I wanted was attention.

When we reached the intersection marked on the map, we were face to face with an amazing old estate.

"This place is spectacular!" I said, as much to myself as to Ruth. "It really doesn't look much like a fraternity. The people who built it must have been worth a fortune." I looked around to take it all in.

Everything was big, including the stone wall surrounding the estate. The driveway was a long cobblestone road that passed through a covered breezeway between the main house and a carriage house before circling back down to the main road.

"I'm afraid I might turn an ankle," Ruth said as she slipped off her stiletto heels. She carried her shoes, holding the straps with one finger, and we began the hike up the long uneven driveway. Without her heels, Ruth had shrunk considerably—she was all of five foot two.

My heart picked up speed. I was here! I hadn't chickened out and I was not alone. This was shaping up to be a really great day.

Vicki Renfro

April 15, AD 35

A secret village exists on the far west side of Britannica, on an island known to few. Mona is an ancient setting of thatched and stone buildings surrounding a temple where Druids have studied mysticism for as long as anyone can remember. We feel safe in the knowledge that the Romans have not yet discovered our stronghold, and life goes on much as usual.

McCollum has summoned me to see him. I present myself, as is the custom, and he motions for me to take a seat. "There is a young lady by the water's edge," he begins, recalling the girl waiting at the boat landing with all her earthly possessions in a bag beside her. "She arrived with the sun and is requesting a position as your apprentice. This one calls herself Rutiah."

McCollum has not seen me face to face for some months now, and seems taken aback by how fast I have grown from a child into a woman. We both know the time is quickly approaching when I must choose my position among the Druids.

"This girl knows her place is at your side," he continues, "for she remembers the previous lifetimes she has spent in your service. May I suggest that you accept her request and train her well? Soon you may come to recognize Rutiah too, and you will treasure the fact that she had the wisdom to search you out."

As I start to respectfully decline, McCollum adds, "If you open your heart, Hilsbeth, Rutiah will claim a part of it as her own."

April 15, 2010

I shook my head to dislodge the strange daydream of ancient times I had lately found myself drifting in and out of.

"So, here we go, Ruth," I said, heaving the brass doorknocker high and dropping it with a resounding bang. "Can we kinda stick together?" I asked, hoping she hadn't had enough of me already.

"It's you and me, Hillary," Ruth said, her response loaded with hope. We faced the door, waiting. "What's behind door number one?" she giggled.

I'd only known Ruth for ten minutes and I was sure she was a great person, but the best thing about her right now was that we were together.

The big oak doors swung open with the low groan of ancient hinges carrying too much weight, and we laid our eyes on two of the most perfectly dreamy boys I had ever seen. Ruth and I looked at them and then at each other, trying to keep our smiles under control.

The young man who stood across from me was tall and slender, with dark brown hair. Although his hair was styled to be brushed back from his face, there just wasn't enough gel in the world to hold that much hair in place. It fell forward, obscuring the most astonishing blue eyes I had ever seen.

When I finally remembered to close my mouth, I lowered my eyes to his chest and noticed that the navy suit he wore was a little outdated. But who was I to criticize? After all, I was the one who had missed the "formal attire" notice. Sadly, I was totally underdressed.

The boy across from Ruth was slightly shorter and thicker, but had the same great smile and deep blue eyes. The two could have been brothers.

As they stepped forward to take our hands, they introduced themselves. "My name is William," the taller of the two said, looking down at me. "Will for short"

Thank God he didn't say Bill! Doing the Bill and Hillary thing would just have been too weird. Okay, don't judge me here. I decided to introduce myself as Chelsea. I have a little alter ego who feels more feminine using Chelsea rather than Hillary. After all, Chelsea's still a Clinton. My parents probably wouldn't mind at all.

"Hi Will. I'm Chelsea," I said, having trouble looking directly into his eyes. "I live in the freshman dorm on Putnam Street. I haven't declared a major yet, but I think I'll do something in mathematics. I scored high on my SATs, and—" I stopped talking abruptly, not wanting to embarrass myself. I caught him smiling at me. "I'm sorry, I'm a little nervous and I think I'm rambling," I said as I felt a hot blush crawl up my neck and over my cheeks.

Will softly laughed as he took my arm and led me across the breezeway, into the carriage house.

Ruth and George were only a few steps behind us, but for all practical purposes, they could have been on Mars. Will's blue eyes had me hypnotized.

Entering the carriage house, I could feel my feet move forward, but my eyesight was slow to catch up. It felt like walking into a dark movie theater when the previews are about ready to begin. I could tell we were in a large room by the echo of Will's shoes against the stone floor, and when we stopped to let our eyes adjust to the dim lighting, I noticed a familiar scent. Out of all the scents it could possibly have been, it was my favorite—lavender. Of course there was no way Will could have known how much I loved lavender. As a kid, my mom put it in my dresser drawers underneath my clothes. Even though I'd always been a tomboy, I liked the smell, and as silly as it was, I now began to feel myself relax.

As I looked around I saw the elaborately beamed ceiling, aged to the color of rich mahogany. In the stones of the high arches and alcoves I could actually see the chisel marks made by the workmen who'd built the place a hundred years ago. I caught my breath and slowly shifted my attention to the masterfully built stone wall, and to the floor on which I stood. Ancient wagon tracks were etched deep into some cobblestones, while others were worn flat by centuries of foot traffic. The old stables still lined one wall even though it was clear that they were no longer in use. Candle flames lit the room, and I suddenly realized Will was still holding my arm.

I imagined this was very similar to how I might have felt at the high school prom I never attended.

An antique table in the corner held a huge bouquet of fresh-cut lavender, which I had smelled earlier. A delicately laced white tablecloth was draped over a different table, which was beautifully set with china for four. It was perfect. I'm not one to complain, but this obviously was not the big party I'd been expecting. As Will helped seat me at the small table, he was already rushing to address my obvious concerns.

"George and I are the only upperclassmen who live in this house," he explained. "When we saw the Spring Fling notices, we applied to host a party and we asked for only two guests. Who would have thought the University would agree to it? I guess we slipped past an inattentive clerk. At the time we did it, it seemed logical to us."

And well, I guess it seemed logical to me too, because I was enjoying Will's company a lot. He sat down next to me, and within moments we were deep in conversation. I hadn't realized until then how much I needed someone to talk to, and talking to Will felt like talking to an old friend, even though we had only just met.

I wanted to spend the next few hours memorizing the curve of his smile. His teeth were all slightly out of place, but as a whole, his smile was magnificent. His face was remarkably expressive, and even though it seemed foolish, everything about Will was slightly familiar.

"I'm sorry about my endless talking," I said, trying to sound convincing. "I'm usually pretty quiet."

"I'm not sure if I believe you are a quiet person, Chelsea," Will replied, caught by surprise. "You may be interesting and charming, but I'd have to argue with 'quiet.'"

As he reached to brush his hair away from those gorgeous blue eyes, I noticed his hands for the first time. *This guy doesn't do physical labor*, I thought as I self-consciously lowered my callused hands from the table to my lap. His fingers were long and graceful and his nails well groomed, especially compared to my uneven ones, and unlike mine, his fingers weren't marred by miscellaneous scars and dry knuckles.

I've done a lot of physical labor in my life, and my hands showed it. I've always thought of my body as a tool. After spending eight months away from the farm, I managed to heal all of my bumps and scratches, but no amount of healing would ever make my hands attractive. As I searched Will for visible scars, I only found one. When he threw his head back to laugh at another one of my lame stories, I spotted a zigzag scar under his chin. Oddly enough, it made me feel better knowing that he had taken a tumble or two in his life.

Will put his hands under the seat of his chair and scooted closer to me. I liked the idea of him making the first move because I was much too shy. I suddenly became acutely aware of my inexperience in the ways of romance, and my nerves began causing an array of uncomfortable symptoms. I felt my insides vibrate and I became a little dizzy, and Lord knows vomiting or passing out right then would not have been sexy. A weird humming sensation was making me overheat, and I felt sweat dripping down my armpits. Placing a hand on my chest to try to slow my pounding heart, I noticed my condition had a curious relationship to my proximity to Will. Not knowing what else to do, I launched into the first story that came to mind.

"As a child I thought I had magical powers." Out of a lifetime of stories I couldn't believe this was the one coming out of my mouth!

Will looked at me with thoughtful deliberation. This story had caught his interest.

"It started when I was only about two or three. I would follow my mom out into her garden, and as the plants began to grow, I somehow got the idea that it had something to do with my daily visit. I would lie on my belly for hours, jabbering away at the buds, coaxing them to bloom, and I swear they would bloom before my very eyes.

"Then, when I was four, I noticed the hands rotating around on the clock in the kitchen. I decided to conjure up my power to discover its secrets and I learned how to tell time. Then I used my powers to decipher the lines and circles in books, and I learned how to read," I softly laughed, embarrassed that he might think me simple.

"I always felt I had the ability to be something special in the world if I used my *powers* for good. I guess that's how a kid's mind works. You know..." I said, rolling my eyes. "'I've come to save the world' kind of stuff." I looked down, not wanting to meet Will's eyes. Telling my childhood story had made me feel foolish.

When I looked up he was still smiling at me. "So how does this story end? Do you save the world?"

"Kids grow up and leave their childhood fantasies behind," I shyly admitted. "Maybe I can use my mathematical powers to discover an algorithm or a formula that might make a difference," I said jokingly.

"I have no doubt in your abilities, Chelsea," Will said, leaning close and lowering his voice for effect. "The important thing is to not forget what that child knew. Children innately know the truth."

Will's head turned abruptly at the sound of approaching footsteps. George and Will froze momentarily as the door opened. They both looked slightly embarrassed, but mostly they looked as if they had been caught. A man entered the room, his long coat flying behind him like a black cape, and they quickly stood to face him.

The man was well over six feet tall, extremely fit, and about ten years older than my father. From the rush of explanations that came from Will and George, I quickly learned the man's name was McCollum and that he was clearly in charge of the household. Despite the somewhat odd circumstances, he spoke calmly and looked kindly at Ruth before his eyes slid slowly toward me. As he furrowed his eyebrows, I could tell that something about Ruth and me held a weird fascination for him. For a fleeting second, I thought I even saw a smile.

"I beg your pardon, ladies," he said as he bowed in our direction, "but these two gentlemen must excuse themselves. There are still thirteen in this household who cannot swim."

There was tension in the room, and when I met the old man's eyes, it was as wonderful as it was awful. Don't ask me what I mean because I can't explain it. I only knew it felt like he was looking directly into my soul.

When did swimming become an emergency, I thought to myself, and as if I'd said it out loud, McCollum turned to me. "You must leave now. This is a home of profound spiritual studies." Before I could formulate my next thought, McCollum raked his fingers through his hair and walked out shaking his head.

Everyone knew the party was over. The atmosphere had changed so completely that Ruth and I just followed Will and George out. As I stood bewildered on the long cobblestone drive, preparing to walk back to my dorm, Will came within ten feet of me and stopped. His face appeared overwrought, like he had a million things he wanted to say, but he said nothing.

Ruth tugged on my arm, and I turned to shrug her off. When I looked back, Will was gone.

CHAPTER
TWO

AFTER WILL and George left us standing alone on the driveway, Ruth and I walked bewilderedly back to campus. We didn't have reason to hurry. Our Spring Fling party was over practically before it had started.

As for me, I had an endless loop of questions and emotions cycling through my mind. *I really like him! Will I see him again? Does he like me too, or does he think I'm crazy?* I kept trying to place McCollum, feeling that I would recall if I'd met a man who dressed and looked like he did. Then I realized nothing really mattered because Will hadn't asked me for my cell number or e-mail. He didn't even know my last name! But still, there was no denying that the worst disappointment was how things had ended.

We walked in silence for the first block or two. Ruth, who was still carrying her heels asked, "Do you think Will and George are really students?"

"Don't you think they have to be?" I answered, even though the whole party had seemed a little *Alice in Wonderland* to me. "I bet we'll see them around campus."

"I'm a Music and Performing Arts major," Ruth admitted. "I don't think I have them in my classes. I can't imagine either one of them singing a show tune."

For the first time, we laughed. Ruth and I were friends now, there was no question about it. We both felt the bond we'd formed by sharing an adventure together. But the interesting thing about our friendship was that *this* was our first conversation.

Life's funny that way. Circumstances had thrown us together, but in hindsight I could see the perfection in all of it. We needed each other for a few hours, and when we didn't anymore, something better took its the place. Ruth and I talked and laughed about stuff like we were a couple of kids on a playground.

"Slug bug!" Ruth yelled, and she hit me in the arm so hard she knocked me off the sidewalk. I looked around to spot the car, but like in the TV ad, it was nowhere to be seen.

"Next time don't hit me so hard, okay?"

"Deal. I guess I forgot my own strength," Ruth said, flexing her muscle, her high heels hanging from her fingertips.

"This is where I get off," I said when we reached the front door of my dorm.

"Me, too," she replied, amused.

As luck would have it, Ruth lived in my dorm, one floor down. It had been a great day. I smiled to myself, knowing I wouldn't have to eat breakfast alone anymore because I now had a friend!

Getting up at sunrise was an old habit of mine, mostly because as a kid there was just no ignoring Dad's rooster cock-a-doodle-doodling outside my bedroom window. I suspect now that I'm in college it's a good habit to have. I could enjoy a leisurely breakfast and still make it to my 7:30 class early enough to have my choice of seats.

Half the girls in the dining hall at 6:00 a.m. were still in their robes and slippers, which led me to wonder if they were here for the education or the social life. With my full class schedule, I had to be fully showered, dressed, and ready to roll by breakfast. Caffeine had become a mandatory food group.

Ruth came in a little worse for wear. I waved her over to the seat I'd saved, and when she sat down, it was apparent that she didn't fall into the *morning person* category. I don't think she'd even combed her hair.

We had stayed up late the night before, comparing the details of our somewhat separate experiences in the carriage house, and Ruth seemed to have had the same experience as me. She'd told George her whole life story and didn't know one single detail about him. Other than their address, their first names, and the fact that they were really nice guys, we didn't know anything at all about them.

As the days went by, Ruth and I stopped talking about Will and George. After all, what was the point when we knew nothing about them? They were slowly being replaced with talk about our looming finals and worry about my grade point average. I had to apply for financial aid in the fall, and my final grades would be a "make it or break it" deal.

Finally, May twenty-seventh rolled around, the last day of school and the end of my freshmen year. I gotta tell you, I was ready for a few months without the pressure of studying. Thumbing through the stacks of papers by my computer, I decided to box up about half of them to deal with when I got home, and throw the rest into the recycle bin. It didn't take long to come across that Spring Fling invitation I had sentimentally saved. I pulled it out of the pile of paper, thinking about the fun we had that day, and then shrugged it off. I hadn't heard word one from Will. So much for the connection I thought we'd made. Maybe in the fall I would take a class in *Character Judgment 101*. I placed the invitation in the pile to recycle.

Ruth's timing was impeccable. She picked that very moment to poke her head through my door to say her good-byes. I couldn't help but hold up the invitation and comment, "Wonder what they're up to this summer?"

"Oh, there's always the next Spring Fling!" Ruth said, rearranging the bags she had slung over her shoulder. Deep down, I knew Ruth could let it slide off her back more easily than me because she knew that life goes on. Due to my inexperience, I was willing to go careening full speed ahead with my naive hope that Will really liked me. I'd been stupid enough to hold onto the hope that I would see him again. I really needed to learn to see "boys" as a Friday night distraction and get on with things.

"I just came by to say goodbye before heading home. I figure a two-hour drive and I'll be in Kansas City with a home-cooked meal and Mom doing my laundry!"

"I'm sure gonna miss you this summer," I said as I flung my arms around her. "We need to get together before next fall!"

Our final hug brought me to tears. Over the semester Ruth had become my light in an otherwise bleak landscape of friendships. Not seeing her for an entire summer seemed unthinkable.

CHAPTER THREE

May 28, AD 35

The sun is dawning, and in the Druid tradition, we have all gathered in meditation to welcome the new day. My mind is always restless and resists this silent practice, but as my consciousness surrenders, I know my soul finds the peace that is elusive during my waking hours. I stretch my limbs as I return to my body, bringing the blood flow back into my legs as I stand and quietly leave the temple to carry on with my day. As usual, one will remain alone, sitting motionless for most of the day. Terrance spends an immeasurable amount of time traveling in the ethers, only bound to this earth by the thinnest of threads. While not in meditation he tends his small garden, digging his hands deep into the soil and pounding his herbs into fine powders in an attempt to attach himself to his physical form, lest he just float away.

We never realized the value of his endless hours in meditation until late one night, under the cover of darkness, a stranger from a faraway land moved toward McCollum's tent. Not one of our posted guards noticed the movement, but Terrance did, and he ran to warn McCollum of the intruder. That was the evening McCollum discovered that while Terrance was in the depths of his meditative state, he draped his expanded consciousness over the entire Druid community. He felt the ebb and flow of every Druid soul as music. Anyone other than a Druid sounded like a dissonant chord. Luckily, McCollum's visitor had come in peace. The soothsayer, Eduardo, had traveled as quickly as possible from Portugal to inform McCollum of his visions and to offer his mystical abilities in defense of the Druids.

From that night forward our primary defense was a single sentinel named Terrance who sat alone in the Temple, monitoring the pulse of our community while he communed with the gods.

May 28, 2010

I left campus before dawn to make my hour-and-a-half drive home. As long as I was home in time for my favorite meal of the day, breakfast, and in time to catch Dad before he went out into the fields, everything would be perfect. I drove up our long dirt road toward the barn and there he stood, blond hair blowing in the wind and dust billowing off his jeans as he beat them with his ball cap.

I pulled up and threw the car in park. Getting out, I yelled, "Hey Dad, have I missed breakfast?"

"No, Kiddo. I'm just dusting myself off so I'll be presentable. This spring has been a dry, dusty one. Come here and give your old dad a hug."

My father was a handsome man. His irresistible smile made his crow's feet crinkle and his light blue eyes twinkle with mischief. His blond hair, which was always longer than what was in fashion, caught the wind.

"Hop on Kiddo, I'll take you up to the house," Dad said as he lifted me up into his tractor.

As I cuddled up next to him on the single seat in the cab, I laid my head on his shoulder, closed my eyes, and took a deep breath. I relaxed to the smells of barley, dirt, and cow dung, all mixed together into one marvelous scent that will always mean home.

When I opened my eyes I noticed a note taped to the dash. Dad spent a lot of hours in the field, and he always wrote a few words down to give himself something to think about. The latest quotation seemed to be from Rolling Thunder, once a Medicine Man of the Cherokee Nation. I leaned over a little further to try to get a better look, and then Dad began to read it to me. He had a deep, slow, melodious voice that made you want to close your eyes to listen.

"Understanding begins with love and respect—for oneself, for one's world, and the Great Spirit which is in all life, in all things. One can perform no greater service for this world than to be mindful of his

acts, even his thoughts and speech become a part of the condition of the world."

We sat for a few minutes, not talking, just slowly making our way up the bumpy dirt driveway toward the house, both of us deep in thought.

"I was only a kid about your age, out for a Sunday drive through the rolling Flint Hills," Dad began. "I don't know how I ended up in Council Grove, and I'm even less sure why I stayed. It was evening and I should have been gettin' home, but the Indians were holdin' a regional meeting under that old tree they still call *Council Oak*."

I knew which tree Dad was talking about. I had driven by it many times on my way to college. The top of the old tree had been blown off by a lightning strike decades before, but it was still the largest tree in the area, spanning some ten feet across at its trunk. The Indian tribes had been meeting at that particular tree for a lot longer than anyone could remember.

"I picked a place near the back," Dad continued. "As far as I could tell, I was the only white boy in attendance. They'd been building a ceremonial bonfire all afternoon, but by evening the wind was blowing so hard, they couldn't get it lit. That's when I saw Rolling Thunder for the first time. He was an ordinary looking man in jeans and a worn western shirt, but when he stepped forward, I realized there was nothing ordinary about that fellow at all. He turned his head until the wind blew his hair away from his face to determine the winds direction. I wasn't sure what he was going to do, but all eyes were on him. He stepped in front of the bonfire, raised his arms, and opened his palms toward the wind. I'll be damned if that wind didn't slowly stop blowin'! The young braves quickly lit the fire as Rolling Thunder lowered his arms, and the wind gusted up again."

"Were you just blown away by that, Dad?" I asked.

"My amazement has never ebbed, Darlin'. An experience like that, seeing something supernatural first-hand, has the tendency to make you wonder how many other things exist in this world that you haven't seen yet. It makes you want to keep your mind wide open, so you don't miss anything."

"Have you ever seen any other miracles, Dad?"

"Those crops growin' out there in my fields … and you," Dad said, so softly I almost missed it. "Miracles happen every day, some large, some small. You just have to be lookin' for 'em."

When Dad pulled the tractor to a stop a few yards short of the chicken coop, Mom was already on the porch. I hopped off of the fender and ran to the front porch to give her a big hug. She was a tiny thing—only four foot eleven, with jet-black hair and ivory white skin—and still a beautiful lady. She had always been outgoing, the high school cheerleader type, which made her an unlikely match for my father, the quiet farm boy. They'd first met in kindergarten, but it took another fifteen years for them to fall in love.

"Hi, Mom, how've you been?" I asked, and rested my chin on the top of her head as we hugged.

"I'm great now that you're home, sweetie. Come in. I have breakfast ready. Tell me all about school." She stopped to wait for Dad, who sometimes seemed to have one foot in this world and the other in the ethers. "Hurry along, Terry! Come back to Earth," Mom teased.

Vicki Renfro

CHAPTER
FOUR

NOTHING ON the farm had changed just because I went away to college. Mom was still in the kitchen, Dad was in the fields, and Kenny, my younger and extremely athletic brother, was still addicted to playing baseball. When the high school season was over, everyone in town, including Kenny, gathered on Friday afternoons down by the overpass to play a game of baseball. The dirt parking lot on the north side of the overpass was set up with a diamond.

The third-base line ran ten yards from a metal building housing a business named "Guy's Nuts." As a kid I never thought twice about that name because Mr. Guy sold chips and nuts, but as an adult I found humor in it. If Mr. Guy were still alive, I'd ask him if he was naive or just that gutsy.

The overpass was a highway over the train tracks, but for our town, it separated the infield and outfield. On the south side of the viaduct lay the outfield. The men with the best arms filled those positions, but anyone was allowed play.

There were even places for older folks on top of the overpass. Their job was to relay messages between the infield and outfield and periodically stop the game due to traffic.

Spectators sat on chairs or blankets because in Kansas the chiggers can eat you alive. And when the locusts began to chirp, that was Mom's signal to pass around the mosquito spray. Over the years the whole system had become very well organized, but my favorite part will always be seeing all the farmers out there playing ball in overalls.

When we pulled up to the baseball field in Dad's big pick-up truck, I wasn't disappointed. I spotted a few kids I'd gone to high school with, along with both sets of grandparents.

If I understood it myself, I would explain the situation with my grandfolks. The thing was, my respective sets of grandparents were seldom seen within twenty yards of one another. They never spoke beyond a cordial hello, and I think that was only for appearance's sake. Today was no exception, with one set of grandparents at one end of the field and the other as far to the other side as they could get and still be considered "at the game." I spent a few innings visiting with each of them and then found a place on a tailgate to catch up with my high school friends.

We all watched Kenny score a home run in the middle of the fourth inning. The ball cleared the overpass, and judging by the hollering of the folks on top of the viaduct, it must have gotten lost in the weeds. The spectators all jumped to their feet to cheer as Kenny crossed home plate because home runs were few and far between. This was because the bases were ten yards farther apart than on a normal diamond, in order to make up for the outfielders not being able to see the infield. Because of this extra distance, only the fittest players were able to make it all the way around the bases without stopping at least once to take a breather.

Late in the eighth inning Dad stuffed a book he'd brought to the game into his back pocket and asked me if I'd like to walk down to the train tracks to see Ol' Ben. He knew the answer by the smile on my face, and soon we were walking along the dirt road.

"What's that book you've been reading?" I asked. "It must be pretty interesting to take your attention away from the game."

"I think I've found my next note for the tractor dash. Let me read it to you and see what you think." He pulled the half folded paperback from his jeans pocket and opened it to the page he had marked.

"Our mind is our predicament. Life is not suffering; it's just that we

do suffer rather than enjoy it. We must let go of our attachments and just go for the ride freely, no matter what happens."

He turned to look at me as he folded his copy of *The Way of the Peaceful Warrior* and stuffed it back into his pocket. "What do you think about that?"

"I think 'letting go' is harder than it sounds." I took another swing at a small stone that I had been kicking down the road.

"Dad, you said this morning that you need to pay attention so you don't miss things. Does that include dreams and déjà vu?"

"I imagine it does," he replied, "although I'm not an expert on either one."

"Well, they both have been happening to me so often lately that I'm beginning to feel a bit crazy."

"You're not crazy. I can assure you of that," Dad said as he put his arm around my shoulder. "If you want an answer, put the question out into the universe. You will hear the answer if you are patient and listen very carefully for it. It might sound simple, but it always works for me."

I must have been about nine years old the day Dad met Ol' Ben. A teenager had come running up to the game, yelling that some drunk guys were at the old man's place giving him a hard time. Dad walked off the field alone, picking up a bat as he went. As I watched him go, he began at a jog and then broke into a dead run toward Ol' Ben's boxcar. It scared the crap out of me, but fifteen minutes later, he was back in the batter's box taking his practice swings.

To this day Dad stands by the story that when he got to the boxcar, all it took was a talk with the two inebriated men. He claims they left without any trouble, and the details have always been Dad and Ben's secret. But whatever took place caused a very special bond to form between them.

As we reached the path that led to Ben's front door, I noticed that his boxcar had undergone some changes. His path was now graveled, and a swing hung from the Oak tree in his front yard.

I couldn't help but remember the old days, when Kenny and I were forbidden to come down here. I didn't know if Mom was more afraid of the train tracks or of Ben. I'm sure Mom had a hard time trusting an old indigent man whom no one knew. I can understand that now, but as a kid, that was what made Ol' Ben interesting.

The sound of Dad and me walking up the path brought Ben to the door. He looked quite a bit older than the last time I'd seen him, but his almost toothless smile remained welcoming, and he invited us in. Ben took my hand between his two very warm, wrinkled ones. He felt boney and frail, and I wondered how many years he had left. I sat in a chair near the door so I wouldn't get that claustrophobic feeling the long dark boxcar sometimes gave me. The air was usually stale because of the lack of ventilation and windows.

As I looked around at odds and ends that people had dropped off, I noticed the old TV Dad had given him a few years before. The boxcar was comfortably furnished even though nothing quite matched. It had been hard for Ben in the early days because he couldn't read, but since the arrival of the TV, he'd learned about the world beyond the fifty square miles he'd lived his life in.

Silently, I listened to Dad and Ben having their regular conversation.

"How are ya doing, Ben?" Dad asked. "How's your health, your eyes? Are you getting enough to eat?"

I knew food wasn't a problem after I spotted the Methodists' round-robin meal delivery list. I also noticed a stack of church bulletins under the coffee table, and smiled at the realization that the church ladies hadn't figured out that Ben couldn't read.

Ben was hard to understand without his teeth, but as he mumbled away, Dad seemed to understand every word. After a while we stood to leave, and I could see the affection Ben had for my dad and Dad for him. I said goodbye and waited for them to finish their hug. Dad was the only person Ben hugged. I figured it had something to do with that afternoon with the baseball bat.

On our walk back to the ball field, we began talking about how some people need very little to be happy, while others will never be happy no matter how much stuff they accumulate.

Dad had always told me that you find all of the important stuff inside. It's still an abstract thought to me, but I hope that someday I will grasp what he so fully understands.

Vicki Renfro

CHAPTER
FIVE

June 15, AD 35

We call them Dreamers, the ones whose souls travel far from their bodies while in trance. Our encampment is aware of the incredible value of a Dreamer like Terrance, who has the ability to warn us of approaching danger. We are thankful that we have two of them.

Kathryn loves to run free in the forest because she is far too full of life and uncontrollable energy to sit still in the temple for morning meditation. Her meditations are much more chaotic and full of dance than we are used to, which sometimes causes us to gather at the forest edge just to catch a glimpse of her. She is so graceful that the magic of her movements can bring a grown man to tears. Even the small woodland creatures are mesmerized by her tenderness.

Kathryn discovered as a child that as she danced, her body spinning and leaping as if it were not bound by gravity, she could feel herself expanding beyond her body. Now grown to adulthood, she has perfected the technique. While dancing in trance, her life force grows far beyond the limits of her body and travels into the surrounding countryside to bring her visions of what is happening miles away. The Druid warriors have found this to be an invaluable tool for defending our dwindling population. Between Terrance's powers and Kathryn's, the two of them can watch over the whole of Mona and warn of an invasion in time for an evacuation.

June 15, 2010

Last spring Kenny found a baby crow. It was the only survivor of three that had fallen out of their nest and was covered with maggots from the unfortunate death of its sibling. My brother, bright kid that he was, took the little crow home to Mom, maggots and all. She was ecstatic to accept his gift, but when he announced that he wanted to name the bird Kate, after her, she thought that was going a little bit too far. She soon settled on the name Giuseppe, or *Gus* for short.

Soon Mom became Gus's flight instructor, throwing him up in the air repeatedly until he learned to fly, and even though he was free, Gus never strayed far from our home. I often found myself looking out the kitchen window at Mom and Gus sitting together in the garden. When Mom talked, Gus actually listened with his head cocked to one side. With a loud caw he would answer, making her laugh. Our old dog Bridget lay at Mom's feet, and the old scraggly barn cat purred in her lap, and for the first time I saw a similarity between Mom and Saint Francis.

Mom loved so many things—gardening, sewing, and every animal large and small—but her true passion was dancing. She had once dreamed of becoming a professional dancer, and from what I've been told, she would have made it. But what does a girl do when she's headed for fame and fortune and finds herself head over heels in love with a farm boy? In my mom's case, you have a family and teach the farm boy to dance.

Kenny and I made a point of watching Mom and Dad dance when the Elks Club had live music. They were simply beautiful to see. Dad was a fantastic dancer, but his dancing was nothing compared to Mom's. She could be as graceful as a ballerina or as energetic as a hummingbird, dancing double time in circles around him—her joy just couldn't be contained.

During the summer the days were either unbearably hot or full of violent thunderstorms. Today was another hot one, and the sweat under my ball cap had begun its journey down my face to settle into a mud ring in the crease around my neck. I had been getting so sunburned that my only option was to wear a long-sleeved shirt.

For weeks I had been weeding Mom's half-acre garden, and

daydreaming had become my main form of entertainment. Lately, my daydreams had become a continuation of my nightly dreams, which was a wonderful escape!

As a Druid, I am absolutely adored by a blue-eyed boy, and as I reach to kiss him, I smell the lavender he's rubbed on his clothes to cover the smell of sweat ...

The ringing of the lunch bell yanked me back to reality. I stretched as I stood and clapped my hands together to remove the dirt from my gloves. When my stomach growled, I looked at the sun to estimate the time of day and then laughed at how utterly unsophisticated I was.

As I neared the house, I heard the phone ring. We still had a landline due to cell service being so sketchy in the rural areas. "It's Ruth," I heard Mom yell, so I turned my walk into a run, reaching the phone in seconds flat.

"Hi, Ruth!" I said. The full weight of how much I'd missed her hit me like a tornado when I heard her voice.

"I've been thinking that you might be ready for a road trip to the big city," Ruth said, bubbling with excitement. "The party of the summer is next weekend, and Hillary, you just have to be here. We'll have so much fun!"

"Actually, I could use a road trip. Let me talk to Mom and Dad and see if I can get away." In my mind I was already on my knees, begging Kenny to help me out with my chores for the next few of days.

"The party isn't until Saturday night, but it would be great if you could come early. We'll need to do a few things to prepare," Ruth said, with a devilish edge in her voice.

I thought about asking a few questions, but decided it might be more fun just to let things unfold.

"Oh, more good news," she added. "That house we wanted to rent in the fall became available, so I put down the deposit."

Things were just getting better and better!

It was an easy drive to Kansas City and I had detailed directions that would take me straight to Ruth's front door. As I got closer to her neighborhood, I noticed the homes were increasing in size, and some of them were actually estates!

Oh Ruth, I thought, *are you in trouble! You should have told me you had more money than the U.S Treasury*! I rolled up to a gate that said Witherspoon. Sure enough, this was the place. I pulled forward and backward a few times to maneuver the driver's side window close enough to the keypad to press the call button. Ruth had never let on that she came from money—and I mean *money* with a capital *M.*

I wondered how this had never come up during any of our hundreds of late-night talks? I knew we had our differences. Yes, she said "floral" when I said "stripes." Our tastes were definitely at opposite ends of the spectrum. Ruth said "drama" when I said "calm down." But after all, Ruth was a drama major. I pressed the button, not knowing what to expect next.

"Hello," a familiar voice said. "Can I help you?"

"Heck yes, you can help me! Do you have my best friend Ruth Witherspoon in there or am I at the wrong house?"

Ruth screamed. "I've been sitting on pins and needles waiting for you to show up. Just come up to the house and I'll meet you out front!"

The gate slowly began to swing open and I pulled forward past an array of security cameras. I thought about looking at my odometer to see how far it was to the house, but decided instead just to enjoy the grounds, which appeared to have been perfectly manicured by a staff of gardeners.

When I reached the house, Ruth ran out the front door, hands waving wildly in the air. What a relief to see she was still the crazy Ruth I knew from college. As I got out of the car, she almost knocked me over.

"No way I could have missed you any more than I have! It would just be impossible. We've got so much to cover," Ruth babbled, only stopping to catch her breath.

"I've missed you too, girl," I said. "This looks like it may shape up to be a hell of a vacation. I feel like I'm staying at the Ritz!" I looked at the house and then sideways at Ruth.

She smiled at me with a shrug of her shoulders. "It's just home to me. Come on! I'll show you your room and then we're going to have our nails done. I already have the appointment set up ... my treat."

It didn't take me long to realize that primping was why Ruth wanted me in Kansas City a few days early. First it was French manicures and pedicures, then hair styling and tints, a facial, and massage. By the day of the party, we had run out of things we could do to make ourselves more attractive, so we spent the day picking out what we would wear to the big party.

It was a good thing Ruth had a sister my size, because nothing in my bag was dressy enough. With the plan being to look like a full-blown socialite, I picked out a basic black gown with a high neckline in the front and a plunging back. I felt more comfortable not seeing what part of my dress was missing.

Ruth put black eyeliner and mascara on me to show off my blue eyes and painted my lips red. "Oh my God, how am I going to keep from getting this all over myself?" I asked Ruth as she told me to blot. Ruth, of course, had a finish coat for my lips that she claimed would make me "kissable" for hours.

Ruth only laughed at how naive I was—her motto was "bold is beautiful," and she was living up to that for this party. Her dress was a blood-red number, slit up one side. The bling on her wide belt was almost blinding and couldn't have been more fitting for her. Her hair was cut to just below her ears and tinted deep brown, almost black. With makeup, jewelry, and her four-inch spiked heels, she looked stunning.

"Don't you dare leave me alone tonight, Ruth," I warned her. "I don't want to be left stranded in a room full of strangers."

"Oh, don't worry, Hillary," Ruth replied. "All of the guys will be flocking around you, so that's where I'll want to be."

By the time we walked to the waiting limo in front of the house, I was feeling incredibly nervous. I asked Ruth no fewer than a million times about the party, but she just kept saying, "You'll see. It will be fine."

CHAPTER SIX

July 13, 2010

ABOUT THIRTY minutes later we pulled up in front of the Hotel Raphael. "Old world charm appeals to old money," Ruth said as she turned to get out of the limo. The Raphael Hotel was 1920s chic, which added even more mystery to the evening.

The limo pulled up to the hotel's enormous entry doors. "Nice to see you this evening, Miss Witherspoon," the doorman said with a nod as he opened the door for us. It was becoming less surprising to me that everyone knew Ruth by name.

All my attention was focused on the task of balancing myself on my borrowed stiletto heels. Frankly, I was quite proud that I hadn't embarrassed myself by turning an ankle. "How much longer before we can find a place to sit down?" I whispered softly in Ruth's ear so no one else could hear.

"Oh, stop your complaining, girl. We're just about ready to make our grand entrance." I could hear the amusement in her voice. Ruth was really enjoying this. I followed her to a table just outside a banquet room.

"Fill out that form," Ruth said, pointing at a paper on the table.

"Why?" I whispered, feeling mortified and trying to stay next to Ruth as I watched a parade of Kansas City's young and wealthy stream by.

"We're going to have a few calling cards printed for you," Ruth said as she moved away. "Corny, I know, but just go with the flow. Fill out the form and hand it to the guy behind the table. He'll print them for you."

"What about you?" I said as I struggled to catch up.

"Mine are printed and right here in my handbag. I keep some on hand for these goofy parties. Here have a look." She pulled one out and handed it to me.

The only thing printed on her card was "Ruth" in a funky script on textured paper with her cell number. I suppose nothing else was needed. Everyone in this elite group knew one another.

As I retrieved my cards at the far end of the table, Ruth put out her hand. "Let's see what you've put together," she said, her curiosity piqued.

"Okay," I said, handing her one.

She read, "Hillary, friend of Ruth Witherspoon." I thought Ruth would never stop laughing.

As we walked into the ballroom, I gazed across a sea of half-covered breasts and black tuxedos. These were the beneficiaries of the 2008 tax cuts, the richest 2 percent. The girls moved in first. Most of them knew Ruth and were thrilled to see her. After the hellos and questions about school and family, they came to the second reason for ambushing Ruth—to check out what they saw as the new competition—and they all turned toward me.

I felt like a deer in headlights, but Ruth had been expecting this and was enjoying herself immensely. With a smile she introduced me. "This is Hillary, my best friend from college. She's the one with all the brains." Ruth said this with a tone that must have left them wondering if I were a future Nobel Prize winner.

Nametags would be nice, I thought as I struggled to remember everyone. I looked from face to face, and it dawned on me that these girls were very similar to the voluptuous ones from the dorm shower room back at college. There were definitely no farmers in this group.

Ruth turned to walk away and grabbed my hand with a tug. "We don't want to spend our night around that group of girls," she whispered. "They're the biggest gossips in town. Let me introduce you to my friends."

We skirted the edge of the room until we got to a table full of significantly less uptight people.

"Ruth, come on over here and give me a squeeze. I haven't seen you in months!" A big bear of a guy grabbed Ruth as she rounded the end of the banquet table, and I watched her curl into his embrace. "How the hell are you?"

"Wait a minute, I thought you were my girl?" the next guy waiting in line bellowed at Ruth.

"I'll always been your girl, Clint." Ruth replied, melting into his arms. "How's your Dad doing?"

As I took a step to follow her, I felt a hand on my arm and turned to see a tuxedo-clad young man who probably caused traffic jams on a regular basis.

"Hello," he said, "my name is Bennett." He was tall, muscular, and heart-stopping. He had a look about him that convinced me he was always the first male to reach the new girl in the room, but I was flattered anyway.

"Hi, I'm Hillary, a friend of—"

"Ruth's," he finished for me. "I saw you come in and run the gauntlet through the greeting line of girls."

"Yes, that was a lot of fun. Do you know them?"

"All of them, all of my life," he replied. "Some better than others."

I gave him my flirtiest smile and began to answer the usual questions, but this time I remembered to ask questions. I didn't want to go home again without knowing anything apart from the name of the guy I met. Bennett came from money—very, very old money, and lots of it. His family had fought for the North during the Civil War, and had therefore been able to retain their property, position, and wealth.

All in all, I liked the guy. He was nice and attentive, and he seemed willing to entertain me all evening. I noticed Ruth was enjoying herself, too, as she began to regale her friends with stories about college. It wasn't long before I heard the group roaring with laughter.

"We've been military men for centuries," Bennett continued. "But I'm attending law school first. I'm at Yale, and when I'm finished there I'll see if the military holds any interest for me. My family historically has done it the other way around—service before law." He put his arm out for me to take. "Would you like to dance, Hillary?"

Finally, something I felt comfortable doing! I flashed on my years of dancing with my father and realized that for someone else to dance like Dad was too much to hope for.

"I'd love to dance, Bennett."

As we walked to the dance floor it felt like everyone in the room was watching us. When we finally melted into the crowd, Bennett placed his other hand on the skin exposed by my backless dress. I struggled to keep my composure.

The song was a waltz, and he danced wonderfully. My dad would have been impressed.

"You're different from the other women here," Bennett said, and it sounded like it might be a compliment.

You can say that again, I said to myself, while saying to Bennett, "What makes you think that?"

"You seem comfortable in your skin. Tonight isn't a competition to you." The song ended and we stood, waiting for the next song to begin.

I smiled and thanked him as I glanced around the dance floor. I noticed for the first time that many girls were looking over their dates' shoulders to peer at Bennett and me.

"Wow, this group has me scared. If I make one wrong move, these girls might attack," I told Bennett, making him laugh.

When the evening came to a close, Bennett asked if we could see each other again, and I said, "I'd like to."

I spotted Ruth walking toward the exit, surrounded by a group of adoring friends, so when Bennett slipped his arm through mine and escorted me out of the ballroom, I knew she was just ahead of us. He slowed as we approached the hotel's front entrance and directed me off to the side.

"I really had a good time tonight," he said, and bent to kiss me softly. I could feel my heart beating so hard that I was glad my dress was low in the back and not the front; he would surely be able to see my chest throbbing as my heart prepared to explode in my chest. It didn't help that I could feel the warmth of his hand pressing on the center of my naked back.

"Come on, girl!" Ruth said, as she suddenly appeared and tugged on my arm. "You'll see him again," she whispered. "Our limo awaits." I gave Bennett a smile over my shoulder and let myself be pulled away.

"Thanks for saving me. I think I was speechless. I couldn't think of anything to say to him."

"What I saw didn't look like *talking*," she teased as we got into the limo.

I collapsed into the soft leather seats and felt the magic of my princess evening disappearing as I started to drift back into my farmer's daughter reality. "Wow," I said, "that was like living a different life!"

"Not for me," Ruth said. "That's why it was fun to take you. That group gets too self absorbed without a little outside influence to keep them in check."

When the alarm clock buzzed, it felt like my head had hit the pillow just a moment before, and I woke with the previous night's smile still plastered on my face. Ruth was blissfully snoring three feet away from me. As usual, we had stayed up too late. "Come on Ruth, rise and shine, and tell me what it's like to grow up rich and why you never told me that you were before I pulled up in front of your house."

"I couldn't," Ruth answered with feigned defiance as she rubbed the sleep from her eyes. "You might not have liked me, and you never would have agreed to come to K.C. for the party if I'd told you beforehand."

"Give me some credit! I would have liked you rich or poor. But you're right about the party. I would have been afraid I'd fall for a guy like Bennett. He's a little out of my tax bracket." I sighed. "I've never known anyone who came from old money. Where I come from, 'inheritance' means the farm."

Ruth sat up to fluff her pillows. "Okay Hillary, I just couldn't pass up the chance to see you dressed like that. I knew you'd get some well-deserved attention, and now those girls will have something new to gossip about." Ruth laughed as she made herself comfortable. "It looked like you and Bennett were having a pretty good time from where I sat, and upsetting a lot of girls who would have given just about anything to be in your place!"

"Yeah, I had a great time, but you've got to explain how rich is rich when it comes to your group of friends? I can't imagine how some of those people were raised. In fact, I can't imagine how *you* were raised. I never saw the country club girl in you," I shook my head, trying to make all the pieces fit together in my brain.

"I wasn't here most of the time, only summers," she reminded me. "Remember I told you I went to a prep school? I just didn't say it was a private boarding school on the East Coast. Even so, it was a far cry from this life, and it kept me a little more grounded than the other folks in this neighborhood."

"Come on girls, breakfast is ready," we heard Ruth's mom call from down the hallway.

"You heard her, Hillary. Just put on one of my robes. It's just us and Mom today."

She tossed me a white chenille robe and kicked a pair of slippers out from under the bed in my direction. I threw the robe on as I hurried out the door to keep up with her. I wasn't about to get lost in Ruth's house. That would be too embarrassing!

Ruth's mom reminded me of mine in some ways. She asked if I slept well, and if we'd had a good time at the party … but when she gave my breakfast order to the kitchen staff, the similarities ended.

We gossiped about the party through most of breakfast. Ruth described all the dresses in detail, and shared gossip about new relationships and breakups. Then she told her mom about my evening with Bennett.

"Well, is he just as good looking as ever? He's always been a handsome boy. I don't think I've seen him yet this summer. How's he doing at school?" Ruth's mom spoke without taking a breath and would have continued on her roll if Ruth hadn't interrupted her.

"From what I was able to gather from Clint—because Bennett was occupied," Ruth smirked in my direction, "Bennett's a powerhouse at Yale, top of his class, and will probably join his father's firm after graduation. But last night he only had eyes for Hillary. You should have seen the girls. They were beside themselves with envy. It was great!"

We had barely finished breakfast when the phone rang and Mrs. Witherspoon hurried off to answer it. "Hillary dear, it's for you," she said, handing me the receiver. "He said to get Ruth on the line, too."

"Okay, Mom," Ruth said, and went to pick up the other extension.

"Hello, this is Hillary," I said, and heard Bennett's voice in reply.

"Good morning ladies. I'm calling to ask Hillary out to dinner tonight. First, I need to know if that's all right with you, Hillary, and secondly if it is all right with you, Ruth," Bennett was being very diplomatic.

I saw Ruth giving me an exaggerated motion for "Say Yes."

"I'd love to, Bennett, if it's okay with you, Ruth," I said with a shrug back.

"Pick her up at eight," Ruth said. "I guess you can have her for a couple hours, but you'll owe me, Bennett." She hit the *off* button.

"Are you still there, Hillary?"

"Yes, I'm still here."

"Tell Ruth we'll be going to the Rozzelle Court Restaurant. I'll see you this evening then?"

"Yes, I'll be ready by eight." Ruth was hovering so close to me that I was afraid she was going to make me laugh.

"See you then," Bennett said and hung up.

"I'm supposed to say we're going to the Rozzelle Court Restaurant. Is that so you can dress me accordingly?"

"I imagine so, but lucky for you he's picked a casual place. It's more comfortable there, no nosey onlookers. It's still early, Hillary, how about a Jacuzzi to relax the old bones?"

A Jacuzzi sounded like heaven to me. Spending the previous evening in heels had made my feet and my lower back hurt. I thought the jets on my arches would be just the ticket.

Eight o'clock couldn't have come soon enough. For two hours Ruth had me switching outfits, making me feel a bit like *Barbie*. But as usual, she had me looking perfect by the time Bennett arrived. I tried madly to hang up the piles of discarded clothes while Ruth insisted, "Don't bother." I wondered as I walked out to Bennett's car just who was going to clean up my mess, and hoped my feet could take another night in heels.

July 24, 35 AD

My name is Marcus Flavius, and I am a General in the greatest army Caesar has ever sent forth. Rome did not expect the tribes in the east to be such fierce fighters, but that is not the battle. My destiny lies far to the west. I am to ensure that no Druid survives to see the dawning of another sun.

We have all heard of Hilsbeth, the leader of the Druid warriors, for the Roman soldiers know the names of the ones they fear most. Stories are whispered around campfires of the strange aberrations that occur while locked in battle with the Druids. It is said that soldiers' minds conjure images of mysterious foes who then vanish, becoming nothing more than smoke, taking with them the afflicted soldier's sanity. I've heard these stories from sources I trust, which leads me not to doubt them.

This day we know the Druids are in the forest, on the other side of our future battlefield, and without even having seen them, fear strikes at the heart of every Roman soldier. Although I would never admit it, even to my closest comrade, their extermination from this Earth will not be of my liking. During restless nights, a mysterious and striking woman invades my dreams, and I become intoxicated. Only recently have I realized she must be Hilsbeth. All other women have become weak and pitiful in her shadow, and I close my eyes and wait for her to come to me. I would like nothing more than to know her in the flesh, to feel her body against mine, to breathe in her breath ... but I know that when our paths cross, that will most probably not be the outcome.

July 24, 2010

Bennett drove up in one of his father's many cars, a sporty BMW convertible. He had left his car at school and flown home for the summer. I couldn't help but notice how much of a gentleman he was. He chatted with Mrs. Witherspoon just enough to make her happy. He took my arm to help me down the front steps and opened the car door for me. Definitely not your average college student! He closed the door and I buckled in while I watched his blond hair catch the sunset as he walked around the car and eased himself into the driver's seat.

As we slipped easily into conversation, I found myself surprised that I wasn't put off by how much he loved power and money. Really, I couldn't blame him. He had grown up with plenty of both, and having been born into it, it fit him like a finely tailored suit. He teased me about being raised on a farm, but it was good-natured. He was trying to rattle my cage, but I was in far too good a mood to second-guess his intensions. I'm sure my being a farm girl made me unique in his eyes.

When we parked I noticed The Rozzelle was in the Nelson Art Gallery, and I realized this evening would prove to be a double treat. I wasn't sure what I was looking forward to most, the gallery or the dinner. As we entered the large hall, I was immediately drawn to the area on the right, and I was glad to see Bennett follow when I motioned to him. A dimly lit room displayed an exciting collection of early artifacts from the United Kingdom.

When I was a kid, our family spent a fair amount of time out west, exploring old Indian ruins on our summer vacations. It was during those trips that I began to believe that artifacts could talk. It made sense to me that if you listened very, very closely they should be able to communicate their history. I thought it would be so cool if I were able to receive long-forgotten knowledge, so I conveniently neglected the fact that I had never heard so much as a whisper. I guess old habits die hard.

I felt my hands open by my side as we entered the room, so I was ready to receive information. I mean, why not? I would never develop the talent if I didn't practice.

Bennett seemed to be as interested in the Roman artifacts as I was in the Celtic ones, and he immediately became absorbed with a display case near the entrance. With Bennett occupied, I took the opportunity to walk slowly down the center aisle with my hands open. When I realized I was totally alone, I closed my eyes, breathed in the musty smell, and felt the cool air run through my open fingers. Soon I became aware of a sharp pain in my chest and a gush of something warm running down my body, pooling around my feet. I noticed a familiar scent that was not pleasant—the *iron* smell of blood that I distinctly remembered from Granddad's hunting trips.

I didn't want to open my eyes and take a chance the magic would disappear. After all, this was the first time I had ever *felt* anything. When I sensed a hand on my shoulder, my eyes flew open. To my relief it was Bennett, but even knowing that, it took me a few minutes to separate him from my other experience. It was that déjà vu feeling again—I could almost have sworn there was another hand on my shoulder a moment before his. As we walked out of the room, I shook my hands in an effort to leave the darkness behind us.

"I didn't mean to frighten you, Hillary. Are you okay?" Bennett asked, slipping his arm around me. I nodded yes, and we walked through the rest of the exhibits barely talking.

The decor of the restaurant replicated fifteenth-century architecture, and it was lovely. As I started to think more about Bennett and less about the artifacts, I realized that I was in pretty good company.

During dinner I learned that Bennett, even with a full social calendar, still found time to achieve a 4.0 grade point average. "It runs in my family," Bennett said. "My father is a lawyer, as was my grandfather. I learned the law from dinner conversations when I was growing up. Law school is only a formality."

"We talk about the latest farm report at our dinner table," I said. "How many cents per bushel." I laughed, but I wasn't kidding. "We live in two different worlds."

"Do you ever wonder what you'll do after college?" I could tell Bennett was asking a sincere question.

"No, not yet," I said. "I figure life will form itself into a future plan if I give it time. I'm not following any family legacy, so I don't have to rush things. After all, I'm only nineteen, still just a kid."

"Following in my father's footsteps has always been the plan for me. I've never given it a second thought. My father pays for everything now, so I'll have a lucrative future … and that's the way it has been for generations, each indebted to the last. Not that my father sees it that way. In my family, we're pretty much driven by money." Bennett looked at me. "Maybe I should pull back the blinders and see if there is something more rewarding out there for me."

I sure didn't know him well enough to become his counselor, so I replied, "We're still young, Bennett. We have plenty of time to make mistakes and make up for them."

"Have you ever thought about moving far away, tossing in the towel? Have you ever been to Rome? How about it, Hillary, want to just disappear with me?"

First of all, I didn't have a towel to toss in—there was just $200 dollars in my savings account. But as long as we were kidding around, I said, "Would you consider Scotland? That country intrigues me."

I watched the twinkle in his dark brown eyes and felt the pull of my heart as I began to fall for him. But somehow I knew it was more like jumping off a cliff. With this guy, my heart was bound to be broken.

"It's nice spending an evening with a beautiful woman with whom I have absolutely nothing in common. It is a very refreshing change." Bennett leaned back in his chair sipping his espresso as he gazed into my eyes.

"Good evening, Marcus," an older black gentleman said as he delivered dinner. "It's nice to see you're still coming home to Kansas

City."

Bennett smiled up at him. "How has life been treating you, Wallace?"

"Just fine, just fine," he replied. "Tell your folks hello for me, and that they are due for a visit to the museum."

When we were once again alone, I couldn't resist asking Bennett why our waiter had called him Marcus.

"My given name is Marcus Bennett Taylor, Bennett being my mother's maiden name. I'm the end of the line on my mother's side of the family, and I've always tried to honor that by using her name as my first. Marcus is a family name of a different kind, from the maternal side of my father's family." He looked at me most seriously and said, "My grandmother insists that our family tree leads straight back to Roman nobility, and if you knew my grandmother, you would also know never to argue with her. That side of my family tree is pure-blooded, hotheaded Italians. The short story is that by my generation, with the mixture of my mother's ancestry, I've never felt like the name Marcus actually fit me." He pointed at his blond hair.

As the evening came to a close, Bennett asked if I would spend one more afternoon with him.

"I want to show you our family's hunting cabin. It's not far, and I'll bring a picnic. If Ruth has you for a couple of days, maybe she'll agree to let me entertain you on Wednesday?"

"I'm sure Ruth won't mind," I said, smiling because I didn't need to be convinced.

CHAPTER
SEVEN

I HAD an incredible time with Ruth. We shopped at the Plaza—well, Ruth did—and dined at Crown Center. But by Wednesday, I was looking forward to going into the countryside with Bennett.

The drive to Bennett's cabin took about two and a half hours. It was farther than I had expected, but I didn't mind. We laughed and listened to music most of the way, and just as Bennett had promised, he had packed an incredible picnic … although it looked much more like it had been packed by a gourmet restaurant.

At about noon we arrived at the sprawling spread that the Bennett family affectionately called *their cabin*. I would call it a second home. We found ourselves spending time on a huge wrap-around porch. I sunk into one of the luxurious cushions that lined one of the many teak rockers, kicked off my shoes, tucked my stocking feet under me, and relaxed, taking in a spectacular view of the Flint Hills.

"There's a storm on the way," Bennett said, and I followed his eyes to the west. Darkness was beginning to gather on the horizon, and I could see the lightning striking against the grey sky as we sat in sunshine. That's the thing about Kansas—with the open landscape, you can literally see for miles. The storm was still a long way off, but it was definitely gathering momentum, and the temperature had dropped.

"Let's go inside," Bennett said as he pulled me up from my chair and held my hands in his. "I'll gather up the remnants of our lunch. If you grab the glasses for me, Hillary, we'll go in and sit by the fire." The "fire" was a modern gas insert he lit by flipping a switch.

As the fire roared to life, so did my panicked thoughts. I'd had hours to think about being alone with Bennett and what I might do if things turned romantic. My heart thumped like a rabbit's every time he was close enough to touch. Breaking the news that I was a virgin would be a huge turn-off. So I kept my mouth shut and struggled to stay in the moment, waiting to see where things might go.

"Which direction is the restroom?" I asked. I was enjoying the cozy fire, but when nature calls, you really have no choice but to respond.

"Down the hall on the right," he yelled from the kitchen. "Do you want me to show you?"

"No, I'll be fine." I got to my feet and made my way down the long, dim hall. The bathroom was just as beautiful as the rest of the old, elegant hunting lodge.

After I'd finished, I quickly glanced in the mirror as I turned to leave, and I noticed that I didn't look half bad. I turned out the light and headed back toward the living room. Still in my stocking feet, I walked down the hall and felt a sudden squish, and then something wet and sticky between my toes.

"Hey, Bennett, I think you might have a problem. Can you come over here? I don't want to track whatever I just stepped in around the house."

Flipping on all the lights as he came to the rescue, he stopped in front of me. "Oh no, we must have a leak," he said, running off and coming back with a hand full of rags. "My father and uncles just got back from a hunting trip to Arizona. They bagged a wild javelina. That's a pig," he added when he noticed I didn't understand. "I think it must be in here."

When I looked at my feet it dawned on me that I was standing in a stream of blood that was coming from under a door. Bennett opened the door slightly, and quickly closed it before much of the odor from the broken walk-in freezer could escape into the cabin. The blood I was standing in made my stomach weak. I could smell it, and it felt warm as it soaked my socks.

"For some reason, my uncle likes to save the blood for black pudding. He claims it's some old bullshit family recipe. I can't stand the stuff myself. I am sorry about this, Hillary. I can't believe this is happening. Let me carry you back to the bathroom so you can get cleaned up. I'll find you some clean socks."

He swept me up into his arms and carried me back the way I had come.

"Turn on the light for me, Hillary." He sat me on the counter top and turned on the water. "Just put your feet in the sink and I'll bring you a towel," he said as he disappeared into the hall.

I stripped off my bloody socks and held them under the warm water to rinse them out. As I watched the blood run from my feet into the drain, the smell and the feeling of warm blood gave me a flash of the Nelson Gallery and the Celtic exhibit. I got that déjà vu feeling again, but I'd be damned if I could understand why. The smell of blood seemed to be the trigger, but why?

I turned at the sound of footsteps, and there was Bennett, standing with a pair of large cotton socks in his hands and an apologetic smile on his face. I finished soaping my feet with the washcloth he'd handed me and watched the last of the blood flow from between my toes. As Bennett began to talk, the déjà vu faded away like an interrupted dream upon awakening.

"That smell and the blood-soaked carpet can take the romance right out of an afternoon," Bennett said. "I called my father. He's sending a repairman for the cooler and a cleaning crew for the carpet before it gets any worse. I guess we should head back to K.C. before they get here."

I put on the socks, stuffed my feet back into my shoes, and followed Bennett out to the porch. It was cooling down fast, and I could smell the ozone from the storm in the air, which was a far cry better than the smell that had permeated the cabin.

The rain poured down on us as we drove home, with the wipers barely moving fast enough to keep up. It was one of those *raining like cats and dogs* storms. The sky was pitch black except when it was lit by one of the frequent lightning strikes.

Bennett had called Ruth to let her know to expect us, and when we arrived she was waiting at the front door with two umbrellas. She ran down the front steps with one umbrella open to protect her from the rain and handed me the other as I opened the car door.

"Come in whenever you're ready. I'll be in the kitchen." She ran back up the stairs and disappeared through the giant entry doors.

I closed the car door and turned to look at Bennett. "I had a great time today."

He looked as though he didn't quite believe me. Chuckling, he said, "Let me make this up to you! What if I call Ruth later and you both meet me at the country club for brunch tomorrow?"

"You have nothing to make up for, but that sounds great," I said, with more enthusiasm than I'd intended to show.

"I'm enjoying our time together, too. I'll see you tomorrow." He leaned in and kissed me with those warm, full lips. I closed my eyes, not wanting to pull away, but in the back of my mind I could picture Ruth waiting for me in the kitchen.

"I'd better go. I'll let Ruth know you'll call her later to make the arrangements."

"Just have her bring you to the club tomorrow around noon." Of course Ruth belonged to *The Club*, I thought, not as surprised now as I would have been a few days before.

I opened my door and the umbrella and raced for the front door. Bennett's horn beeped and I turned to see his car disappear down the drive.

Ruth couldn't help but notice the socks.

"What else of his are you wearing?"

"Everything except the socks is mine. Now tell me the truth—am I an idiot to think a guy like Bennett could truly care about me?"

"Wake up, Ruth. We only have a couple of hours to get ready for *the club*." I had been awake for hours, daydreaming. "Bennett wants us there by noon."

"I told him we'd be there at one. Fashionably late makes more of an impression."

I washed my face and watched the mascara from the night before roll down the sink toward the drain. "What miracles are you going to perform on me today? I really need help. Look at the bags under my eyes!" We'd been up late every night since I'd arrived, and I was looking the worse for wear.

"Not a problem, Hillary. I have a caffeine cream for circles under the eyes."

"No thanks! I prefer to drink my caffeine," I teased.

We arrived at *The Club* at 1:00 p.m., but by the time we parked and got to the clubhouse, it was 1:15. I spotted Bennett sitting with Ruth's friend Clint. "This works out handy, doesn't it?" I said to Ruth in a low voice.

Our seats were in the shade of an umbrella that overlooked the pool, which looked over the rolling hills of the golf course beyond. Once again, I was very fashionable in clothes borrowed from Ruth's sister. Today was my last day in Kansas City, and I wanted to make a lasting impression on Bennett.

I had become a better flirt since meeting Bennett. He made me feel significant. When we talked and laughed, somewhere in that fairytale place in the back of my mind I became a hopeless romantic. We could manage a long distance relationship … I'd never been to New Haven, Connecticut … My parents would love him … I'd like a long Italian vacation …

Then, as if on cue, I heard a female voice over my right shoulder. Bennett looked up and stood.

"Hi, Bennett," a dark haired beauty said while pointing to a younger version of herself. "I'd like to introduce you to my cousin. She's visiting from New York." The cousin was the whole package: long, silky hair, bedroom eyes, and a body from Victoria's Secret.

Bennett stepped forward to shake the young girl's hand. I watched his eyes as he reached with his other hand to tuck a fallen strand of hair behind her ear. It was one of the most intimate acts I'd ever witnessed in public! The intensity of their eye contact was reminiscent of Brad Pitt and Angelina Jolie in *The Smiths*. Everyone knew poor Jennifer didn't stand a chance. The chemistry was just too strong.

Damn it, how could I have been so stupid? The reality of my situation became crystal clear. My chest felt as though someone very large were standing on it while I tried desperately to appear as if nothing were bothering me. My heart was breaking, and I was fighting tears. Call it what you like, even another frickin' growth opportunity, but I just wished I could disappear.

I had plenty of time to try to pull myself together. Bennett couldn't seem to say goodbye to his new friend. I plastered a smile on my face when he finally sat back down at the table, and I noticed Ruth was saying goodbye to Clint and picking up her bag. She was going to get me out of here before I crashed and burned. I loved her for that. We made a hasty retreat, giving Bennett zero opportunity to respond.

The following morning, Ruth and I made arrangements to see each other back at school. She knew I was crushed, and I could see how bad she felt for me.

"Come here, honey." She opened her arms and I gladly walked into them. "I'm sorry I told you to trust that jerk."

"That's what I love about you," I said. "You're loyal to the end. But really, you don't have to hold it against Bennett. I'll be okay."

"I know you'll be okay. I just hate to see you like this. I'll make it up to you in the fall. Not sure how, but I'll work on it."

With a mixture of regret and thanks, I said good-bye to Ruth and her family before I headed home.

I was so deep in thought that I didn't notice the hours passing. Before I knew it, I was making the turn up our dirt road and I could see our old farmhouse sitting in the distance. I pulled up in front and stopped, not having the strength to worry about unloading the car. I just wanted to get past my parents and up to my room before they noticed my puffy, red eyes.

Of course Dad was in the kitchen, so I kept my head lowered.

"What's up, Kiddo?" he said, taking a closer look at me when I wasn't my usual cheery self. "Are you okay?" He stood up and walked over to me.

With one big exhale I decided full disclosure might help.

"Oh, Dad, I feel like an idiot. I fell for a guy in Kansas City. I thought he cared about me, but not so …"

"Oh, Kiddo, it happens to the best of us. When you open your heart, love usually has a lesson or two to teach you. The most interesting one is that true love never depends upon whether you are loved in return." He lifted my chin to look into my eyes. "We all want it to mean that. It's hard to believe the answer to all questions in life is just to love, regardless. Even when we don't see how, life has a way of working things out. After all, it's about the journey, and Kiddo, you're barely out of the starting gate."

CHAPTER EIGHT

August 10, AD 35

Hidden among the huge roots of an old oak tree sits the most peculiar fellow. He's very small and round, not at all the lean warrior physique the word "Druid" usually brings to mind. Because his Druid lineage has never been broken, he carries all the physical traits of the ancient line. He has a shock of white hair falling forward over his thick eyebrows, and his fingers and toes are slightly webbed. As far back as memory can recount, his kind have spent their time communing with nature amid the standing stones. So, it's no wonder that Gillian draws his paranormal powers from nature itself.

Gillian earned his position as a Druid warrior not by his ability to fight, but through his skill in weaving his magic into fog to cover the Druids' position, and his supernatural ability to draw the twilight in before its time. Gillian's magic is the kind that can turn the tide of a battle. During it all, he remains totally invisible—not because he possesses the power of invisibility, but because no Roman soldier views him as a threat.

Their inability to see Gillian as lethal has cost more than one Roman soldier his life. Seeing him as only a forest dwarf, they underestimate what he can do with his pocketful of small, perfectly shaped stones. He prefers using these stones to hunt for dinner. With a snap of his fingers he can send a stone flying at such speed and with such accuracy as to strike a rabbit (or a Roman soldier) dead in his tracks.

August 10, 2010

The last few days of summer passed quickly, and before I knew it I was moving into my very first apartment. Excited to see Ruth in the flesh again, I was looking forward to one of our long talks in our PJs, drinking coffee with way too much cream and sugar in it.

Ruth and I had rented the second floor of an old house, within walking distance of campus. I knew Ruth could afford more, but this was the limit of my finances.

Of course my old clunker would be parked on the street so Ruth could park her expensive high school graduation present inside the garage.

Ruth and I agreed to meet at the coffee shop. We wanted to pick up the keys together since this "home away from home" was a first for me. Independence, here I come—or as much independence as someone could claim with their parents still footing the bills.

Kenny and a couple of his buddies were waiting for us on the bench out front, enjoying watching the college girls walk by. They had pulled a U-Haul full of apartment stuff for me and volunteered their labor.

"Oh, did I forget to tell you our apartment is on the second floor?" I teased as we all walked back to the truck. They really didn't care one way or the other; they were there to taste the adventures of college life.

It only took a couple of hours to get everything moved into the apartment. It wasn't even noon when we finished setting up the bed frames, so we all decided to check out what was happening on campus. I had noticed a bulletin on the community board for flag football sign-up, and being a tomboy, I thought it might be fun to find a team. Shortly after walking toward the intramural fields, Kenny and his buddies decided to dump us and head over to the girls' dorms to check out the sunbathers.

"I talked to Bennett before I left K.C.," Ruth blurted, broaching the subject of Bennett Taylor for the first time.

"Really?" I said, as we approached the fields.

"Yeah, he told me to say hello, but I wasn't sure if I should bring him up again after … you know," she said, trying to read my reaction.

"It's okay, Ruth. I've done plenty of thinking about him during the past couple of weeks, and my heart isn't broken anymore. I was kind of swept away—I mean, he's a great looking guy with everything a girl is looking for—but something wasn't quite right … well, besides the fact that he dumped me!" We both laughed and let the subject change as we approached the intramural fields.

Ruth stopped to take a seat in the bleachers to guy-watch. She wasn't the least bit interested in exercising to the point of sweating.

"I need to track down one of the coaches, Ruth. Are you going to be okay here alone?" She waved me away like I was a buzzing fly, so I began my hike in the direction of the sign-up tables.

It took me about fifteen minutes to work my way to the front of the line. The girl behind the table shaded her eyes and looked up at me.

"There's only one team left that has openings for girls," the girl informed me, "but that coach is taking a break right now. I think he actually went across the street to have a smoke," she said, turning up her nose at the mention of cigarettes.

I thought about walking across the street to interrupt the coach and his groupies—I really wanted one of those spots—but I decided to take a seat on the curb and wait for him to come back instead. *How long does it take to smoke a cigarette*? I wondered, as I sat overheating in the sun. My best alternative to baking alive was to scoot down the curb and into the shade of a tree. I knew I would be invading someone else's personal space by moving, but decided it was a better option than drowning in my own sweat.

I slid over, and for a few minutes I sat staring straight ahead, thankful to be cooling down. But due to the weird jerky movements in my peripheral vision, I couldn't resist looking at the guy next to me. When I glanced over I found him to be almost as wide as he was tall, although he wasn't fat. He was more like a boulder with arms and legs, topped with unkempt black hair with a streak of white falling over his cherub face I noticed he was smiling right at me.

"Hi, my name's Gilbert," he said as he stretched out his oversized hand.

I shook it willingly, but as I pulled my hand away from his, a bottle cap stuck to my palm. I opened my hand and stared at it.

"Oh, that's my defense system," Gilbert said, as he tossed a bent bottle cap down the sewer grate near us. He then pulled another cap from his pocket, and with a snap of his fingers he shot and hit an empty Coke can across the street with amazing accuracy and ferocious speed.

"My name's Hillary, and wow, you're quite a shot," I said as I pointed toward the can he'd dented. "Are you here to sign up for flag football?" I asked as I watched him shoot another bottle cap into a plastic bottle lying by the curb.

"Wish I could, but no, I'm not allowed to play anymore. Last year, I was making a run toward the goal line when a member of the opposing team grabbed me by the shorts. He ripped a big, gaping hole in the back. Mind you, it was only my backside showing and I'm not particularly shy. What was I going to do anyway? I couldn't make my shorts magically reappear, so I went for the score and got a standing ovation. I'd never had a standing O before, so I celebrated my fifteen seconds of fame by taking a victory lap.

"Unfortunately, the faculty didn't find it as funny as I did. Someone got puckered and they decided to call it 'indecent exposure.' I'm lucky they didn't expel me. So no, I can't play flag football."

Gilbert pulled another handful of bottle caps from his pocket and continued. "I should spend more time studying anyway. I'm in the PhD program. Quantum physics is my field." His pockets were bulging with bottle caps, and I began to hope he wasn't drinking as much beer as that collection of bottle caps suggested.

"Well Gilbert, I'll probably see you around campus then. I'm a mathematics major, so we share some of the same buildings." I stood to stretch my legs.

Somehow the coach had snuck past me, and people were already lined up waiting to talk to him. I decided it just wasn't meant to be, and Gilbert's story of losing his shorts in front of the student body had made flag football seem much less appealing anyway.

During the summer I had received a letter from the university about student aid and opportunities to work on campus, so I arranged an interview at the campus library.

Since it would be my first job working for someone other than my parents, I wanted to make a good impression. I typed the application, rehearsed every possible scenario over and over in my mind, and arrived early for my interview. When the secretary called my name, I stood up and walked into the director's office with confidence. I kept reminding myself—*back straight, firm handshake.*

It wasn't long before it became obvious I had the job—and I mean *obvious*! The man interviewing me, Mr. Delaney, was an old family friend.

"I played college basketball at Emporia State with your Uncle Paul," Mr. Delaney said, recalling those days fondly with a smile and a faraway gaze.

But as he continued on and on with Kate this and Kate that, it dawned on me that he had a huge crush on my mom, and time had done little to diminish his feelings. He was reminiscing as though it had been the best time of his life.

"Your Uncle Paul and I were the stars. You should ask your mom about it. I spent a lot of time over at their house."

Mr. Delaney was tall, but I don't know if I would say he had *star quality.* I had some serious questions for my mother.

We spent my interview chatting about what my mom had been doing for the last twenty-some years. By the time I assured him for the third time that my parents were still happily married, he'd weaseled a promise from me to bring Mom by to see him the next time she was up for a visit.

My new job wouldn't be anything demanding; just swiping student ID cards during the late shift at the checkout counter. But even at minimum wage, it would be nice to get a paycheck and not have to rely on my parents for spending money. After all, isn't part of the college experience supposed to be growing up before you're thrown out into the real world to make it on your own?

CHAPTER NINE

THEY NEEDED me to start work ASAP, so I scheduled my orientation for the following morning. When I arrived, I found four nerdy ... sorry, *studious* looking students who all appeared to be upperclassmen.

"My name is Anne Marie," the administrator said as she handed us each a packet of forms to fill out. "I am the one you will receive all of your work assignments from. At the beginning of your shift, report to my desk. I am located outside the research offices at the end of the main hallway."

As she continued, it slowly began to dawn on me that this was a much more interesting job than the one I thought I had applied for. Dear Mr. Delaney was a smart guy. He must have gotten me this position. Now Mom would be sure to thank him when she was on campus for parents' weekend. I was almost more excited to begin my new job than to start classes.

On Monday, I arrived at the library a little after three o'clock for my first day of work.

"Good morning, Hillary," Anne Marie said, handing me a packet. "Here's what I'd like for you to do first. When you finish this, which should take you the rest of the afternoon, you can come back to see me. If it's after 5:30, someone else may be here and they can let you know if we have any other urgent requests."

I took the packet and laid everything out on a reference table in the corner of the library. The packet contained a detailed map of the entire library and a list of books I was supposed to find. When the first book was located, I had to scan the requested pages and e-mail them to the university that had placed the order. Then I had to find the second book, and so on, until I got to the end of the list. The map gave me a pretty good idea where to start looking, so I took off on my first search.

Libraries can be musty places, especially in old areas where most of the books aren't often opened. The third book on the list was one of those books, and it proved to be nearly impossible to locate. It wasn't on the first four floors of the building like all the others, but on an odd "half floor" at the library's far north side.

Wow, now this reminds me of childhood! I thought as I stepped onto the glass floor of the room. The old library in my hometown had a glass floor just like the one I was standing on. I still don't understand *why glass*, but this room was long and narrow, with a ceiling so low it made me feel claustrophobic.

It took me a few minutes to find the book because someone had put it back in the wrong spot. As I reached for it, I remembered something else from childhood. You had to tap your fingers on the edge of the bookcase to discharge static electricity before touching anything on the shelf, or you'd get a hell of a jolt from the glass floor.

I tapped and pulled the old dusty book off the shelf, and because the binding was so limp and broken, it fell open … so I read:

This book comes to you as a friend who knows you, not for what you seem, but for what you are and are capable of becoming.

Never had a book introduced itself to me before! It made the book seem like a living, thinking entity rather than print on paper. The warm feel of the old leather fascinated me, so I closed my eyes and let it fall open again. The pages were worn and faded to yellow, but the print was still very legible. My heart fluttered as I began to read again:

Science and religion are united in the conviction that all forms of life express one principle. Science calls it energy or light. Religion calls it God. Beginning logically with that premise, we may see that this is not the way of the world but a way that discloses a new world; not merely an imaginary world, but a tangible world that exists right here and now.

I wanted to sit down and take more time to become better acquainted with my new friend. I held the old book ever so gently in my hands because it seemed so fragile, as if it were a very wise old sage, bent by the years, but not yet broken. Then suddenly I remembered I was at work, and wondered how long I had been standing there holding the book rather than taking it down to the office to scan.

I made a mental note to come back to this area again; the room seemed to be a very special place. I guessed hardly anyone even knew about this part of the library. All the books were old and probably out of print. Certainly none of them could be found online, which made them feel even more unique and special.

I turned the book on its end and noticed that a considerable amount of dust had built up since it had last been opened, so I blew softly to clean it off. It occurred to me to check the date the book had been printed, so I'd know just how old my new friend was. When I flipped to the front, the date said 1925—it was not far from its hundredth birthday.

"I'll have to bring Dad up here when I get a chance," I said out loud as I closed the book. Turning to leave, I couldn't help but look behind me. For a moment I could swear I felt the presence of someone else in the room, but the room was empty.

It took me about thirty minutes to scan all the pages that were listed on the request and to get them e-mailed to Professor Edwards, the person whose name appeared at the top of the form. Then I returned my new *friend* to its rightful place on the shelf and moved on to the rest of the books on my list.

CHAPTER TEN

I WAS glad to get off work in time to stop by the Student Union for a newspaper. It was a beautiful day, and with time to spare, I found a place in the sun and took a moment to catch up on the news.

A group of students were congregating across the street, and my attention was drawn by the sound of their angry voices, one joining with the next and then the next. It soon became obvious that someone was stirring the pot, and not in a good way. When the crowd moved away, two people remained, a student and a man who appeared to be around thirty. Both looked agitated and ugly.

Returning to my paper with a shiver, I felt a bit blue and wondered why my cheerful mood had suddenly turned dark. It actually seemed as though a cloud of gloom was descending on the Student Union, causing me to feel uncomfortable. Standing, I walked out to the road where the recycle bin was located to toss my paper in.

Glancing back toward the Union one last time before heading home, I saw that the angry man from across the street was now standing where I had been sitting just a moment before. He was dressed in old black jeans and a black faded t-shirt, with dark, thinning, shoulder-length hair hanging limp. His face was broad and pale, and he was smiling directly at me as if we were friends. But I had never seen him before today. I quickened my pace as that feeling of déjà vu filled me, searching my memory for any way I might have known him.

I arrived at the apartment just in time to try Ruth's first attempt at Mac n' Cheese.

"Ruth, I really like this. Was the recipe on the box?"

"My mom had the kitchen staff put together a college cookbook for me as a joke," she said, "but I think it's going to come in handy. Take a look, and let's pick out something for dinner tomorrow." She tossed it across the table.

"I don't think there are enough green things in here to make for a balanced diet," I said. "We'll have to fit a salad in every now and then." I took the little book into the kitchen along with the dishes, and filed it away on the shelf for safekeeping.

"I'm going to get ready for bed and check my e-mail," I said as I headed to my room. "See ya tomorrow, Ruth." Shutting the door behind me, I opened my backpack and pulled out my laptop. I thought for a moment about sitting at my desk, but decided to pile up my pillows and climb into bed. I just wanted to check my e-mail, make sure I had all my materials for tomorrow's classes, and go to sleep.

The first e-mail was from Mom and Dad, sending me encouragement, telling me Kenny had made it home safe, and sending their love to Ruth.

The second e-mail was a welcome from the president of the university, with an invitation attachment for an upcoming Student Body Fall Mixer.

When I saw the third e-mail, I yelled, "Hey Ruth, get in here."

When she came through the door, she took one look at me and started in, "What kind of PJs are those, Hillary? I'm going to have to give you a lesson on—"

Before she could finish, I interrupted her. "I mean it. Get over here!" She climbed in bed beside me, slipped under the covers and looked at the screen. "Not that one Ruth; the third one." The subject line read, *Chelsea, is this you*? It was from Will.

"Open it Hillary! If you don't do it NOW, I think I'll explode." Between the two of us, we may have sucked all the air out of the room. I opened the e-mail.

Dear Hillary,

Before I write a lengthy letter, I'd like to confirm that you are indeed the person I seek. Do you refer to yourself as

Chelsea? This has been a puzzle that my friend George and I have been trying to solve for some time now. Please reply, if indeed you are the one I have been searching for. Also, please let us know if you have any connection through which we can contact Ruth.
Sincerely,
William Emerald

We exhaled slowly.

"Wow," I said. "I did make it awfully hard for him to find me by lying about my name. I wonder how they did it. How the hell did they find my e-mail? Are we listed in a school directory?"

"Heck if I know or care," Ruth said, delighted. "But feel free to give George my e-mail!"

"I think I'll wait and reply tomorrow. I'd like to compose a letter that doesn't sound as giddy as I feel right now. Besides, I don't know what to say!"

"Maybe just say, *"Yes, it's me!"* And then see what Will has to say."

"I think that's a fine idea, but I'm still going to wait until I'm not so tired. I'll do it at the Union tomorrow between classes."

"We'll have that PJ talk tomorrow," Ruth said, leaving my room. "You need something besides that ratty old t-shirt."

I smiled at her, turned off the light, and rolled over in bed. My heart was beating so hard I could hear my pulse in my ears. When I finally began to calm down and drift off, the roar of my pulse became the sound of rolling ocean waves.

August 23, AD 35

As the tide rolls in and out, I turn my face to the sun. This is how I like to begin the day. I breathe in deeply and I open my palms to receive what the universe has to offer me. I'm not sure of the cause, but the result is as sure as the sun rising in the east. The energy, which lies outside of me, begins to fill my body through my fingertips, and when it reaches my mind, I begin to know things that are beyond mere human understanding. I feel the power pulsing in my veins and begin the rituals to harness it ... when I realize, today is my day to rest. So I let myself become the tide, flowing in and out, and the rhythm rocks me to sleep.

August 24, 2010

I rolled over to turn on my computer, first to make sure I hadn't been dreaming about the e-mail, and second, to save Will in my address book. *What a great surprise*, I thought as I closed my laptop and got ready for class.

My 7:30 physics class was in a large auditorium, and while I had the option of doing it online, I truly enjoyed the energy of being with other, like-minded students.

After I got situated in my seat, I looked down toward the podium to check out the grad assistant who was supposed to be doing the tutoring. That's when I noticed Gilbert sitting on the stage. Well, he *had* said he was in quantum physics. The poor guy was fidgeting with his folding chair, trying to figure out what to do with his hands. It actually looked like he'd made an attempt to get a comb through his hair, although I think he failed.

I left class a few minutes early and ran down the stairs to see if I could catch up with Gilbert before he got away. When I rounded the last corner I saw him exiting the auditorium. "Hey, Gilbert," I yelled, a little louder than necessary. Everyone in the hall turned to look at me. This was the first time I had seen him standing, and he was probably only five foot four.

Gilbert turned around on tippy-toes to see over the crowd of students exiting the class, and smiled when he caught sight of me. "Hi, Hils," he called back, and motioned for me to work my way through the crowd.

"Gilbert, I'm in your class," I said when I'd reached him.

"It's great to see you again so soon." He lowered his voice and continued, "But actually Hillary, here you should call me Mr. Dutton."

"Well, Mr. Dutton, I am wondering which night your study group meets, and if I can attend?"

"I'd love that, Hils, but I don't have a schedule. My groups are mostly on request out of desperation the night before an exam. My office number is posted on the board." He pointed to the list and sure enough, there was his name. "It's my cell number. I have a hard time spending a lot of time stuck in that cubicle they call an office when I can be in the sun. I think more clearly outside.

"Call me any time, or just come find me. I'm usually sitting on a bench outside the Union. I can always count on getting a cup of old, bitter coffee from the cafeteria. It's an acquired taste," he added, lifting one side of that uni-brow. "If you don't mind being tutored there, you can drop by anytime. It's as good as anywhere, as long as the weather holds out."

The bells chimed in the tower.

"I've got to get to my next class now," I said, "but I'll call you as soon as I need help. Thanks."

"See you around, Hils." Gilbert turned on his heels and headed in the opposite direction, quickly disappearing into the crowd.

I sat through my next class not paying much attention to the instructor. My mind found its way back to Will and the letter I had been composing in my mind, and within moments I was back in that carriage house looking into those beautiful blue eyes. When class was over, I looked for a place to sit down in the sunshine. I made it as far as the first bench outside the front door of Becker Hall, opened my laptop, and began typing before I either forgot what I wanted to say or chickened out completely.

Dear Will,

Yes, I do refer to myself as Chelsea, although I would not have if I'd known our night would be cut short without time for a more formal goodbye. My given name is Hillary Rubner, and I would be delighted to receive a lengthy letter from you at your earliest convenience.

Please let George know I have attached Ruth's email address.

Awaiting your reply,
Hillary
P.S. How did you find me?

I instantly began going over things and second-guessing myself. After all, what did I know about him? Zero! And that was the honest truth. I thought about everything that had happened that evening, and he remained a bit of a mystery. I closed my eyes, took a deep breath, and clicked *send* ... and it was gone before I could change my mind.

I started checking my e-mail every chance I got, like a crazy woman, but there was no reply. I checked it first thing in the morning and again before I left for class. I checked a half a dozen more times before 3:00, and finally decided I should try to get hold of myself. I headed toward work and tried to put Will out of my mind for a while.

"Hello, Anne Marie. Do you have a list for me today?"

"Sure do, Hillary. It's right here. We have more requests from Dr. Edwards. His list gets longer every week. Hope you don't mind, but they're all in the same area of the library as last time," and she slid the packet toward me.

"I like looking through those old dusty books," I said, pretending to cough. Anne Marie laughed and I was off on another afternoon scavenger hunt.

As I walked up the stairs, I began putting together an imaginary picture of Dr. Edwards. It provided entertainment, and the picture got a little more defined the deeper I dove into his research subject matter. I thought of him as an elderly man, probably because of the old books he requested. *I hope he smells better than some of these antique books*, I thought as I picked up another one that was musty and slightly mildewed. I imagined him to be small in stature, with a grey mustache that curled up at the ends, a bit disheveled on the outside, but with a brilliant mind. His office had no light other than the one on his desk, and his books and papers were like walls around him, stacked from floor to ceiling on every surface available. When he left his office in the evenings, he always covered his bald spot with a fedora. That last part might have been a little over the top, but I had plenty of time on my hands to daydream as I walked around the library. "Well, Dr. Edwards, what will you teach me about today?"

I read the request form, pulled the book from the shelf, and just let it fall open. I had acquired a habit of reading a few pages from each book I pulled for him. It was food for the imaginary game I played with myself.

Vicki Renfro

In our action-oriented society, when a man lies down to sleep, he is effectively out of the picture. He will lie still for six to eight hours, not behaving, thinking productively, or doing anything significant. We all know people dream, but raise our children to regard dreams as not real, unimportant. Thus most people are in the habit of forgetting their dreams, and on occasions when they remember them, they usually regard them as mere oddities.

What are we to make of a person who takes exception to this general belief, who claims to have experiences during sleep or other forms of unconsciousness that are not only impressive to him, but which he feels are real?

My mind drifted back to the dreams I so often had, and I realized that they were of the *feels real* type. Intrigued, I gingerly held the book in front of me and let it fall open again.

His unequivocal knowledge will change his position relative to nature and the universe. He will know death is not final, but a passing from one body into another. He will understand how this is possible, and that there are an infinite number of variations in the spectrum. He will then realize what the dreams have been trying to tell him all along.

I read on for a while, trying to digest the information, and wondered if my dreams were giving me insight into past incarnations. I wanted to talk to Dr. Edwards in the worst way because based on his research about reincarnation, my guess was that he was an expert.

I found the elevator that took me to the second floor. It was getting late, and it was time for me to head home. With only one more book to find, I exited the elevator trying to recall my dreams.

It was a pleasant surprise to find Ruth busily cooking a fragrant meal from her little cookbook.

"Let me guess," I said, sniffing the air and tossing my backpack onto the couch. "Tuna casserole."

"Probably, but that's not what they call it in my book. We would never have anything called *casserole* at my house, and if it was actually a casserole, the staff always called it something French." Laughing, she pulled a tuna casserole from the oven.

"Hey, Hillary, did you send that e-mail to the boys?" Ruth asked casually as she walked through the kitchen door holding the dish with her hot-mitts.

"'The boys!' Is that what we're calling them? And yes, I did."

A gush of excitement came bursting forth from Ruth, and she ran to the table with the casserole dish out in front of her. As she tossed it on the table, she almost screamed.

"Well don't keep me in the dark! I've been dying to know what you decided to say!"

"Well, I hate to disappoint you, but there's not much to tell. I'll let you read the e-mail I sent if you promise not to give me grief. It's the best I could do. And last time I checked, I didn't have a reply."

"Well, get your laptop over here," she ordered. "We can do this while we eat."

I was not looking forward to tuna on my keyboard, but Ruth was out of control.

"Okay, okay! Calm down," I said as I turned on my computer.

"We have to get a faster connection," she said tapping her fingers on the tabletop. "Open, open, open!"

Once I opened my mail, I clicked on the letter I had sent to Will. Ruth turned the screen to face her and read it out loud with her mouth half full.

"Don't talk, Ruth. Didn't your parents teach you manners? Swallow that first."

She chewed in a frenzy and swallowed hard. "You gave George my e-mail address! I've got to check my computer!" she exclaimed, running off to her room. She returned with the laptop balanced in one hand, and turned it on with her other hand.

"Sit down, before you sprain something." I moved her plate swiftly out of her way.

"I've got mail!" Ruth clicked on her inbox, and her face fell. "I've got mail from my mom. Damn it anyway."

"Oh, give it a while. Maybe they haven't even seen each other yet. The only thing we know for sure is that somewhere out there in cyberspace, there is an e-mail I sent to Will. Maybe it hasn't even been opened yet."

I was being as cheery as I could for Ruth's benefit. I guessed she liked George more than she had let on. We finished dinner with both computers keeping us company, open and ready for e-mail, but by bedtime nothing had happened.

"Sorry Ruth," I yawned. "I've got to get some sleep, and I still have some work to do on a paper. I'll see you in the morning."

"Okay, I'll do the dishes," Ruth said. "I'm not tired yet." She swept her computer up and walked into the kitchen. I picked up mine and headed for my room.

CHAPTER ELEVEN

I LOVE being in bed *alarm free*, under a pile of covers and sleeping until I wake up naturally. Tomorrow was Saturday, and unless something changed drastically between bedtime and 8:00 a.m., my big plan was to sleep in and dream to my heart's content. I'd been a lucid dreamer for as long as I could remember, but without much ability to remember them. But since I'd discovered *the mystic messages from the books*, I intended to pay more attention.

Excited about my otherworldly adventures, I slid my computer off my lap, fell back on my pillows, pulled my covers up around my chin, and bade the world good bye.

September 23, AD 35

My dear mare is sleek with sweat and I can hear her pant as I lean forward, low over her neck, forcing her to run faster. Together we rarely lose a race. And today in particular, we will not lose to Liam. Liam is my best lifelong companion, and I am out to prove to him that I am the better horseman. Pulling ahead, I slowly turn to smile at Liam, watching his hair blow back from those amazing blue eyes, and hear ...

September 24, 2010

"You've got mail!"

I was reluctant to wake from my dream, but decided to roll over anyway. Through one open eye, I looked at the time. It was 4:00 a.m.!

I considered closing my eyes and returning to my mare. She needed to be rubbed down, and I still needed to gloat over winning the race. I was not ready to leave the boy, my best friend … what was his name? As I tried to remember his face, the dream faded quickly, and I was unable to hold on to it.

As I re-entered this world, I remembered what had woken me up. *Damn it, this better be good!* I shook myself awake and pulled my computer onto my lap.

This was actually great! The e-mail was from Will, and the subject line read, "My reply to follow."

I threw off the covers, pulled down the old t-shirt I was sleeping in, and gathered my computer to go find Ruth. I almost ran headlong into her and her computer as I opened my bedroom door.

"Hillary, I got an e-mail and I'm afraid to open it!" Ruth blurted.

"No, you're not!" I said. "You've just been spending too much time in those drama classes of yours! Besides, I've got one, too."

We both began jumping up and down like we were on a bed of hot coals.

"Who first? You or me? Let's flip!" Ruth blabbered, totally out of control.

"Do you have a coin in those pajamas of yours, Ruth?" I asked.

Believe it or not, she did. I was totally surprised by the fact that her pajamas had pockets. I mean really, what for? Beyond the occasional coin toss?

"Heads, I go first," Ruth said as the coin flew into the air. "Damn, it hit the floor."

I watched it roll under the coffee table and knew instantly this was going to turn into a long ordeal.

"Don't do anything, Hillary! Let me see if it's heads or tails." Ruth was down on all fours, trying to see the coin in the dark.

I flipped on the light and Ruth said, "It's tails. How could that be? Statistically it should be heads, shouldn't it?" she asked, looking up at me.

"Get up, Ruth. You're wasting time. I'm opening my e-mail."

"No, wait for me!" she cried as she scrambled to her feet and raced to sit beside me.

"For heaven's sake, don't make me hit delete by accident. Let go of my arm!"

She dramatically locked her arms to her side as I clicked the e-mail.

Dear Hillary Rubner,
You are cordially invited to attend the Fall Mixer
"Under the Full Moon Celebration"
With William Emerald
September 30
Location: the Campus Commons
11:00 PM
Please RSVP
Lengthy explanation to appear in person
Sincerely Yours,
William "Will" Emerald

I saw Ruth's hand move, and then I heard a click.

"We'd better be going to this party together," Ruth said as her e-mail opened. "Wait for it … YES!"

Dear Ruth Witherspoon,
You are cordially invited to attend the Fall Mixer
"Under the Full Moon Celebration"
With George Elliot
September 30
Location: the Campus Commons
11:00 PM
Please RSVP
Sincerely Yours,
George Elliot II

"Cool. What does one wear to a full moon celebration? Ruth, are you listening?"

"Nope, I'm composing an RSVP."

"Are you going to send it now?" I asked in frustration. "They'll know we were up at 4:00 a.m. reading their e-mails. Do you really want them to know how geeky we are?"

"Oh Hillary, they're going to find out soon enough," she said as she hit send. "I don't want George Elliot the Second to get another date."

"Sweet dreams Ruth. I'm waiting until morning." I escaped back into my bedroom and floated off to sleep, hoping to return to my dream.

I slept until the smell of coffee drifted into my dreams.

"Okay, okay, I give!" I yelled as I made myself vertical.

"Get out here and drink this coffee before it gets cold. I've got a salt bagel with butter for you. I'm waiting."

Imitating a zombie, I opened the door and walked slowly toward my coffee cup.

"Oh, cut it out Hillary. You've slept ten hours. Get in here and write your RSVP. They'll probably wait for both answers before they e-mail us again."

"Okay Ruth, let me wake up and get my thoughts straight first."

She went into my room and walked out with my laptop. "Here you go," she said, setting it down by my bagel. "I've turned it on for you."

"This might take me some time to write. Stop breathing on me. Go sit down and I'll let you read it before I send it. Shhhhh." I pulled the computer toward me and stared at the screen.

It took me one hour and three cups of coffee to type nineteen words.

Will Emerald,
I gladly accept your invitation. Please advise me of the
location of the meeting.
Yours truly,
Hillary

"Ruth get in here, I'm going to send it. And I don't want any crap about how long it's taken me to write this!"

Ruth read it over my shoulder and laughed.

"Shut up, Ruth! This was all I could think of to write."

"That's the same thing I e-mailed to George last night, and it took me thirty seconds to come up with it." Ruth shook her head as if to imply that I was simple.

"I think we should walk over to the Commons today and scope it out. No one will be there on Saturday." Her tone changed when she saw me roll my eyes. "Seriously, Hillary. This way we'll know which way to make our grand entrance for the biggest effect. The thirtieth is next weekend."

"Okay, but I need a shower first." I took my coffee into the bathroom and set it on the counter. The hot water ran over my head for a good ten minutes until it turned cold. If Ruth wanted a shower she'd have to wait twenty minutes for the water to heat up again. I dressed and went out on our little deck to let the sun dry my hair.

The day was a clear and sunny one. The sky was an intense blue without a cloud in sight. Squirrels were chattering at the top of their little lungs, totally pissed off that I dared invade their territory. The robins hadn't started their flight south yet, which meant mild weather would be around for a while longer. Then, I heard a familiar bird song, or rather a squawk. I leaned forward and searched the trees until I spotted him. On the topmost branch of the tree in the neighbor's yard was a big black crow.

"Hey there, buddy. Do I know you?" He flew to a tree that was closer to me and cocked his head. "Are you Gus? Did Mom send you to find me?" He just cawed and flew away. Over the summer I had become fascinated with Mom's crow, and I absolutely believed it was within Mom's talents to turn her crow into a carrier pigeon.

I pulled my hair back into a ponytail. "Come on Ruth. I'm ready to go," I yelled as I walked back into the apartment. Ruth was waiting at the front door, keys in hand.

The University Commons was about a one-mile walk from our house, on the other side of the Union parking lot. It was a large and inviting open park area accented by a bell tower. By the time we got there the bells were ringing 2:00 p.m. Ruth had thought ahead and brought a blanket so we could lie under one of the old oak trees.

"Hillary?"

"Yes, Ruth?" I answered, lying back on my backpack pillow.

"Do you think they are as dreamy as we remember?"

"Hope so. Don't you?"

"Yes."

"We only have a week to wait—that is if they e-mail us back."

Ruth sat up. "I hope they're both great. Then we can double date. Have a double wedding."

"Don't get ahead of yourself," I laughed. It was just like her to take this to the extreme. "We are already double dating. They seem to come as a pair."

Ruth got up to take a walk around, and by the time I caught up with her, she was reading the Full Moon Celebration poster that was taped to the lamppost. "Look at this," she said, pointing at the poster. "It's going to be a pagan thing. I love pagan."

Reading it over her shoulder because of the four inches I had on Ruth, I felt my mood darken and my skin crawl with déjà vu. Across the open space, not twenty yards from us, I noticed the man from the Student Union sitting down on a park bench and waving.

"Don't look now, but when we go back to pick up our things, tell me if you recognize the guy on the bench."

"Are we leaving already?" Ruth whined as we walked to our blanket. "Am I supposed to know him?"

"No, I've just seen him around campus and something about him seems off. It's no big deal. I just get a creepy feeling … like I know him, and I wonder if maybe I recognize him from Kansas City or something."

Ruth turned as nonchalantly as a drama major could, letting the breeze blow her hair away from her face. Leaning down to pick up her backpack, she agreed that he was seriously creepy. "It's like he sucks the wind out of your sails. Come on, let's get out of here."

Once we cleared the parking structure, our moods lightened and Ruth said, "What were we talking about?"

"What normal people will be wearing to the mixer. If I see Gilbert, I'll ask him. Or maybe I'll ask around the library. I really don't want to be dressed like Goddess Hera if everyone else is in jeans."

CHAPTER
TWELVE

"WHAT ARE Will and George doing?" Ruth said in a huff. "Are they trying to worry us sick or just dump us? It's Tuesday and we don't have a place to meet them yet. Do you think we're going to hear from them again?"

"Yes," I said, not knowing if I really believed it myself. "They're probably busy. I'm sure they feel like there's plenty of time. Saturday is still a long way away. I'm planning on going to the mixer whether we hear from Will and George or not. Life goes on, Ruth. Don't get your panties in a twist over a couple of guys we don't really know. There will be hundreds of other people there."

The whole town was crazy with the upcoming celebration. All the off-campus stores were looking for a way to join in and make a buck. There were sidewalk sales with clothing, food, and all kinds of trinkets. It seemed like the new-age store had their entire stock out on the street.

"Come on, Ruth," I said. "Stop pouting. Let's get a soda and go shop." Shopping always cheered her up, and my first paycheck was burning a hole in my pocket.

At dusk, the old-style lampposts lining Manhattan Avenue began to light. It seemed like the restaurants were purposely blowing the smell of their food out onto the sidewalks to make us hungry. We both got a piece of pizza to go and walked up and down the streets, looking at everything.

"What's this?" I asked Ruth, a string of wooden beads hanging from my hand. "They come in different sizes."

"I don't think you want to know," she said as she looked up to check out the store's name.

My eyes followed hers to a sign adorned with a half-clad female that read, *Toys for all Reasons.*

"Yuck!" I dropped them back into the fur-lined box and wiped my hands with my napkin.

"I don't think, as a virgin, you're ready for those yet," Ruth said. "But maybe some cute pajamas. Do you want to look?"

"No, let's go," I blushed and hurried off to the next booth. "Hey Ruth, look at this." I wanted to hurry her along. "It's an astrology place. Have you ever had any of this done?"

"Yeah, my sister and I love this stuff. Do you know what time of day you were born?"

"No, why would I need to know that?" I asked.

"Why don't you e-mail your mom and have her send you a copy of your birth certificate. We can come back another day for a star chart, but for now this looks interesting." Ruth picked up a box of cards. "I kept a box of cards similar to these under my bed at boarding school. We used to do readings for each other after lights out. It's always better by candlelight."

She handed me a box of Goddess Oracle Cards to check out, and as I read the instructions, she handed another box to the clerk.

"What scents do you like?" she asked, sniffing each candle one by one.

"You pick. You're the one who knows what you're doing."

Ruth settled on a spicy scent, along with a stick of sage, and gave them to the clerk to ring up.

"We might need to smudge the house before we do this. No telling what spirits are still hangin' around an old house like ours!" With Oracle cards in hand, Ruth seemed to cheer up a bit. "Let's get home and I'll give you a reading!"

We didn't even need the porch light to see the keyhole in our door lock. The front of our house was brightly lit by the approaching full moon. I flipped on the lights and headed toward the kitchen to put on a pot of coffee.

"Not coffee, Hillary, tea," Ruth ordered. "The bags are in the second drawer."

Ruth's mom (or staff) had sent her back to school with a fully stocked kitchen. Who knew we had tea? I opened the drawer and found it stuffed with exotic looking boxes.

"What kind should I make?" I asked.

"Hmmmm. I'm thinking gunpowder green tea, with a splash of the coca that was grown in Machu Picchu for the high priests. That's a good combo for tonight. See if you can find a bowl for the sage ... and bring the salt shaker, too."

"Next thing you're going to say is that you have a Ouija board," I said jokingly.

"Not with me. It's at home in Kansas City. Bring that stuff over here and let's get started." Ruth lit the smudge stick and started to walk from room to room, waving it and shaking the ashes into the bowl. "Bring the salt, Hillary. You need to shake a little in the outside corners of the rooms."

"Ruth, you're going to get us in so much trouble. The sage smoke smells just like pot!"

"If the cops come, I'll do a reading for them, too," she said, mumbling some kind of chant under her breath.

"Where did you learn all of this stuff?" I asked.

"Quiet. I'll tell you in a minute." We made one circle around each room, opened the closets and shower curtain for a quick wave of sage, and ended at the dining room table.

"Thanks Ruth. Now all of my clothes smell like pot. I don't think a ghost was hiding in my closet."

She ignored my comment and ordered me to get the tea while she set up the candles and cards. When I returned with our steaming mugs, the cards were in a stack on the table with a crystal sitting on top.

"Where'd that crystal come from?" I asked.

Ruth shrugged. "Everyone has a crystal or two lying around, don't they?"

"I don't," I said, and then remembered: "My mom has a few in her jewelry box at home, but I don't think they have anything to do with card readings."

"Maybe ... after she put you to bed when you were a kid, she snuck out behind the chicken coop to dance around the Maypole with all the other pagan farmer wives ... always keeping the crystals in her pockets to gather goddess energy!"

Ruth's visuals always cracked me up. "How do you know so much? Are you a pagan?"

"No, I'm a Catholic. Haven't I ever told you about the boarding school I went to?"

"Are you still a virgin?" It was out of my mouth before I could stop myself.

Ruth looked straight into my eyes and said, "Not as much as you are. I haven't gone all the way, but I've played on the fringes."

"I didn't realize virginity came in degrees. I thought it was either yes or no," I said as we both began to laugh. "Just deal the cards."

"You're right handed, so hold the deck of cards in your left," Ruth instructed. "That's your *receiving* side. It will take a couple of minutes for your energy to permeate the cards. You can drink your tea while I light the candle and turn out the lights."

"The candle smells great," I said as I strained my eyes to read the small print, "but the room's a little dark. Will you be able to see the cards? I think we need to turn on the kitchen light or something."

Suddenly, the room was filled with a weird, bluish glow. "I think this will work better. It's a little less direct." Ruth had turned on our computers and put them in opposite corners of the living room.

"Is this supposed to be spooky or enlightening?" I asked, truly not knowing what Ruth would do next.

"Uplifting and informative! We'll get better lighting next time, but for now this will have to do."

"Now, tap your right knuckles on the top of the deck to clear all the old energy out. Really Hillary, just do it. I had Angel Cards at school, but I figure this deck works the same way."

I followed her instructions.

"Now, shuffle the cards and ask a question at the same time. Stop whenever you feel you are finished."

"Well great, you should have told me earlier that I had to come up with a question," I said as I finished shuffling. "What kind of question do I ask?"

"Ask anything. I know what I'd ask ... wink, wink."

"You'll be relentless if I don't. I'll ask about Will, but what?"

"Let's see," Ruth said as she tapped her nails on her teacup. "Let's ask how Will feels about you!"

76

"Okay, but I'm not sure I like this. I feel a little bit like a stalker." I wondered what right I had poking around in Will's head. "Let's get going, Ruth, before I change my mind."

"Put three cards on the table, side by side, and then tell me what the one on the left says. It's what Will is feeling right now." I turned them over and Ruth picked up the handbook, ready to reveal its meaning.

It didn't look good for Will's masculinity when his first card was The Butterfly Maiden. At the bottom it said, *you are experiencing enormous changes right now*. "Is this card supposed to be me or Will?"

"It's Will. Just picture The Butterfly Maiden with blue eyes and wearing pants." Ruth began to read from the little handbook.

"As you go through this period of change, it's normal for you to wonder if the future is safe. To bring in your desired newness, you must first allow old parts of your life to fall away."

"Will's ready for a change. Let's see from what. What's the middle card?" Ruth glanced down to see what the card was. "This one is Will's current situation."

I picked it up before Ruth could get her hands on it. It was a pink card decorated with young girls. "Oh, this should be interesting," I said as I read what was on the bottom. "*You are good at helping, counseling, and healing children.*"

Ruth thumbed to the proper page and announced:

"One can be gentle and a fierce protector simultaneously. Your vigilant focus on keeping harmony within the household stems from your desire for children to maintain their youthful awe and sense of wonder."

"Don't get worried yet, Hillary," Ruth said with a snicker. "Will might still end up having some testosterone. The card on the right is the future outcome. Let's see what he decides to do about his babysitting job." I took a playful swipe at her. "Come on Hillary, what's the last card?"

The card had a bluish girl on it with her finger up to her lips.

"Take some quiet time alone to rest, meditate, and contemplate."

"Oh … Will is just a wild man," Ruth said as she found the correct page.

"Shhhhh, dear one. Go into that space of silence deep within you. Now is the time to retreat into silence and spend time alone. Do not try to make any decisions now. Just allow your mind to rest and re-center. You'll know soon enough when it's time to take action."

"Well, now I know why he hasn't called," I said as I looked up at Ruth with a big smile on my face. "I hope he's re-centered and ready to take action by Saturday or I'm stood up."

Ruth picked up the cards and held them in her left hand.

"Let's see if George is going to be a good or bad influence on poor, sensitive Will. If Will is looking for a change, maybe George can facilitate it for him."

I rolled my eyes at Ruth. "I'll warm up the water for more tea." I headed to the kitchen and noticed that it was already after midnight, and I was beginning to feel sleepy.

When I returned with the teakettle, Ruth already had the cards laid out and was reading from the handbook.

"Look at this, Hillary. The night I met George, he was *honoring the cycles of his body, energy levels, and emotions.* Now, *he's stronger than he thinks and his strength ensures a happy outcome.* And Saturday night he's going to *be honest with himself and his heart's true desire!* I'd say George is going to be a very, very bad influence on softhearted Will!"

"Well, let's hope that George and his *desire* can get gentle Will to the party. Maybe the full moon can bring out Will's wild side."

Ruth laughed at me and said, "I think the Goddess has matched us correctly. I do deserve the wilder one."

"And the shorter one," I added.

CHAPTER
THIRTEEN

SEPT 19, 35 A.D.

Tall, broad-chested Liam looks like a powerful Druid warrior, but he is not. He spends his days totally involved in the teaching of children, oblivious to the world around him. Without his full attention, these young adepts might never be able to unleash the full potential within them. Liam encourages their innocent, pliable minds to follow him into other dimensions by letting them hitch a ride into the heavens on his life force. Once there, they play in this magical world, bringing back with them to the Earth plane supernatural talents not known to mere mortals. The powers are first felt as a vibration, but as the children learn to trust themselves, they manifest according to each child's desire.

During the hours their souls take flight, the young students' bodies sit limply next to Liam's, in the silence of the temple. There is only one person Liam trusts with the monumental responsibility of guarding these helpless children—his lifelong friend, Georog. Battle-scared and a giant among men, Georog has a ferocious love and loyalty for his fellow Druids and would happily lay down his life in defense of his brethren.

September 19, 2010

I was sound asleep when I heard it … or thought I heard it. I tossed off my covers, walked to the living room, and switched on the lights. Ruth was madly running between computers, trying to figure out which was hers.

"Yours is over here, Ruth, and it looks like you have mail." We had forgotten to shut our computers down when we stumbled off to bed.

"Here's yours, Hillary, and you've got mail too! Who should open first?"

"Like I have a choice. You go first. You look like you're going to have an apoplexy."

She opened New Mail and clicked.

I will wait on the South side of The Bell Tower
11:00 pm September 30th
Under the full Moon
George

"What's yours say, Hillary?'

"The same as yours, but without the full moon thing."

"Oh George, you *are* a little wilder than Will," Ruth said with satisfaction. "Get your party on, Hillary." She danced off to bed.

The rest of the week passed rather unremarkably. I talked to other employees at the library, and they seemed neutral about attending the Fall Mixer.

Ruth, on the other hand, had a group of friends who were going fully dressed—or undressed—for the occasion. Ruth's friends viewed the Fall Mixer as a full-on costume party, and were attending in pagan garb. I planned on finding the happy medium between the two groups.

We painted our toenails Saturday morning. After all, we were wearing sandals, and while I'd feel funny with the same color on my fingernails, I love dark polish on my toes. This took most of the morning—painting, drying, and repainting.

Later we visited the cosmetics section of the drug store.

"Okay Hillary," Ruth said, motioning me toward the hair product aisle. "Your hair needs some fullness. This'll work."

Willing to take Ruth's advice, I read the label of the bottle she handed me, "'*Sex It Up.*' Just hilarious, Ruth."

"No joke, it's really good. You'll like it."

My two-item bag didn't compare to Ruth's very large bag, and as if she weren't loaded down enough, she insisted on one more stop—the bath shop.

"This is a make-or-break deal," Ruth explained as we both picked out a scent before heading home. "We need a body mist, not perfume."

Figuring we needed a nap so we'd be able to stay up until 1:00 or 2:00 a.m., we set our alarms to wake us in two hours … but neither one of us could sleep. Instead, we decided to go out for Italian food and strong espressos. I had a double shot, but Ruth was already so wired I tried to steer her toward water.

"You know we have to set up some rules, Hillary," Ruth proposed.

"Rules! Like putting a sock on the door handle?" I laughed.

"Nooooo," she said, drawing it out for effect. "You know last time …" I nodded my head *yes*. "We got home and didn't know a thing about George and Will. This time we have to ask some questions. I'd at least like to know enough to look them up online."

"Have you tried searching them already?" I asked with a sneaking suspicion.

"Yes, and I can't find anything. I need to know where they're from, maybe their high school, something traceable."

"Wow, I thought the Tarot cards were invasive! You did a search?"

"Yes, my sister and I started checking on people as soon as we learned how to get online. It's fun."

"I'm not ready to do a full interrogation, just a little small talk."

"Okay," Ruth said grudgingly. "Let's get the dinner bill and head home."

"I'm nervous," I admitted as we walked slowly back to our apartment. "Are you?"

"You really have to ask? You can't see me shaking?" Ruth said as she unlocked the door. "I have a lot of guy *friends,* which is how most of my dates end. I hope George doesn't want to just be friends."

"I guess we won't know anything for another few hours. Let's leave early, so we can walk across campus and back toward the tower. I want to make sure they are at the tower before us." By now I could tell nothing was going to relax Ruth.

It wasn't long before I was slipping my red party toes into my sandals and locking the door behind us. We had talked about everything twice, so it was a silent walk to campus. We could see the smoke from the bonfire through the trees as we walked toward The Commons. It wasn't what we would call a bonfire down on the farm, but it would pass for one tonight.

Ruth and I skirted the crowd. Some of the students looked as if they had been here all day, and it was looking a bit like Woodstock. The full moon was definitely having an effect. We were meeting Will and George another block to the east, so we slowed our pace, knowing that we would soon intersect the sidewalk directly in front of the bell tower. We finally reached the point of no return and turned down the walk toward the tower as the bells rang eleven times. By the moonlight we could see two figures standing by the stairs. They walked up to meet us, their smiles brilliant.

CHAPTER FOURTEEN

"WHAT DO you prefer?" Will asked, stopping directly in front of me and looking into my eyes. "Do you like Hillary or Chelsea?"

"It usually depends on my mood, but tonight I think it's better that I'm Hillary." I was a little embarrassed that I hadn't been truthful about my name the first night we met.

"Okay, *Hillary* … would you like to sit?" He motioned to a moonlit park bench just outside a ring of students. It looked very romantic, but my mind and body were far too revved up with the excitement of seeing Will again to sit still. I smiled inwardly as I began to feel the same humming sensation in my body that I'd felt in the carriage house, and I now knew it was related to my proximity to Will.

"I think I'd like to walk for a bit."

During the first few uncomfortable moments, we strolled silently through groups of students who were obviously eager for the midnight show to begin. We found an open space to stand about twenty feet from the stage, and as the silence between us began to grow to a deafening roar, the floodlights dimmed and the lights came up on the stage. The dancers were astonishingly talented, so I tried to concentrate on the show, but I found myself worrying about what I was going to say when the music was over.

At intermission, the student body erupted into applause as the stagehands moved the old sets off stage Dand the new ones on. This gave us time to become more comfortable with one another, but now came the hardest part—talking.

"What have you been up to?" I asked, knowing how lame it

sounded.

"I did promise you an explanation. Would you like me to answer your questions, or do you want me to start where we left off the last time we were together?" Will's voice was just loud enough for me to hear over the crowd.

"You can just start. I'll let you know if I have a question."

Will looked up at the moon and seemed to gather his thoughts.

"George and I live in a fraternity house with our brothers. We just aren't affiliated with the university. We're a fraternity dedicated to the study of *knowledge* instead of *learning*." He paused to look for my expression, and I motioned for him to continue.

"Last spring George and I stepped outside the boundaries set by what we'll call our *fraternity*, and found we really enjoyed ourselves." He seemed to smile to himself. "Our home is not a seminary," he said, as if reading my mind. "We've just chosen to remain hidden from the rest of the world."

I could tell he was trying to pick his words carefully, so I remained quiet while he gathered his next thought.

"George and I have been going out at night, *literally* going over the wall after everyone in our house is asleep. We started by walking the alleys around our neighborhood about a year ago. It's amazing what people throw away these days; perfectly good stuff. That's when we found the computer that our neighbors left by their trashcan. Computers are a technology we don't have inside our household because they are a distraction that pulls you away from discovery of self, but I must admit that we were excited to find one so easily.

"It took us a while to figure out how to use it, and one night the most amazing thing happened. We discovered if we sat close to the house next door, the computer would connect to the World Wide Web. We began by typing in subjects we'd like to know more about, and eventually we got to be more proficient. We keep our computer hidden in a protected area near our house, but not near enough to be discovered by McCollum.

"It took a while longer for us to figure out we could actually use the computer to look for you and Ruth. We didn't have much to go on. As it turned out, I didn't even have your real name." He winked to ease my guilt. "We found a number of girls named Chelsea, but none were you. It was a fluke we found you at all. George was the one who came up with the idea of looking for a Hillary after it came to him in a meditation.

"Two weeks ago we saw the Fall Mixer poster on one of our midnight walks and thought it would be a nice place for a reunion with you and Ruth. Yours was the first e-mail we've ever received on our computer. Please believe me when I say that we're really not uneducated; just impaired technologically." He laughed softly, and the sound of his laughter made me break out in goose bumps.

"Is that why we always get our e-mails from you in the middle of the night? Because you and George have jumped the wall?"

"Yep, we've broken out, so to speak."

"Are you over the wall tonight?"

"Yep, we're over the wall tonight, too." I could see mischief in his deep, blue eyes. "It's not that we can't leave. It's just better that we set a good example for the younger boys. It's important that our actions don't interrupt their studies. This journey is meant for George and me alone."

As the second half of the show began, Will said, "Come on, let's walk for a while." We turned, and he took my hand to guide me through the crowd. "It will give you a chance to think and decide if you'd like to see me again."

We walked to where two sidewalks intersected and took the one that headed away from the crowd, weaving through small groups of students along the way.

"I met my teacher many years ago. I was only nine. From the first time I laid eyes on him, I felt like I was home, like I had always known him, but from where … I could never quite remember. When I was ten, my parents sent me to study with McCollum. It was the only thing I'd ever wanted to do. At first I visited my parents between terms, but as my studies required more and more of my time, my visits became less frequent. Now this is my home, and it's been years since I've seen my parents face to face. We write and love each other, but they know my life has taken a different path."

I wondered how that could possibly happen, because I couldn't think of any circumstance that could keep me from visiting home. But then his next sentence was the beginning of an explanation.

"I guess you could call our house a monastery, but that's not exactly correct either. We're not monks.

"George was already there when I arrived, and we've been friends since the first time we laid eyes on each other. Over the years I learned that he is much more than a friend, although it is hard to explain." Will took another slow, deliberate breath and turned to face me.

"Imagine you're a college student … that should be easy for you," he said, trying hard to make sure I understood. "You're tired at the end of a long day of classes, so you sit down on the couch in your apartment and gaze out the window at the beautiful sunset. Or maybe you find yourself listening to the hum of the refrigerator. When your roommate walks into the room sometime later, she asks you what you're doing. Your reply might be something like, 'Boy, I must have *zoned-out* for a while,' because you know a lot of time has passed. But you also know that's not exactly correct. You were floating, traveling somewhere beyond the walls of your apartment.

"That's what began happening to me at a very young age. The difference is that I found myself yearning to be in that other peaceful place all the time, so I would let my mind go more and more often. My parents saw it as daydreaming, or maybe even a touch of autism, but neither was the truth. I began to wonder if I were going crazy.

"It went on like that for years, and I kept it to myself because nothing like this was happening to the other kids. I had no one to talk to, no one who could help me understand what was happening to me. My father told me to stop daydreaming, and my mother was quite worried. You see, to most people the world is a finite place. There is a beginning and an end to everything. They build their world around the physical and psychological things they see every day. My world wasn't like that. I lived in other places, too, that were full of infinite possibilities."

As I looked up at Will, his eyes were twinkling as brightly as the stars above him. He was slowly letting me into his world, and I was pleased by the realization. He pulled my arm through his, and we continued our walk … and he continued his story.

"What we do at our house is try to nurture that other place, the place that isn't finite … the part of the mind that is outside the box, the part of us that is willing to accept that the world is more than what it seems. Most who study with McCollum felt like I did as a kid. I mean really, I couldn't go to school and tell the other boys, 'I just came back from a trip to another dimension' or 'I can see things other people can't see.' I would have gotten my ass kicked! Luckily, we all found each other, George, me, and the rest of the boys.

"It's wonderful to see the look on each new boy's face when he realizes that he's not crazy but gifted, and not alone in his experience of life. Do you remember the man who broke up our party last spring? McCollum's our teacher." Will looked embarrassed.

"Oh yes, he leaves quite an impression," I said quietly, not wanting to break his train of thought.

"Do you remember him saying we had boys who couldn't swim?"

I nodded. "That's always puzzled me."

"It's a euphemism. We call the place where everything has always existed—all of it, the past, present, and future—*the River of Knowledge*. When we use these words, it's easier for the younger boys to understand, although the kids coming to study with us today are much more advanced than George and I were at their age. Last year there were thirteen who didn't have the ability to *Swim in The River*. Now there are only three who haven't entered *The River*. McCollum only expects a few more boys to find us in this lifetime.

"Don't be freaked out, Hillary," he said, trying to read my expression. "People tend to incarnate within the same groups, lifetime to lifetime. Your great grandmother may be your daughter someday. Your mom could've been your sister in a past life. We're not special in that way. We just arrange to meet a little more consciously."

"Do you recall your past lives?" I asked. I stopped him in the moonlight, so I could see his face more clearly. For the first time I noticed how quiet it was. We had wandered away from the festivities and were almost to the other side of the campus.

"Yes … parts. Not all … not yet," he stumbled. "I sometimes see my friends as they were in previous lives. Other times I experience only the emotions, that feeling of déjà vu. I remember only the parts of the past that I can bear at the moment because I still have to continue my journey in this life. When we have time I'll tell you more, but not now, if that's okay."

"Of course," I answered, dying to know everything. The more he talked, the more mystical he became. I had heard of regression before, but nothing like this.

We turned and walked in silence back toward the party, because really … my mind was just saying "WOW." I was speechless. Will looked at me sideways as his hair fell forward, and asked in a soft voice, "Well, have you heard enough to make you want to run, yet? Do I sound like I'm a lunatic?"

"No, I think you sound like my dad," I said, squeezing his hand.

We made a full circle around the Commons and back to the bell tower, where we found that Ruth and George had not moved from the spot where we'd left them.

"Well ladies, our pumpkin is about ready to depart," George said, pulling Ruth to her feet. "We need to get home before we're missed, but we have time to walk you home, if you'd like our company."

"I think we'd like that," Ruth answered for both of us, and I agreed with a nod.

"Lead away, ladies." George gave a gallant bow. "We may have found you on the computer, but we don't have any idea where you live."

Ruth and George walked ahead of us while Will and I followed about ten yards behind. Once at our front door, Will stopped me so we could talk alone for just a while longer.

"Well Hillary, do I get a thumbs up or down? I'll respect whatever you decide."

"I'd like to see you again," I started. Before I could add another word, he bent down and brushed his lips against my cheek. He wrapped his arms around me and pulled me close. It took my breath away. I could feel his warm breath as he began to whisper in my ear.

"What would you do, Hillary, if you were certain you were in the presence of your immortal self? How much time would you give to such a Being?"

I held still, trying to comprehend the depth of the question. My immortal self ... it was too big a question. I couldn't think while he was holding me so close, and the humming sensation was returning with vengeance. So I said, "Can I get back to you on that?"

Will laughed at my response, and I felt his breath as a soft burst. "I'd love that."

He kissed my forehead and turned to leave.

"I'll e-mail you soon, Hillary." I watched him walk away in the light of the full moo

Part Two

CHAPTER FIFTEEN

October 1, 2010

It took a while to shake off my dream state as I slowly opened my eyes. The endless rewinding of the same dream disappeared into the background, and I found myself back in my college existence.

Still wearing my ratty old t-shirt and socks, I dragged myself out of bed and walked into the living room.

"Come on Ruth, get up. I need to talk."

Ruth looked at me from the kitchen door.

"I'm up and the coffee's on. You seem grumpy."

"Not grumpy, disoriented. What happened last night?" I asked.

"Are you serious, Hillary? I don't know about you, but I had the best time of my life! I haven't been able to stop thinking about George."

"I slept so deep," I said, sitting down with my head in my hands. "Like I was drugged or something. My dreams were all in slow motion and they kept repeating over and over again. They were some kind of medieval thing with people dying and wizards casting spells."

Ruth handed me a cup of coffee and moved on to the topic in the forefront of her mind. "You ready to compare notes?" she asked.

"Sure, tell me what ya got."

"I've been up for a while with nothing to do, so I decided to see how much info I could get online."

"You did a search for them?" Her expression gave me the answer. "Wow, I'm glad you didn't ask me first. I'd have said 'no way.' But since you didn't ask me, sit down and tell me what you found out. Are they real?"

"Well, let's start with George. I know he's not a New Orleans jazz musician or the George Elliot born in Jasper, Indiana in 1841. And I'm pretty sure he's not the geek with his personal info all over the Internet. I didn't actually open those pages because I don't want that guy to find my contact info," Ruth said with a shudder. "So no, I found nothing concrete on George."

"As far as Will goes, there's an emerald forest, emerald mountains, and Emerald William. I checked that picture out and he's a *she*. Maybe if you can give me a few more details about Mr. William Emerald, we can run a trace. Maybe I should use another search engine. My sister was telling me—"

"Wait a second. This is giving me a headache. Why don't you just start with last night? What did George talk about?" I finished a big cup of black coffee and felt my eyes begin to open as I motioned for Ruth to continue.

"We were right about Will. He is a teacher for the younger boys in their house. George says it's his Dharma. He's always been the teacher. It's his gift, and it has been as far back as McCollum is able to see. I'm pretty sure George was talking about previous lifetimes. He was a little hard to follow sometimes. I'd think he was talking about a few years ago, and then I'd get a feeling he was referring to something a couple lifetimes ago. He would tell me a story about them as kids, and then all of a sudden he would mention a country that doesn't even exist anymore, like Prussia."

"So," Ruth took a deep breath and continued, "if we begin with the premise that George is sane, that leads me to believe that he's known Will for hundreds, maybe thousands of years, and Will has always been the same guy. He's a teacher with a mystical way of opening each child's mind. Whatever ... I got a little lost with a lot of that stuff. The short story is that Will's a real sweet guy."

"What about George? Is he the wild one?" Then I heard my stomach growl. "Ruth, I need something to eat before you get started again."

"Go get dressed, Hillary. We'll go out for some real breakfast."

I slipped on my jeans from the day before, put on the first sweatshirt I came across, and pulled an old ball cap over my unwashed bed-head. I finished off my ensemble with a pair of sunglasses I found stashed in my top drawer. With any luck, no one would recognize me.

Inhaling the fresh air as we walked brought me back to life. I was finally wide awake and was beginning to get my head wrapped around what we were talking about.

We walked into a café and my stomach did a summersault as I ordered a scramble with cheese and an extra, extra-large iced tea. The guy behind the counter raised his eyebrow at my somewhat pale color. I must have looked terrible.

"I believe enormous hydration might be my only rescue," I explained.

"Let's sit at the table in the back corner, Hillary. I don't want anyone to bother us or overhear us talking. People will think we are on drugs or something."

We sat, and I downed half of my tea while Ruth picked up our conversation where we'd left off.

"George told me they've been sneaking out at night for the last year. For eleven years, they've been immersed in their studies at the very house we went to for the Spring Fling party. I think George is a little burned out and is looking for a new adventure. See Hillary, you've got to trust the cards. The cards are always right. George is the wilder one."

I rolled my eyes and then realized the movement was wasted, since Ruth couldn't see through my sunglasses.

"Did George talk about what they study?" I wanted to know Ruth's interpretation without prompting her.

"I get the idea that they are somewhere between Buddhist Monks and Samurai warriors," Ruth said. "It's not that he actually said it. It's just a feeling I have. What did Will have to say?"

"He talked about altered states, how we can slip into them by accident, although I think the people in his household do it on purpose. He calls it *the River of Knowledge*. Then he talked about reincarnation and immortality. I thought he was talking about George and himself, but at the end it seemed like he was saying that I was immortal, too."

"Today I feel immortal," Ruth laughed. "But yesterday I would have said no! As for reincarnation, I've always believed in that. Please, don't tell my very Catholic mom. She'd freak!"

"Will said that he's known George for lifetimes, and they and their fraternity brothers had planned to meet in this lifetime. How does that happen? I've never heard of people remembering that kind of stuff, not without hypnosis or outside of a psychiatric ward! Do you think they're crazy?"

"Look what the cat dragged in," I heard someone say behind me. I was pretty sure the statement was directed at me, because I looked exactly like something the cat had drug in. I turned to see Gilbert gazing down at me.

"Looks like you were at the bonfire a little too late last night, Hils. Were ya drinkin' the firewater? You seem hung over." Gilbert put his coffee cup on our table and pulled up a chair.

"Hi Gilbert. This is Ruth, my roommate. Ruth, this is Mr. Dutton, the teaching assistant in my physics class."

"I couldn't help but overhear your conversation," Gilbert said. He sat down, but never quite sat still. "Sounds like studies of ancient Vedic teachings mixed with quantum physics to me. Who are these guys you ladies were with last night?"

"Don't give me that crap so early in the morning, Gilbert. You *did* mean to overhear us, and what does any of this have to do with quantum physics?" I repositioned my sunglasses. I felt a twinge of guilt about treating one of my professors with such little respect, but he was the one butting into my business.

"A little testy this morning, are we?" Gilbert asked, looking at both of us. "Is it because you didn't get enough sleep, or do you really not understand the relationship between quantum physics and the human journey?"

I lifted my shoulders in a shrug. "Explain it to us, Gilbert," I said, figuring he might be able to shed some light on the subject.

"Where do you want to start? Do you want to know from a scientific or religious point of view?"

Ruth didn't seem to have a preference. She just leaned back in her chair, as if settling in for a professor's lecture.

"Okay, let's start with the religious viewpoint. After all, it is Sunday."

"Which Christ figure should I pick? Buddha? Krishna?" Gilbert mumbled to himself, and finally looked up to engage Ruth and me. "Let's pick Jesus. We all know who he is, right?" Gilbert took a swig of coffee and began.

"Here on Earth, there have been a number of beings who have reached the level of Christ. The one that westerners are most familiar with is Jesus, so let's talk about a few things Jesus said, like, 'the kingdom of heaven is within.' That's a good place to start."

I sarcastically thought, *Maybe we should have picked science.*

"What is the human life? I think it begins when *spirit* enters *density* here on Earth, density being the tactile world, things like touch, smell, hearing, what we see, and a spirit consisting of awareness, sense of self, the ability to experience feelings, to love and be loved."

We both nodded our heads to indicate our understanding, even though I was sure we were both clueless.

"Religions would like us to think that Earth is God's great testing ground to see if we'll be naughty or nice, if we will choose good over evil when given the opportunity. To help us, religion tries to control our behavior with the threat of condemnation. You know, burning in hell for eternity versus hanging out on a cool cloud with benevolent spirits. Now *that's* where the ultimate conspiracy story begins, ladies."

Gilbert leaned forward and lowered his voice for a dramatic effect.

"Let's start with this lifetime. You're born, you grow up, and things seem like they're rolling right along. You know, shit happens, good and bad, but it's largely out of your control. I don't have the right job. I don't have the right body. I don't have the right lover." He nodded his head yes, indicating that this was a foregone conclusion.

"The reality on this earthly plane is that the average person's attention span is six to ten seconds. The human mind is crazy with thoughts twenty-four hours a day. Most people can't stay on the same subject long enough to see anything clearly."

I had to agree with Gilbert. "So what's the point? What are you suggesting?" I asked.

With his fingers steepled to hold up his chin and still his hands, he continued. "You ladies should do what I do—*manifest* your life! Take a few extra minutes when you wake in the morning to figure out what you'd really like to create in your life today ... *consciously*, with deep and intentional thought, rather than blindly accepting that it's out of your control. Don't worry about the coffee being made or what you're going to wear; just think about what you'd like in life. It's similar to planting a seed in a garden. Don't worry about how it will happen. Seeds always sprout. You just have to decide what it is you'd like to grow, plant your dreams firmly in the soil of your mind, and then watch them unfold. If you're attentive and water them every day, you will begin to see miracles. That's how you start ... baby steps.

"Then, as you grow, job opportunities will appear and a cute guy will smile at you from across the room. The most amazing miracle for me was the day I realized that I could be happy by just *making that choice*. People don't believe it. I can tell by the tension in your face, Ruth, that you want to argue right now." Gilbert egged her on with the smug smile on his face, so Ruth let him have it.

"Come on, Gilbert," she said defiantly. "Sometimes bad things happen. You can't just pick happiness."

"Okay," Gilbert said calmly, "let's take an example. What really pisses you off, Ruth? What isn't going your way? What's happening in your life that wouldn't be better if you just *chose* to go with happiness?"

"You're saying I should be happy about losing the lead in my theater production. I'm the best choice, and I got passed over because of politics," she spat.

"Yes, I am saying that. I expected a more thought-provoking example, but let's go with the 'lead in your play' for now. Next time you go to class, make a conscious choice of happiness and watch to see what unfolds. Happiness is really YOUR choice." Gilbert put up his hands to stop Ruth's interruption.

"The most important part of this experiment is to NOT be connected to the outcome. You have to let things unfold in their own way. Don't mess it up by trying to control it. You need to be an observer of what you are creating by making the choice to be happy with whatever transpires."

Gilbert smiled, eyes twinkling, "When you start on this path, all you can see is where you are standing at the moment, but as you become the creator of your life and look back from the mountaintop, you'll understand that it was never about that one place in time. Life is about the whole vista, everything we have planted along the way."

Ruth attempted to argue, but Gilbert cut her off again.

"Get back to me on what happens. You'll be amazed," Gilbert said confidently. "Plant a seed in your garden of self creation when you wake up tomorrow. Next time I see you, we'll talk.

"If it were that easy, everyone would be doing it," Ruth said with conviction.

"It *is* that easy. It just doesn't occur to most people to think about consciously making a *choice* to be happy no matter what the outcome is, let alone to consider making it a lifelong practice. Most people on this plane of existence build their lives around being happy *if* a certain outcome happens. I will be happy *when* I get my next raise, *when* I can buy a bigger house, *when* this hot guy asks me out. Their state of well-being is predicated on specific outcomes that they think will make them happy when they're achieved. It is work to claim control over your life, and even harder to take responsibility for it all. Most people find it easier to blame things on the other guy or bad luck. They don't want to consider that it's their unconscious creation."

"Okay Gilbert," I said. "What does this have to do with Will, George, or Jesus? I think you're getting off the subject."

"It's exactly the same subject at its infancy. These guys are just a lot further down the road. So … let's jump ahead on the evolutionary path. Now that you have become the creator of your life, you're one of the lucky few who view life as more than happenstance. This state is called 'free will.' Doesn't the Bible talk about that?"

He took a sip of coffee.

"The reality is that your moment-to-moment existence is altered by your love of life. Each of us is meant to be successful, happy, and fulfilled. We are already perfect in God's eyes. Our journey in this lifetime is to reintroduce our divinity—the magic of life—back into the equation. 'The kingdom of heaven is within.' Jesus told us that! So if you can become the creator of your own life, then God the creator must exist within you, too. And even better, if God, the *divine creator,* exists within each of us, then we have the capacity to bring into existence the life of our choosing. Can you begin to see that? And if your two guys are for real, they already have this *creator* stuff down."

I gave him a "standing O." As I sat back down I said, "Gilbert, that was a great lecture. Where can I sign up to be God?" I laughed.

"Hils, as a quantum physicist, I have to say that you already are God," Gilbert answered with all seriousness. "You just need to awaken the part of you that has forgotten."

Ruth and I sat silently, just trying to take it all in.

"Well ladies, I expect I'll see you around campus and we can talk again. Maybe then we can have a conversation about neurons and peptides, the places where science and religion intersect." Without another word, Gilbert stood, spun on his toes, and walked away, leaving us feeling like we'd been hit by a hurricane.

Vicki Renfro

CHAPTER
SIXTEEN

October 1, AD 35

He is not of Druidic descent. He came to us from a distant desert, a master of immense knowledge quite different from our own. But truth is truth, and McCollum granted him entrance to our Druid stronghold even as he entered under the cloak of darkness, evading all on watch except for Terrance's ever-vigilant, meditative eyes. McCollum's intention was to learn everything this stranger had to teach him, and over the months they have spent together I've watched an enduring bond form between them. Eduardo came as an alchemist, but now he is a mystic of extraordinary ability. McCollum has also grown in power, which seems to be magnified when the two of them are together.

The Druid community has only witnessed their shape-shifting abilities from afar. Their two figures stand atop the bluff, their cloaks billowing from the extreme heat created between them. As they weave their illusion, a spiraling plume surges high into the sky. McCollum and Eduardo appear to take flight with it, only to descend earthward as the most hideous monster the mind can imagine, eyes aglow as it screams with the howls of the dead. Even the Druids fear that if McCollum were to lose control, this creature would devour us all. But still, we thrill at the fear this sight will inspire in the hearts of the Roman legions.

October 1, 2010

My daydreams momentarily made me forget that I was still sitting in a coffee shop. I looked over at Ruth and determined that I must not have been *gone* for long because she was sitting much in the same state as me.

"I think I'm going to go to the library, Ruth. I'm feeling a little naive about quantum physics and I think I know where I can pick up some information on the subject. Do you mind if I leave you alone?"

"No problem," she replied, smiling. "I wore my big girl panties today."

I refilled my coffee and headed to the library. Stopping for the pedestrian signal at the light, I felt a person walk up behind me. I looked down and back to see a pair of scuffed black boots and faded black jeans, and knew instantly who was wearing them. Seemingly out of my control, a heavy feeling descended over me.

"Hi, Hillary. My name is Jackson Black."

"How do you know my name?" I demanded.

"It wasn't difficult," he said quietly. "I asked around campus." He moved closer to me. "Don't you feel it, too? We're kindred souls." I took a step sideways and he moved to close the distance. "We are allied in this world, connected. We must talk!"

"No, I'm … I'm on my way to meet my boyfriend," I lied, trying to ditch him.

"I'll find you later. You know I will," he said in a loud, controlling voice as I crossed the street and began to jog away. But even with increased distance between us, I had a hard time pulling my mind completely free of him. He left a nasty residue on me that made me feel dirty. I pushed through the automatic doors and hurried into the library restroom to wash my face and hands.

I knew where to look for the information I needed, and headed up the stairs to the glass floor room. I wondered how I would find the exact book I needed; there were so many to choose from. Entering the dimly lit area, I decided to just pick a book off the shelf, open it to a random page, and trust that it would lead me in the right direction.

I strolled along the first row of shelves, lightly running my fingers along the front of the books, all the time thinking of what Gilbert had said and asked for a book that would help me understand. I decided to reach for a small, green book that had slipped farther back on the shelf than the larger books around it. *Prosperity* wasn't the mysterious title I was hoping for, but I figured I should stick to my plan. It fell open to page 93, and I sat down at the reference table in the corner.

You can do anything with the thoughts of your mind. They are yours and under your control. You can direct them, coerce them, hush them, or crush them. You can dissolve one thought and put another in its stead. There is no other place in the universe where you are the absolute master. The domain given you as your divine right is over your own thoughts only. When you fully comprehend this and begin to exercise your God-given dominion, you begin to find the way to God, the only door to God, the door of your mind and thoughts.

I was surprised by my ability to quickly find a book on what Gilbert had been talking about. I flipped to the front to find the date this gem had been put into print—1936—and I let it fall open one more time.

By doing this, you place yourself under a divine law of demand and supply that is never influenced by the fluctuations of the market or the opinions of men. Every time you send out a thought of whole hearted faith in the I AM part of yourself, you set in motion a chain of cause and effect that must bring the result you seek. Ask whatsoever you will, and your demands will be fulfilled; both Heaven and Earth will hasten to do your bidding. But when you have asked for something, be on the alert to receive it when it comes. People complain that their prayers are not answered when, if we knew the truth, they are not aware to receive the answer when it comes.

I was so deep in thought that I didn't hear him enter the room, but my peripheral vision caught his movement, startling me.

"I'm sorry, I don't mean to disturb your reading," he said when he saw me jump. "This part of the library is my favorite, and I always try to visit when I'm in town."

Deciding I should trust the interruption, I turned my book face down on the table.

"Hi, I'm Hillary, and this is my favorite spot, too," I replied, taking a better look at the guy. His six-foot-four frame filled the room, and I could tell he had a muscular body under his sport jacket, but he didn't intimidate me. His gorgeous, long, dark hair had been pulled back into a ponytail. Based on the slight graying at his temples, I figured he was around forty-five, fifty tops. His eyes were kind, and if this was his favorite spot in the library, his choice in reading material made him an okay guy.

"Are you just here for today?" I asked, not knowing quite how to strike up a conversation.

"I'm actually here for a couple of days," he answered as he pulled a book from the shelf. "On Wednesday I'm attending a seminar at Menninger Clinic in Topeka."

"I didn't know they gave seminars at Menninger Clinic. I thought it was a facility for the mentally disturbed."

He gave me a kind smile.

"I attended my first seminar at Menninger's in 1981," he explained. "I initially went there to visit a high school friend with one too many personalities knocking around in her head. On my way to her room I saw a lecture notice pinned to the bulletin board near the nurses' station. That was the first time I saw the name Yogi Shanti."

When he saw the blank look in my eyes, he continued.

"Yeah, I guess that might be somewhat before your time. It was the time of sex, drugs, and rock n' roll," he said, nostalgically. "It was shortly after the second British Invasion, the one the Beatles began, and interestingly enough their popularity was instrumental in bringing the first yogis to the United States. The Beatles met the Maharishi, and all of a sudden everyone was talking about consciousness.

"So later that evening, after visiting my friend, I met my first Yogi. I was only sixteen, and in the eighties it was cutting-edge stuff. At my tender young age, he was very influential. I guess I've never gotten over it, because it's become my life's work. That evening was my first glimpse beyond the concrete jungle we call reality." He reached into his wallet and pulled out a very old and worn slip of paper. "These are the words he opened with that night," he said, handing it to me. "I keep it with me, so I always remember."

I gently unfolded it and read, "*It is important to not take things too seriously. You must see all experiences, including the negative ones, as merely steps on your path ... and proceed.*"

"Please excuse my rambling. I haven't even introduced myself. I'm Lee Edwards ... Doctor. That's PhD, not MD," he said as he reached out to shake my hand.

"Oh my gosh!" I gasped. "I know you. I collect your research materials. That's how I found this area of the library in the first place. You've been my mentor in a way." I shook the hand offered to me. "It's very nice to meet you Dr. Edwards."

It took a few minutes to re-adjust my image of lonely, old Dr. Edwards to this handsome man, who was probably never lonely.

"I've been pulling research for you all semester. To entertain myself, I painted a picture of you in my mind, and you are definitely not the picture I came up with!" A blush warmed my cheeks.

He chuckled, "I hope I'm better, not worse than you imagined."

"You're much younger," I said, and then decided to change the subject before I put my foot in my mouth. "What's your research about Dr. Edwards?"

"I am scheduled to do a few lectures for the psychology department right here on campus. You can get the dates online and come to hear for yourself." Looking at his watch, he must have realized he was running late. "I can never resist visiting this room, but I've got to be on my way."

"I'll look online," I said as I carefully folded the yellowed paper and hand it back to him.

"Take care, Hillary. It's been a pleasure talking to you, and I'm sure we are destined to meet again."

A moment later, I had the room to myself again.

CHAPTER
SEVENTEEN

November 2, AD 35

"I don't think it's safe for you to travel alone, Hilsbeth. You should wait for an escort. You were very nearly abducted by the two roadmen last time you went out alone," Liam insists as I mount my mare.

"Don't be foolish, I reply. "I am always protected. By whom and for what reason I do not understand, but someone watches over me."

November 3, 2010

Waking from another of my daydreams, I shook my head as I slid the book back onto the shelf. I struggled to remember where my mind had been, but once again, the thought had left before I could retrieve the vision.

Gathering my senses, I smiled as I recognized a craving for a hot, glaze-covered donut from a classic bakery run out of the basement of a house known simply as 'Vern's.' Actually, I craved a dozen just out of the fryer. The sun had set, and after sunset was when they started making fresh ones for their morning deliveries. I walked home as fast as I could to get Ruth and the car, but when Ruth was nowhere to be found. I decided to go without her. If I got back in time to serve her Vern's donuts for dinner, she would be in absolute heaven. Ruth was always my co-pilot on this trip, but I figured this time of night I could find it without her help by spotting the long line of students at the side door.

It had been weeks since I had driven north of our apartment, and the extent of road construction surprised the heck out of me. Bumping slowly along a single-lane dirt detour, I headed toward a lady holding a stop sign. I swore at myself for not turning on 6th street.

Out of nowhere, an old red Chevy flew past me at a ridiculously high speed, on what might loosely have been considered the right shoulder. I didn't even see the car's headlights, and I'm pretty good at keeping an eye on the rear view mirror. The car disappeared over the hill in front of me, and I felt immediate relief that I wouldn't be sharing the road with such an idiot.

Turning up the radio to drown out the rattling of my car as I drove over the rough road, I slowed down to look for the turn into Vern's. After one right and one left, my mouth was watering with anticipation.

After parking as close to Vern's as I could get, I locked the car door and headed north on foot.

Walking in the street because there were no sidewalks, my nose caught the smell the donuts wafting on the evening breeze, confirming the house was just on the other side of the street light about twenty yards ahead.

A wiry guy with greasy, slicked-back hair sauntered up to me with both hands shoved deep into the pockets of his dirty jeans. "What's a girl like you doin' walkin' around in the dark alone?" he said. "Ain't ya worried it's not safe out here?"

He didn't seem quite right, so I kept my eyes down and tried to ignore him. I caught two shadowy figures running behind the parked cars and instinctively knew that he had buddies ready to cut me off from behind.

"I'm talkin' to you, girly," he yelled in such a frightening voice that I looked up to meet his eyes. "I'm the one you damn near killed by tryin' to run me off the road. Don't act like you don't remember."

I heard his buddies skid into place on the pavement behind me, and I began looking for anyone who might be able to help me. I knew I'd lost my chance to run when I found my back against a parked car. Panic washed over me as he moved his face so close to mine that I could feel spittle hit me as he screamed profanities.

"You better leave her alone!" a female voice yelled from under the streetlight. Three girls had seen my predicament, but refused to leave the protection the light provided. I didn't blame them in the slightest. "We've called 911! You better run! The cops are on their way."

I said a prayer of thanks, but it still felt like an eternity before I heard two short blasts of a siren. The police car skidded to a stop and shined its headlights on the nasty group of thugs who had surrounded me. A young officer wearing a navy t-shirt, jeans, and a ball cap got out of the unmarked patrol car and held his badge up. My attackers were so stupid that it took them a while to decide to scatter in three different directions. I slid down the car that had been holding me upright and put my head on my knees.

"Are you all right?" the officer asked as he knelt down to check for himself.

"Yes," I said, on the verge of tears.

"We've been having reports about problems in this area and I need to talk to the witnesses. Will you be okay if I leave you alone for a minute?" he asked. "I won't take my eyes off of you."

I looked up and tried to smile. He took off his ball cap and put it on my head, and it felt reassuring. It was warm and it shaded my eyes from his headlights, but I still began to feel ill as he disappeared down the street.

I muffled a scream as someone sat down on the pavement beside me.

"I didn't mean to scare you," said Gilbert. "Are you okay? I was just out for a sugar fix and ..." I must have looked terrible because Gilbert was looking at me with great concern.

"I'd love some company, Gilbert. Help me up." Having a friend by my side made me feel more secure.

As the officer walked toward me with his notebook in hand, I noticed that he wasn't much older than me.

"I need to take your statement," he said, looking at me and then at Gilbert.

"I might be a while, Gilbert. Thanks for keeping me company, but I'm okay now. I'll see you in class." He nodded goodbye and I turned toward the patrol car.

"My name is Officer Hall," he said. He opened the car door and I got in. "This will only take a few minutes."

Handing him my identification, I told him that my assailant had accused me of running him off the road, and if I had to make a guess, I would say they were driving a beat-up red Chevy that had passed me on the road construction.

"Let's get you back to your car so you can go home," he said, snapping his notebook closed and handing my license back to me. "I will call you if I need any more information."

We began walking toward my car, and just when I thought the

evening couldn't get any gloomier, the sky opened up and it began to rain. I pulled the ball cap low on my head to keep the raindrops out of my eyes and tugged my jacket tighter around me. How much more miserable could this night get?

As we approached my car, I saw Gilbert walking toward me with a large bag of donuts and a couple of cups of hot coffee.

"I thought I should stay to take you home, if that's okay with you?" he said. "There's nothing quite like a mugging to whet an appetite!"

"Nothing quite like it," I agreed. "Yes, Gilbert, please take me home … that is, if you're finished with me, Officer Hall."

"Go home and get some sleep, Ms. Rubner," he said, handing me his business card. "You can keep the ball cap."

"Thanks, but no thanks," I said. "Too much of a reminder, if you know what I mean." I took it off and handed it back to him.

"All in a day's work for me," he said as he pulled the cap down on his head with a twist.

Gilbert took my arm, and with friendly support, walked me to the passenger side of my car. I climbed in, thankful not to be driving. Turning the key, he revved the engine.

"Easy boy, there's a cop here." I said. Gilbert just laughed and pulled slowly out into street.

Ruth opened the door and seemed to wonder what I was doing with Gilbert.

"You can drive my car home," I said, tossing him the car key and heading to my bedroom. "I'm going to take a hot shower. We'll talk tomorrow."

As I closed my door I heard the rustling of the donut bag, and I heard Gilbert and Ruth talking softly. I didn't care if they ate them all; my emotions were so frazzled. I was pissed off and frightened and I just wanted to get the night over with.

I showered to scrub the scummy feeling off my skin and dropped my wet towel to the floor before climbing into bed. Piling my pillows up around me, I held one tight to my chest. My mind moved from subject to subject, setting into slow motion the events of the night. I saw the old jalopy speed past me in my minds eye and recalled my relief as it disappeared...only to be confronted by a worse situation once I parked. I tried to make sense of it all, but before long all that was running through my mind was, *why me, why me, why me?* I'm not sure how much time passed before I finally fell into a restless sleep.

November 5, AD 35

While on the road to a nearby village to meet a smithy about forging a sword more appropriate for my adult height, I take a rare tumble off the back of my mare. It happens so suddenly that I have no time to react, and in the fall I cut my leg quite deeply on a sharp stone. It is a stupid accident caused by the wind and a falling tree limb.

After calming and hobbling my mare, I find a nearby stream to clean the dirt and debris from my leg and attempt to reduce the swelling and pain. I return home with my tail between my legs, knowing I'll have to admit to Liam my poor horsemanship.

I cross McCollum's path after stabling my horse, and he notices my limp and asks me to sit with him. I express my enormous disappointment over not reaching the smith and McCollum replies, "Dear one, do not ever question the small misfortunes along your path, because what looks like a misstep to you may look completely different from the heavens. I am on my way to the temple to chant for the souls of a family who were slaughtered for their meager possessions not far from your destination. I thank the gods that you were turned back."

November 5, 2010

Feeling like I'd had a visitation from a kind soul, I slowly woke from my deep sleep. Certain that Ruth had been walking on eggshells for hours trying not to disturb me, I pulled on my robe and walked into the living room. Gilbert was on our couch wrapped in a blanket, still fully clothed. His eyes popped open the moment I stepped into the room.

"Hope it's okay I stayed. I wanted to make sure you weren't too freaked out about last night." Sitting up, he looked at me for an answer.

"I can't figure out why those guys picked me out of this whole wide world. I didn't do anything to provoke them," I answered.

He patted the couch next to him and I walked over to sit down.

"Have you ever heard of *karma*?" he asked.

"Sure," I said. "It's one of the most overused words in the English language, next to *soulmate*." I stole part of his blanket and shook the bag on the coffee table to see if there was a donut left.

"Overused, maybe," he replied. "But you've got to understand, everything is karma. Nothing happens by accident."

"Sure, like all the people in a plane crash want to die?" I said sarcastically.

"Yes, as hard as it is to understand, everything is perfect—even that. It takes a while to get to a point where you can begin to see it, but the world *unfolds* as it should." Gilbert's voice went soft.

"Those are the words on my father's tombstone: *the world unfolds as it should*. He picked the words himself, but all the angels in heaven couldn't have convinced me that statement was true when my dad was dying." He lowered his eyes. "That was the worst time of my life, but since then I've had time to think about it, and I'm beginning to understand what that statement means."

"Gilbert, I appreciate what you are saying and I'm sorry you lost your father. I can imagine how much that must have hurt." I took his hand, thinking of my own dad. "But it's not the same thing. Those guys were disgusting, and I don't want them touching my karma."

"I hope you're not upset to find out that I'm part of your karma, too. In fact, every person you pass on the street—the people in your classes, the ones who wait on you at the coffee shop, even someone as abstract as the person who built your car or lived in this apartment before you—is part of your journey on earth. It's actually all karma!"

I just rolled my eyes. "Tell me something that makes sense to me."

"Okay, here's an idea for you. What if those three thugs last night weren't truly violent, but just bullies? I mean not actually bad to the bone. Maybe they were sent by your spiritual guides just to make you pay more attention. Open your mind, Hillary! Imagine there's another side to this coin. What if you were on a collision course with a destiny that had to be changed in order to save your life?" His voice increased in volume. "In other words, you needed to burn off some of your negative karma. It's like opening a bypass valve to let off steam before *she blows*."

Embarrassed by his enthusiasm, he returned his attention to his toes and said more calmly, "Not all things that look bad *are* bad. I'm just suggesting, Hils, that you try to look at it a different way. Try not to be too frightened. Consider it a necessary experience and someday, in hindsight, it may make more sense to you when you're able to see the big picture." Gilbert moved his hands in a huge circle indicating he meant the all-encompassing BIG PICTURE. "All parties involved last night actually agreed on some level to enable the event to happen, deep in the subconscious. Don't look at me like I'm crazy, Hils!"

Ruth appeared from the kitchen with a pot of coffee and the remaining donuts I'd been looking for.

"Don't take it personally, Gilbert. I get that look from Hillary all the time." Ruth turned to look at me. "Gilbert says that cop was cute. Is he going to get back to you today?"

"I didn't think guys talked about how cute other guys were!" Smirking, I looked into Gilbert's eyes and for the first time saw a very amazing man.

"As long as we are on the topic of who's crazy or not," Gilbert said, looking at Ruth, "How did your experiment go with choosing happiness over being pissed off? What happened in your drama class?"

Ruth seemed a little hesitant to respond, and I concluded she really didn't want to admit that Gilbert was right.

"Okay ... okay, I did what you said," Ruth admitted with unaccustomed shyness. "I planted the seed and went to class happy that I lost the lead. At first I felt phony as baloney, and then I began to see a change. I asked the *less talented* girl who got the lead if I could help her study her lines. Soon another girl asked me to help with her lines and to become her understudy, which my pride would have never let me do prior to this experiment. Before long my professor even noticed my versatility and willingness to work with others. She pulled me aside to say she was in the process of putting together the largest production the department has ever attempted, and she thought I would be the perfect lead. The amazing thing is, getting the starring role takes second place to the new relationships I've made. Hate to admit it to you Gilbert, but it all feels magical."

Vicki Renfro

CHAPTER EIGHTEEN

I SKIPPED all my Monday classes, deciding instead to stay in bed and sulk. I just felt like I wanted to take a sick day and stay tucked in at home, in the dark, with the drapes closed. My emotions were still stuck somewhere between good old self-pity and defiance. *"Get up Trinity!"* I said, imagining myself as Trinity from *The Matrix*. She never gave up and I hoped using her words I could coax myself into being less pathetic.

By afternoon I was bored with my self-indulgence and got dressed to go to work. I'd gotten a voicemail message from the police, saying everything looked random and that they would get back to me if anything changed. So it was time to put everything behind me.

To make sure I got home before dark, I left for work two hours early. Pondering what Gilbert had said about karma, I looked at each person I passed on campus and wondered if I knew them from a previous lifetime or had made a *subconscious* agreement with them.

Once at the library, I picked up my assignments and thought, *Wow, how could there be so much work on the day I want to leave early?* The word *karma* came to mind, and I wondered what the day held in store for me.

Walking up and down the aisles, I picked up book after book, and by the time I finished scanning and e-mailing them, I had a sinking feeling that darkness was falling.

I kept telling myself I wasn't going to be afraid. Those slime-bags didn't know who I was, and Officer Hall would call if I had anything to worry about. *I will not let one event take away my ability to live my life* I decided, and I punched my timecard and walked out of the building.

"Hi Hillary," I heard someone say as the library door slowly closed behind me. "I thought you might need someone to walk you home."

A smile lit my face as I turned around. It was Will. "I'd love that, but what are you doing out so early?"

"George received an e-mail from Ruth late last night, so I came to make sure you're okay." He slipped his hand into mine, and a warm feeling of contentment spread though me.

"No, really Will, aren't you going to be in trouble for this?" I said squeezing his hand back. "You know, being *out*?"

"Actually, no," he explained. "George and I have been talking to McCollum for a while now. McCollum told us the time would be right as we near the winter solstice."

"Right for what?" I asked.

"The time would be right for us to re-enter the outside world, to move out of his household. McCollum believes the remaining people destined to complete our circle are nearby. He can sense them, and having us live outside the walls will facilitate our finding them." Will removed his hand from mine and put his arm around my shoulder.

He was so warm, and as usual, my entire body began to hum softly. Oh, it was a lovely feeling.

"The few we are missing are probably adults now, and if they're given a chance, McCollum thinks our karma will draw them toward us. So, Hillary, if it's okay with you, I'd like to spend my time waiting for them with you."

He said it with such calm that I wasn't sure of the correct reaction. I wanted to scream, "YES! YES! YES!" but decided that might be a bit much. So after counting ten sidewalk cracks, I calmly answered, "I'd really like that."

Will was more handsome than the last time I had seen him. His untamed hair and blue eyes were irresistible, and I couldn't stop staring at his gorgeous smile.

"That makes me happy, because the only house we know of—besides the one we live in now—is yours, and the lower level seems to be available. Before you say anything, there is one more thing." He paused.

"What's that?" I held my breath. Things were improving by the minute!

"McCollum told us recently that the night he saw you and Ruth at our private Spring Fling, he *recognized* both of you. But he needed to discourage George and me from seeing you until more time had passed. He wanted you to be on your own for a while." Will laughed softly. "I suppose he knew that I would try to occupy all of your time. He knows me pretty well."

My heart was beating so hard that I felt a little faint. I had wanted this, and now it was really coming true. Will wanted to spend time with me!

Will interrupted my thoughts. "Your turn to say something, Hillary. Don't leave me hanging here. What do you think?"

We were within a block of my apartment.

"I think I like all of what you've said, even the karma parts that I don't understand. How about coming up to my apartment and we'll talk some more?" I could feel myself blushing, and I really wished I weren't so transparent.

"I think we might be expected. Ruth and George are having this same conversation. We want to make sure both of you agree before we sign the lease." Will's hand slid back into mine and it felt very natural, like we had been holding hands forever.

We found the apartment door unlocked, and when we opened it, two sets of eyes were peering at us with ear-to-ear smiles. "I see you found her all right," Ruth giggled. "Come on in you two. We've got things to talk about."

"Dinner smells wonderful!" I said. "Does Ruth have her little cookbook out again?"

"I'm the cook!" George grinned. "Will's the teacher and I'm one hell of a chef! The smell just makes your mouth water, doesn't it?"

"Well, that's a plus." I looked at Ruth, raising my eyebrow. The table was already set, so we took our places as George brought dinner from the kitchen.

The room was filled with a pleasant easiness, and oddly enough, I wasn't questioning it. It was as though this had always been part of the journey. We laughed and talked lightheartedly through dinner.

Motioning for Ruth and George to sit still, I announced, "We'll wash the dishes. You two relax. It won't take us long."

I was nervously looking forward to being alone with Will.

We stacked the plates, gathered the silverware, and headed for the kitchen. Everything had to be rinsed before going into our decrepit dishwasher, so I filled the sink with hot water. Will moved in close beside me to place the dishes in the sink. Happiness washed over me—and to be honest, almost knocked me over—as I felt the heat of his body along my side. Then, moving behind me, he wrapped his arms around me.

"This is going to make the dishwashing go a lot slower, you know." I inhaled, trying to catch my breath.

"It doesn't matter to me how long the dishes take," Will contentedly whispered in my ear, "Take your time. I'll just wait here."

My need to wash the dishes vanished, and I let my hands drop into the warm water. I just wanted to stay in his embrace forever.

"Your hands are going to get wrinkly," he said.

"I don't care." I turned to face him and his lips found mine, and my body leaned against his. I could feel his heart beating as fast as mine, and nothing else in the world mattered.

I don't think our rosy red lips were a surprise to Ruth and George when we walked back into the living room. We had been in the kitchen for a long time.

"Did you miss us?" I asked as I pulled Will down beside me on the couch.

Ruth and George looked over at us, both blushing, "No, not at all."

"So what's our answer, girls?" George boomed. "Can we live below you? We'll be good neighbors. We promise to be quiet. We'll give you your privacy, if that's what you want." George nudged Ruth as he said this.

Ruth elbowed him with a laugh, "Not on your life." Then, as if to clarify, she said, "I'm talking about the needing privacy part. As for the living below us, my answer is yes."

Everyone in the room simultaneously turned to look at me.

"My answer is yes, too," I agreed, knowing I really meant that I wanted Will to be as close as possible.

CHAPTER
NINTEEN

AS FALL became bone chilling, I anxiously awaited Will's move into the downstairs apartment. We still had our late night e-mails, but we barely had spent any time together over the last couple of weeks. With work, school, and studying, I didn't have a lot of spare time, although I would have made time for Will. Will had also been quite busy. He was teaching his final classes, and although he was as anxious as I was for his new life to begin, I could tell how much he was going to miss those boys. After all, they'd been his family for more than a decade.

The sun hadn't shown itself for days, and the air was damp and cold, making it hard to get dressed and walk to campus. I was sure it would be snowing by afternoon, so after a hot shower I layered on the warmest clean clothes that I had and was ready to face the day. I didn't need my backpack because I only had one thing on my schedule today: the long-awaited lecture by Dr. Edwards that I was attending with Gilbert.

I opened the door to leave, only to find a tin can crammed full of frozen flowers. Picking them up, I walked to the kitchen and unfolded a scrap of paper tucked in the top. *Oh God!* My heart sank. The note was from Jackson Black. "I need only to close my eyes to find you." With disgust, I tossed everything into the sink and hurried out the door.

The walk to the auditorium was bone chilling, partly because of the note I had just received and partly because the temperature had dropped. My teeth were chattering and my nose was so cold it was practically numb. By the time I opened the lobby door and the warm air hit my face, I could barely find my Kleenex before my nose began to run. Gilbert found me in all my glory.

"I saved us a couple of seats near the front," Gilbert said, staring at my red, runny nose.

"Don't give me any crap about this. It's cold outside and I walked. It's not like I'm sick or something." I stuffed the Kleenex back into my coat pocket.

Gilbert had become one of my very best friends over the past semester—sometime during all our long talks after my almost mugging. Yes, he might be a little odd, but in a very adorable way, and it was sweet that he was willing to be my date for the lecture.

We entered the main auditorium through the east door and walked down the aisle toward the stage. I was glad Gilbert had gotten there early because the place was packed. I wondered if it was because everyone was interested in eastern philosophies, or simply because Dr. Edwards was such a hottie. His long, thick hair and wonderful deep blue eyes set him apart from the other fuddy-duddy college professors, and the students clearly liked the image he projected—especially the girls.

Gilbert pointed to our seats and we shuffled in, excusing ourselves along the way. We were front and center when the lights began to dim. Gilbert nudged me and handed me the program. From the bulge in his backpack, it was evident that he had smuggled in some contraband for us to munch on. Gilbert lowered his voice to a whisper as the introduction for Dr. Edwards droned on.

"What do you feel like Hillary? I've got salted and unsalted nuts, Dr. Pepper or Arizona tea, and of course, chocolate."

Gilbert used the applause to cover up the crackling of cellophane and had everything opened by the time Dr. Edwards walked on stage. Dr. Edwards was wearing a sports jacket, jeans, and a white shirt opened at the collar. The girls were holding their breath because he looked *that good* walking up to the podium. The Oakley sunglasses atop his head swept his long hair back from his chiseled face. He picked up the microphone and stepped to the front edge of the platform.

"Buddha—a name everyone has heard, but most know nothing about.

"Buddha, one of the Christs of the East, was born south of Nepal six thousand years before Jesus Christ, and was destined by birthright to become King. He was known as Siddhartha Gautama, and at his birth, Asita, the wisest of the seers told his mother that he would become a *Buddha*—one who has supreme knowledge. Unfortunately, his mother didn't live to see that happen, for she died seven days later, leaving Siddhartha to be raised by his sister.

"His father, King Suddhodanna, in an effort to protect his son from anything unpleasant, built Siddhartha a palace for each season, and in these palaces he lived a lavish lifestyle. At sixteen his father arranged his marriage, and soon another prince was born.

"Even though Siddhartha's every need was more than met in his young life, he became curious about what lay beyond the palace walls. On the night of his twenty-ninth birthday, Siddhartha secretly left under the cover of darkness, giving up his royal life. He shaved his head and sent back his princely garments, becoming completely homeless.

"He became enlightened while meditating under the Bodhi tree when he was thirty-five, revealing the hidden mysteries of the human mind. In this transcendental state of consciousness, as a *completely realized* being, he became the salvation for the suffering."

Roaming the front edge of the stage, Dr. Edwards thought out loud, "How many of us would give up great wealth and a lavish lifestyle for any reason? After all, isn't that the *American Dream*?

"Some of you may have been exposed to the basic eastern spiritual precept that divinity lies inside each of us. *Namaste*, a common greeting in many parts to this world, literally translated means, 'the *God* in me recognizes the *God* in you.' So as *Westerners*, largely raised without a point of reference to the concept of internal divinity, what do we do? How do we begin to make the connection with that all-knowing *Buddha* within each of us?" He smiled widely. "Well, this afternoon we're going to figure it out together."

He gave us a moment to let this idea settle in and then continued.

"Let's be honest with each other. Nothing of any consequence in life comes without intense focus, commitment, and dedication to a path of action. It takes time to break patterns and learn new, fundamental *truths*, but I guarantee every step on the journey of self-discovery will be well worth your effort. We are going to begin today with Buddha's own statement, 'We are shaped by our thoughts; we become what we think. When the mind is pure, joy follows like a shadow that never leaves.'

"So, if this is true, the first thing you have to do is clean up your apartment." The auditorium erupted into laughter. "I'm serious!" he said, laughing along with the student body. "You have to take out the garbage, literally and figuratively. You have to clean up your relationships. You have to clean up your intentions, and what follows is the commitment I spoke of. You must take control of your thoughts and dust off your dreams."

Dr. Edwards dominated the auditorium as he paced slowly from one side of the stage to the other, all six feet, four inches of him.

"You laugh, but I'm dead serious, so please, see if you can follow this train of thought. We're taught as children that God, the *ultimate power*, floats above us in heaven, but I want to suggest again that the *ultimate power* lies within. You are the sole creator of your existence. You are the one who decides which direction your life takes with each thought that you have."

His voice softened, as if he were having a personal conversation with each one of us. "I know this can be difficult, but it is imperative that you hear it. At this moment, most of you let random thoughts run your life, not actually caring one way or another how ugly or disturbing your thoughts might be. After all, you're not voicing the worst of them out loud. You think no one hears them, but you need to recognize that these thoughts *are* being heard. Your subconscious mind hears all of it and then sets forth to bring your thoughts to fruition, to manifest them in the physical world.

"You have good luck and bad luck, and sometimes things just happen ... right? Wrong! You create *today* by what you thought yesterday and the previous day and the day before that. If you want to know what you were thinking last year at this time, look at what you have in your life today! You have to refocus your responses to everything that comes your way so that the universal law of cause and effect will, a month from now, a year from now, result in your life looking like you made a conscious decision to *create* it rather than to become a *victim* of it.

"Take a minute to reflect on what your mind is manifesting for you and decide if learning to be the master of your thoughts is worth the return," Dr. Edwards said, standing with his arms crossed and his feet shoulder-width apart. He scanned the audience, and it felt like he was looking into each of us.

Gilbert elbowed me in the ribs, "Told you so."

"I'm starting to get the idea, Gilbert," I whispered. "It's coming at me from so many directions I feel I'm being beaten over the head with it."

"Well Hils, time to wake up." Everyone in our area shushed us as Dr. Edwards resumed his talk.

"I know this is a lot to absorb, especially if you have never considered any of these ideas before. Sometimes it's easier to let your life run amuck, unchecked, but I think in the long run it's much easier to just create what you want your life to be.

"Don't kid yourself. Your mind is the most powerful computer ever created. It generates what you see, what you hear, and what you feel by its interpretation of the situation. It determines what you're afraid of, the challenges you will face in life, and ultimately your health and well-being. Your mind and your thoughts even determine whom you will meet in the future, and whether your spouse will be loving and supportive, or a dreadful … ah … problem."

The auditorium chuckled as Dr. Edwards rolled his eyes and raised his hands to quiet the audience.

"Now, imagine for a moment a person who walks through life saying things such as, 'It just makes me sick, I hate my life, I'm so stupid, I'll never get this done in time, my homework is too difficult, I'll never get the job, it really doesn't matter anyway,' and the worst thing of all, 'I'm not good enough.' What do you think those thoughts are instructing the subconscious mind to do? If your subconscious is creating, without question what you ask it to, I'd say this person is not far from creating crisis after crisis in their life. Hypochondriacs create what they are looking for—illness. The one who says, 'I can't find my car keys,' won't find them, the same way a person who is *looking* for new opportunities will find them everywhere. It's up to you. You can live your life by *default* or you can live it by *design*."

Looking around, I saw that Dr. Edwards had the audience in the palm of his hand.

"Buddha tells us if a man can control his mind, he can find the way to Enlightenment, and all wisdom and virtue will naturally come to him.

"There is a thread of consciousness in the universe that links everything together, and if you choose this path, you will become aware of the connection of everything and everyone, because in truth ... we are *One*. We are One with nature and with one another, and we are One with the *Universal Power*, the *I AM*, and One with *God*. Awareness of this thread of consciousness is ours to discover.

"Unfortunately," he said, opening his arms to indicate the physical world we live in, "at this lower level of consciousness where we spend most of our time, we are totally unaware of the unlimited beings we really are."

Dr. Edwards stopped to take a drink of water. It was so quiet you could have heard a pin drop. He sucked in air loudly and began to talk again.

"If you begin to grasp the idea of working with your subconscious mind, your life will take a quantum leap forward. It takes unwavering faith in self and amazing passion to take the journey to self-awareness. Now you have to ask yourself, 'Do I want to take the red pill or the blue pill?' One will let you remain asleep; the other will show you just how deep the rabbit hole goes!

"To embark on this path takes trust and courage. I have a friend who was terrified that there would be no one at the end. I promise you there will be someone there, and it will be *you*, a stronger, more loving, and compassionate *you*.

"Each of you will find your own unique journey, sometimes traveling with others, other times remaining solitary. I was led to a guru, a teacher. He schooled me in transcendental meditation, but you must find what works for you. You can use yoga, prayer, long walks in nature, Tai Chi, Chi Gong; the list of techniques that will advance you is endless. Even digging a ditch will work if you use it as *practice* for higher consciousness.

"I suggest doing some research. Find a teacher who can help you get started, but never believe that your first teacher is going to be your last. Also, be wary of teachers who believe they are 'all knowing,' because few humans are. Each teacher is a step on your path, and if you are growing, you will find the next teacher. Your journey will take a lifetime … or more," he slipped in under his breath. "But ultimately you will arrive and realize who you really are.

"I've traveled around the world, and it is apparent that there have been many Christs who have walked this planet, and there are some who walk among us today. I study with one such Being, one who does not get wet while walking in the rain. He is love and beauty, and he exists consciously in dimensions far beyond the one we spend our time in. You will find these magnificent beings when it is your time, when you are ready for them and are at a level that enables you to understand their teachings. You cannot hurry your journey. Just know that when you are ready, the masters will appear. Work on making yourself ready for the mystical adventures that are out there waiting for you.

"This path will lead you to the necessity for self forgiveness. Nurturing self-love within us is mandatory. We all must get to the place where we can move forward in life without the weight of self-loathing and guilt. The *Universal Power* already sees each of us as perfect. You're the one holding grudges against yourself for what you've done or not done. GIVE IT UP!" Dr. Edwards shouted so loudly it startled me. "Offer yourself forgiveness, because at the end of your journey it will become obvious that there is no blame.

"Let me leave you with a quote from my Master, who doesn't get wet in the rain." Dr. Edwards pulled a piece of paper from his jacket pocket, slowly unfolded it, laid it on the podium, and began to read:

"There was a gift that was given at the beginning of all time. It is called life. *You experience life by how you are known by others and by those you love. But it is understood within your spirit's existence that you are much more than that. You are the physical embodiment of the Divine One whose purpose is to bring God to this planet."*

He folded the paper and placed it back into his pocket.

"The *thing* you must realize is that the second coming of Christ that you have been waiting for has already happened. The second coming of Christ is YOU. It's always been YOU. This is the beginning of the Twilight of the Kali Yuga, the Age of Aquarius, the time of Enlightenment; the Mayan Calendar ends in 2012. The time is drawing near for all of you to awaken. WAKE UP! It is your time to shine with a light so brilliant that it can be seen from the heavens. Start your path today. Watch your thoughts. Forgive yourself and grow. I beseech you, the time is now, don't miss your opportunity. The world needs you. YOU ARE THE ONE WE HAVE BEEN WAITING FOR!"

The audience was totally quiet as Dr. Edwards turned to walk off the stage.

Then I heard Gilbert start to slowly clap. I followed suit, and then more and more people began to join in, until there was an uproar of joy in the room. We had just been given a great gift, and it felt wonderful.

CHAPTER
TWENTY

November 17, AD 36

"Come with me, dear one," McCollum says. "I have something I'd like to show you."

It's very cold, so I wrap myself against the wind and mount my mare. We ride for hours before we reach our destination, and when we do, it's nothing but the remnants of a once thriving town. McCollum dismounts, and looking up at me asks, "What do you see?"

I scan the area slowly and begin to speak. "The fields are barren, as if the crops had failed. The people stayed as long as possible because they had built their lives here. Eventually, with nothing to eat, they had to move on, and now their homes sit before us in decay." I explain from a knowing within me. "I feel the sorrow of the people who once occupied this village deep in my bones."

"Come child. Let's build a fire and I will tell you a story." McCollum leads our horses into the remains of an old barn and begins gathering kindling. When the fire is lit, we both sit close to warm our hands.

Looking into my eyes, McCollum admits that I am correct in what I saw. It makes me wonder why we had to ride so far on such a bleak day. Placing more wood on the fire, he settles in.

"Let me tell you the story of the downfall of this settlement, so you will better understand. About ten years ago, a man walked into this thriving village and was welcomed as an additional set of hands to work the land. He was strong, and as he helped plant the crops he also began to plant other seeds in the minds of the villagers. He talked of drought, famine, crop failure, and starvation, and one by one these

worries grew and festered in the farmers' minds. Negativity slowly sucked the dreams of the future from their naive souls. The pride they had once taken in the appearance of their homes soon faded because they were distracted by fear. And as the fear grew within them, it became a self-fulfilling prophecy. Their crops failed because the darkness of their vision caused them to make devastating decisions. Before long, brother argued with brother, and neighbors began to doubt one another's loyalty. You see, Hilsbeth, what happened here is just the reverse of what you saw. The downfall of this town began with the planting of a thought, and when it took hold, there was no one in the village who was powerful enough to stop its manifestation."

"What happened to the stranger?" I ask, afraid of the answer.

"There will always be darkness in our world that preys on the ignorance of mankind. It creates bigotry and hatred, infests the world with fear, and drains the life force from individuals who don't have the vision to see through it. I brought you here today so you'll realize how important it is to hold the light for the ones who are lost. We must never be seduced by the darkness, dear Hilsbeth, but learn to recognize it by the feeling it creates and the destruction left in its wake. We must always instill hope and stand on the side of love, peace, and thoughtfulness. And hold a positive vision, because in time ... I pray light will prevail."

November 17, 2010

I heard Ruth's key in the front door and watched her drop her purse and computer on the couch. "Hard day?" I asked, seeing her exhaustion.

"I think I just haven't been getting enough sleep lately," she said as she headed for the kitchen. "I'm going to make a cup of tea, take a long hot bath, and hit the sack."

I heard her mumble, "What the hell!" and I remembered the flowers I'd left in the sink. She came back into the living room holding the scrap of paper.

"Who's Jackson Black?"

"He's that guy I pointed out at The Commons the other day. Scruffy guy, older."

"Yeah, I remember, but what's with the flowers?" she asked.

"He was outside the coffee shop. He knew my name, and now he obviously has figured out where I live."

"Is Creepy Guy stalking you?"

I thought hard for a minute before answering.

"It's hard to explain. It's like he reaches inside me and takes my joy, leaving me slimed with a dirty feeling. It's not illegal, but it should be."

"He sounds like my Uncle Marvin. He can suck the happiness out of a room just by walking into it. He loves talking about negative stuff. If it's not a pandemic or forecasting the crash of world markets, it is the wrath of God. His family is always depressed."

The following morning I woke to a clatter outside my window. I pulled the blanket off my bed and wrapped it tight around me. It had snowed overnight, and our heat was set at 55 degrees. In fact, this morning our apartment was damn cold. I needed to have a talk with Ruth about setting the temperature at 65 now that winter was here.

I walked over to the window and pulled the curtain back so I could see what the noise was all about. There was a moving truck parked at the curb, and no fewer than ten boys were excitedly moving boxes into the downstairs apartment.

"Oh my God, it's happening! Ruth, it is happening! Get up," I yelled at the top of my lungs while running toward Ruth's room.

"What's happening?" I had obviously roused her out of a deep sleep.

"Will and George are outside," I said. "Well, I didn't actually see them, but I'm sure they must be with everything else that is moving in downstairs." I wasn't able to hide my excitement, and now neither could Ruth.

"Which window?" Ruth asked as she pulled on her robe. "I want to see if I can spot George. Good God, it's been weeks since they've actually been here."

"Come on, it's my bedroom window." I shooed Ruth off my trailing blanket so it wouldn't be pulled from my shoulders.

"By the way Ruth, we've got to set our heat higher on these cold nights," I said as we passed the thermostat and I pushed the heat up a few notches.

"Yeah, yeah … whatever," Ruth called, running into my bedroom. By the time I caught up with her, she had the curtains open and her face all but smashed against the window.

"Look Hillary, there they are," she said, waving wildly at them.

"So much for playing coy."

All self-respect literally went out the window when Ruth opened it and started asking the boys questions. She wasn't going to be happy when she finally looked in the mirror and saw her tousled hair and her eyes, which were still black from last night's mascara.

"What the hell!" I said, and stepped to the window to see if Will was with George. I ran my fingers through my hair, hoping I didn't look too bad.

"How about some hot chocolate for the moving crew," Ruth yelled, and all the little faces looked up at her and then back to George.

"I think that sounds great!" George bellowed back. "Give us about an hour to finish up and you can bring it down to our place. We'll give you the grand tour."

"That doesn't give us much time." Ruth was now in a bit of a panic and in high drama mode. "How about if I start the hot chocolate while you shower, and then you can finish up while I clean up?"

"Sounds like a plan." As I washed my hair, I delighted in the fact that Will was only one floor below me. I'd never been in the apartment downstairs, so I wasn't sure where Will's bedroom would be, but no matter the location, when we both fell asleep tonight we'd be closer to each other than ever. I figured my manifesting skills were getting better, because my dreams were coming true.

It wasn't long before Ruth was pounding on the bathroom door, "It's my turn. Hurry your butt up."

"I'm just about finished," I answered, drying my hair as Ruth busted through the door, slipping past me to get into the shower.

I finished quickly and hurried to the kitchen to see where Ruth had left off. The milk was just warming and the cups were already on a tray. I started to mix in the cocoa when there was a knock at the door. Dropping the spoon on the counter, I ran to answer it.

"What's the ruckus downstairs?" Gilbert said as he stepped through the front door, coffee in hand. "Don't look so disappointed, Hils. You'll give me a complex."

"Come on in, Gilbert. I'm not disappointed. It's always great to see you. I just thought you might be Will." I walked back to the kitchen to stir the hot cocoa, and Gilbert followed.

"The mystery man … what's he doing out in the sunlight?" Gilbert joked.

"He's not a vampire," I said, laughing. "All those kids downstairs are helping Will and George move in. We're on our way down with hot chocolate. Do you want to meet him?" I asked with a smile I just couldn't get off my face.

"Of course I'd like to meet Will. After all, I'm like your big brother," he stated as a matter of fact. "I need to see if he's good enough for you."

We'd never really voiced it before, but I felt that same level of affection toward him, and I believed he was right about the big brother thing.

Ruth was a little out of breath when she emerged from her bedroom.

"I'm ready. How's the cocoa coming? Oh hi, Gilbert," she said looking at me with a questioning look on her face.

"Gilbert's coming down to meet Will; it's big brother stuff," I said, smiling at him and handing him a stack of napkins. "Come on and help me carry this tray. It's all ready to go."

It only took a couple of minutes to get organized and we were off to entertain our new neighbors. As we walked into the apartment, all the little faces quickly gathered around us, waiting patiently for their drinks as they warmed up their hands and toes near the fireplace. I had never noticed that our house had a chimney. It was well hidden by the trees, and since the lower apartment had been vacant the previous semester, we hadn't noticed any smoke. But now my mind filled with romantic thoughts of Will and me cuddled up in front of it.

From across the room I heard George's booming voice.

"I would like to introduce you to our good friends, Ruth Witherspoon and Hillary Rubner. They live in the apartment upstairs."

"And I'm Gilbert, Hillary's big brother," Gilbert couldn't resist adding with a grin.

"You boys can introduce yourselves while they serve you hot cocoa," George said.

They all lined up and did exactly as they were told. I imagined this was a big day for them, being this far away from their home, with their only supervision being George and Will.

Suddenly, I felt a hand slip over mine as Will took the ladle from me and gave it to Ruth.

"I'd like to meet your big brother," Will said as he directed me into the living room. "I was completely unaware that you had an older brother,"

"Well, it's more figurative than literal. Gilbert is my good friend and sometimes my protector. He's also the teaching assistant in my physics class," I looked around for Gilbert, only to discover he was right beside me. "Will, this is Gilbert Dutton. Gilbert, Will Emerald," I carefully watched the reactions in both of their faces.

"Very nice to meet you, Will. I've heard a lot about you." Gilbert stuck out his huge round hand.

"It's very nice to meet you, too, Gilbert. I'm happy Hillary has such a good friend to rely on," Will shook Gilbert's hand.

Will towered over Gilbert, but I was sure Gilbert outweighed him. They looked each other squarely in the eyes and then their hands dropped. Later I'd have to ask what their first impression was of one another. They both smiled, and before I knew what was happening, I was heading outside with Will.

"It's nice of you to bring us the hot chocolate," Will said, walking through the door. But once we were out of earshot of the boys, he turned toward me, and his deep blue eyes burned into me.

"I've been patiently waiting for this day to come for months," he said, "and thank God, it's finally arrived. I haven't been able to think of anything but you. My meditating has gone downhill because you have become the only thing occupying my mind. I'm not complaining! It's just far different from what I'm used to. I've got to settle down, and I think the only answer to my conundrum is to spend more time with you. I hope a lot of time."

I took a breath and ignored my normal tendency to be shy.

"I've been waiting for you, too, Will. I've been dreaming of us spending time together, and now here we are." I wanted to kiss him in the worst way, but couldn't risk it so close to the boys.

"We'll be back in the morning to stay. Can I see you then?" He had to know my answer by the way I was trembling.

"What time? I'll be waiting," I managed to say calmly.

"We'll be here at nine," Will promised, pushing back the hair that had fallen into his face. "I'll come get you as soon as I can."

"Anytime is good. I probably won't be able to sleep tonight anyway, so just come up as soon as you can."

I began to hear voices as the boys emerged from the apartment. The kids were beginning to pile back into the truck bed as George, Ruth, and Gilbert brought up the rear.

"Come on, Will," George yelled. "We've got to get back for evening meditation. It's our last one for a while. The boys are promising to give us a big send off!"

I could tell by the boys' faces that even though today was an awesome adventure, none of them were looking forward to tomorrow, when Will and George would be leaving.

Will turned to catch up with the boys and didn't give me another look, at least not until he was in the truck and driving away. Ruth, Gilbert, and I waved goodbye and then went back inside to gather up the cups.

"What a nice group of boys," Gilbert marveled. "I can only hope that someday I'll have some of them as students in my class. They would be an interesting group to have a discussion with."

"What makes you say that?" Ruth asked.

"You're kidding me, right? You're really kidding me." Gilbert turned to look at me and then at Ruth. "You didn't feel that?"

"What?" Ruth was oblivious to everything except George. "Feel what?"

"Feel the Shakti, the current of energy running through the room. It was tangible." Gilbert looked at us with disbelief. "This is a very elevated group of humans you are hanging out with. I loved standing next to that Will of yours, Hils. You can get high just being close to him."

"I know!" I was excited to have someone to talk to about that weird hum I felt when I was near Will. "When he holds my hand, it feels like I've been hooked up to something electrical. My body begins to buzz, and I'm exhausted when he leaves me."

"Yeah, that's the Shaktipat. I went to see a guru once to receive

Shaktipat. It seems ridiculous to travel a long distance to see a guru and then just sit there without a word being spoken. But you do it for the high. The great ones, the ones near enlightenment, have a more powerful life force than the rest of us. Just sitting in their presence causes your own life force to increase, and it's like no other feeling. It's as if the secrets of the universe are revealed. Unfortunately, it dissipates shortly after leaving their presence. The trick is to eventually learn to create it within yourself." Gilbert shrugged, "Of course there are junkies, people who just want to steal the life force. That's very hard on the Masters. The relationship between teacher and student is meant to be very sacred."

"You're losing me, big Bro. What do you mean *I can learn*? All I feel is stupefied when Will leaves me," I said.

"You need to open up, let that energy flow through you." Gilbert closed his eyes and held his hands palms up to illustrate what he meant. "This is a gift, girls. In this state of consciousness you just naturally become more, understand more! Your body becomes an expanded vessel. It has *more* room for everything—creativity, thoughts ... transcendence. You two have just been too enamored with Will and George to take full advantage of what they have to offer you," Gilbert dropped his hands and gave us a big smile. "Call me, I'll come over and hang out with Will and George anytime ... or even those kids, for that matter! And unlike you girls, I won't waste a minute swooning over them. I'll spend my time with them learning. After all, Dr. Edwards says we have until the end of 2012."

CHAPTER
TWENTY ONE

AT SUNRISE, Will tapped on our front door so lightly I could barely hear it. I ran to answer it in my ratty t-shirt and panties, robe in hand, but he had already let himself in. He was just standing there, looking beautiful and staring at me with those piercing blue eyes. His hair looked like he had just gotten out of bed.

I stopped dead in my tracks and felt my robe slip from my fingers to the floor, and before I knew what was happening, I launched myself into his arms. My legs wrapped around his waist, my arms went around his shoulders, and my face nuzzled into his neck. All my worries about what I didn't know fell away as my sexual inexperience was replaced with the security of pure love.

He turned his head to run his lips lightly over my neck before tenderly kissing me beneath my ear. He let his coat drop to the floor as he slipped his hands under my bottom, so I didn't slip out of his embrace. Slowly he carried me to my bedroom and softly closed the door while still holding me in his strong arms. He sat down on the edge of the bed, with me still wrapped tightly around him.

Moving one hand up to hold my face, he whispered, "I've missed you," and I was completely lost in the moment.

I had waited for this perfect moment all my life, and now I wanted nothing more than to feel his skin next to mine. Running my hands under his t-shirt, he lifted his arms to help me slide it over his head. Warmth radiated from him, and I tucked my head tightly against his neck—scared, but knowing this was *right* for me.

Still holding me against him, Will stood, turning to lay me gently across my rumpled bedding. I watched him as his jeans slipped to the floor. He was beautiful—the dark hair across his chest and the flexing of his muscular legs as he bent to climb into my bed beside me. He made me breathless. I reached down to pull the comforter over us and felt our bodies instantly melt together. As I breathed in the irresistible smell of him, my face against his chest, I found myself saying ever so softly, "I love you, I love you, I love you …"

The rest was like a dream, my body exploding with sensations I had never felt before. As Will rolled on top of me, everything came so naturally. I felt him inside me, moving so slowly that the ecstasy was beyond what I ever had imagined it could be.

"Don't move," I managed to whisper. "I want to remember this moment forever."

The rippling sensation threatened to unhinge us. Will's breath was heavy as he tried to hold everything together, and goose bumps followed my hands when I ran them up his back.

"I can't Hillary," he said softly. "I have to move."

As I felt Will begin to move his hips, my body followed every movement, rising to meet him, each movement provoking one strong emotion after another.

"Oh God, Will …" My mind and body seemed no longer to be connected. I began to lose perception as the dimension our bodies existed in and the room around us dissolved. I wanted to scream because the feeling of pure love was ecstasy. I heard Will's breathing quicken, and then he gasped as he lifted his body, and I felt warm liquid across my belly.

Will lowered his body against mine, holding his weight with his elbows. Pushing my wet hair back from my face, he kissed my forehead, my eyes, the tip of my nose, and then my lips. He rolled off me, still holding me tight. We held each other, not talking, but gently rocking back and forth until we both entered a place where we weren't actually sleeping, but rather, floating.

We held each other the whole day, hidden away in my room, not even leaving to eat or drink. Neither of us wanted the magic of our first day together to end. We spent hours exploring each other, talking about our past and what the future held for us now that we were together. I told him the story of each scar on my body, and in return he told me his.

I don't think we would have ever gotten up if we hadn't been interrupted by Ruth and George outside my bedroom door.

"I don't know George," Ruth said loudly. "Do you think they just evaporated or were beamed up by the mother ship or something? I see a robe and a coat. They must have both been here at some point.

"It would be too bad," George replied quickly, "if on Will's first day in our new apartment, he starved to death, or even worse, died of thirst."

"Okay, okay," Will finally shouted loud enough for Ruth and George to hear. Then, looking at me, he suggested, "Maybe we should eat something."

I laughed the most joyous laugh of my life. I was giddy, drunk with the humming in my body, which I was sure would become a way of life with Will. Gilbert had called it *Will's gift*, the ability to raise a life force, and I knew beyond a doubt that he was right. But there was much more to consider, I thought, as this incredible human being got out of my bed and put on his clothes. William Emerald is the gift—not just his life force, but all of him, from his smile to the depth of his soul. The second gift was that he was mine.

Will reached down and pulled me to my feet. "Come on, get dressed. I don't want you to starve either, and I think our roommates want to say hello!"

We squeezed into the bathroom to freshen up a little, laughing non-stop. My new mantra was *I love my life, I love my life, I love my life*. Dr. Edwards would absolutely have approved of my new self-talk.

Looking as good as possible after splashing water on our faces for a few minutes, we tugged on the rest of our wrinkled clothes. Will put his arm around my shoulder and we opened the bedroom door, only to be greeted with a roar of laughter and applause.

"McCollum knew what he was doing when he wouldn't let you out of the house," George teased. "Are you okay, Hillary?"

I could feel the heat of blush on my face.

Will defended me joyfully. "She's just fine, George, but I do think we should get her something to eat."

"I bet you do. You've burned quite a few calories," Ruth sputtered as she headed toward the kitchen. "Let me see what I can throw together."

Ruth actually had become a very good cook, but it didn't matter what I ate; anything would taste delicious.

Other friends might have gotten annoyed at how Will and I were unable to let go of each other, but Ruth and George took everything in stride. When we weren't totally wrapped around each other, we at least held hands.

After dinner, we adjourned to the downstairs apartment. Ruth and George had been unpacking all day, and the place looked great. The apartment was definitely a shoe-free zone, with the most luxurious rugs spread on the floors. It felt incredibly cozy with the smell of George's spice tea permeating the air and the fireplace blazing.

"The pictures on the walls are mostly Mandalas and gurus," Ruth said. Seeing the confused look on my face, she put her arm around my shoulder. "They are spiritual teaching tools. I'll explain more later, sweetie, when you return to being yourself." I saw a mock look of sympathy between George and Ruth before they once again broke into laughter.

I found a space to curl up by the hearth while Will and George continued talking.

"You weren't around, Will, so I picked the bedroom I wanted," George explained, pointing to the room on the right. "That one is yours."

"You receive with your left and give with your right," Will acknowledged.

"That's how I figured it out." George smiled, and it was evident that the two monks were brothers through and through.

Will pulled me to my feet and we walked down the hall to the room on the right and opened the door. The furniture was stacked against one wall and the boxes along the other.

Holding back a laugh, I said, "Looks like you'll have to stay with me tonight."

Will smiled. "Sounds great. I can unpack tomorrow while you're at class."

We returned to the living room to find George and Ruth sitting by the fire. Joining them, we made a spiced tea toast to Will's and George's new lives, and then we excused ourselves to go to sleep upstairs.

"I think I'll be able to control myself tonight," Will said as he climbed into bed beside me. "I've thought of nothing but the moment we would be together for months. And then, when I saw you, it was totally out of my control. I couldn't have stopped unless you said I had to. I would have, I promise you that," he said, fluffing the pillows.

"I don't think I could have found a way to say no. Every girl wants her first to be perfect." I looked at Will to see what his reaction was. "I suppose I wasn't acting much like a virgin."

"Well, neither was I, and I always wondered if I would know what to do."

My heart stopped for a beat as I took in what Will had just said. "I thought we were perfect! Just think how wonderful we'll be with a little more practice," I said, as I snuggled closer.

"But no more practicing until we are more prepared. I was as careful as I could be under the circumstances. We need to figure out some birth control, and soon. I'm only promising control for tonight—mostly because I'm exhausted." He pulled the covers up to his chin and closed his eyes.

"I'll drop by student health when I'm on campus," I said. I kissed him on the forehead, both eyes, the tip of his nose, and then on his lips. "Thanks for the most incredible day of my life, Will," I whispered.

"Shhhhh. If you wake me up too much, you might have a monster on your hands," he said with his eyes still closed. "Today was so incredible, it's best I don't think about it right now. I'm trying to be good, Hillary," he said, holding back a laugh and opening one eye, "I'm not kidding Hillary, don't get me started."

I'd always relied on my own body heat to warm the cold bed. Tonight, Will was like a furnace, warming my bed for me. I wondered what my dreams would be like with him beside me, and I drifted off to sleep.

December 2, AD 36

We gather near the water's edge around our campfire to listen to McCollum as the sun rises. He has seen in his dreams what he believes may be our future, but deep inside he still hopes that he is wrong. We sit in a circle close to a fire because the air has become cold and damp with the onset of winter. Eduardo sits to McCollum's left, enabling McCollum to draw upon Eduardo's powers of clarity and insight. I, Hilsbeth, sit directly across from McCollum, with Liam and Gillian to my right and Georog and Rutiah to my left. Kathryn and Terrance have been left behind to watch over the Druids in our village, who are not yet aware of our impending fate.

"We must join together to call forth the great power created by the purity of light." McCollum begins. "An ominous darkness is falling over our land, and it is driven by ignorance to destroy what it does not understand. Those who will not bend to the laws and beliefs of this new culture will not be allowed to survive. Most will comply. We will not." As McCollum looks deep into our eyes, one by one around the circle, his voice softens.

"Today we stand alone in the brightness of our being; no others will come to save us from this fate. But our light will remain upon this planet until the time we come again to reclaim it. In the future we—"

December 2, 2010

I heard a ringing and felt the pull to return to my familiar college world. Keeping my eyes closed, I strained to hear the information that was being revealed around McCollum's campfire. Leaning forward, I listened to the one across from me as he spoke of the future. Everything faded as my alarm clock blared in my ear. Angry that I had forgotten to reset it the night before, I hit the off button hard. Confused about where I was, and by the fact that it was still dark outside, I closed my eyes and tried to recall any lingering part of my dream. But it was totally gone.

Forced to merge back into this world, I reached out to touch Will, slightly afraid that our night together might have also been a dream. The bed was still warm where he had slept, but he wasn't there. "Will?" I whispered into the darkness.

"Good morning, my beloved," I heard equally as soft from somewhere on the floor beside my bed.

My heart leapt at the level of affection in just those few words.

"Did you fall out of bed?" I asked, confused by his location.

"Yes, but I did it on purpose. I meditate into the sunrise. It's how I start every day. I didn't want to disturb you."

I scooted off the side of the bed and pulled the comforter with me to cover us.

"Is it all right if I just sit here quietly with you?" I asked. "Maybe you can teach me meditation someday."

"I love that you are here with me. Not only because I would love to teach you to meditate, but also because I am freezing. You and Ruth need to turn up the heat." Will tucked the comforter tightly around us. "For now, just sit quietly and see if you can clear your mind."

He reached out and took my hand. His breathing slowed and I could feel the energy move from his hand into my entire body. Then I felt Will completely change as his energy left me and he went to a place far beyond this physical one.

I stayed as still as I could for what seemed like hours. My joints began to cramp and my mind was anything but quiet. It was racing with thoughts of Will, everything I had to get done today, and things I wouldn't get done because I wanted to spend all my time with Will. Slipping my hand free, trying not to disturb him, I tucked the comforter around him and snuck quietly into the bathroom.

I let the steaming hot water run over my head and down my back until my skin turned rosy red. I usually stayed in the shower until all the hot water was used up, but today I wanted to have some time to talk to Will before class. I toweled off, dried my hair, and peeked to see if Will was back from never-never land yet. His eyes flickered open.

"Are you among us?" I let all the steam flow out into the bedroom.

"Yes, and I'm so happy," he answered.

"I'm happy, too," I said, crawling back under the comforter that covered him.

Will chuckled. "*I am so happy* is an integration phase I use when I come back into my body. You see, when you meditate, your soul becomes almost detached and expands far beyond the limits of your body so it can commune with the beauty of being one with everything. *Coming back* can sometimes cause depression because the human body is very confining after being everything. So it's always best to come back quietly, saying to yourself, *I am so happy, My life is so simple*, although waking up next to you, I can't be anything but happy. Come here and kiss me good morning."

His arms wrapped around me and he pulled me into his lap. Our eyes met, and we had our first, very long and sensual good morning kiss.

"My life seems to be full of firsts, and I'm glad they're all with you," he said, "because I have loved you since the first moment I laid eyes on you, Hillary Rubner."

My breath caught in my throat. I must have looked surprised, because Will quickly added, "I don't want to make you uncomfortable. Tell me if I'm moving too fast, but I figure after yesterday you already must know how I feel."

I reached up to touch his face. "I love you, too, Will Emerald. With everything I am, I love you, too."

CHAPTER
TWENTY TWO

IT'S NOT normal to smile this much in the dead of winter, but I had never been happier. For weeks I'd walked from one class to the next with a huge smile on my face, and today was no exception. People were beginning to look at me like I had a screw loose.

Will continued to teach the boys during the day while I was in class, which also kept him happy. We spent our early mornings and nights together, and that meant neither of us was getting much sleep.

Of course I'd admitted to Will that all I did was daydream about him during our sunrise meditations. He encouraged me to just relax, clear my mind, and use the mantra he'd given me. I truly tried, but my mind always drifted back to romance. It was all so new to me, and sitting next to him, feeling the heat of his body, was completely distracting. I was sure I'd get the hang of meditation soon, since I was putting it first on my list of New Year's resolutions.

Finals were fast approaching, and I found it hard to choose studying over time with Will. We needed a bit of a cooling-off period. I mean, after all, how long could two people go without letting each other out of a passionate embrace? Even Ruth and George had started looking at us funny! I'm sure they were impatient for the time when we could be taken out in public again.

I'd told Mom and Dad I had a boyfriend. I was sure they could hear the emotion in my voice. I wanted to take Will home over Christmas break, but there was something he had to do at the house over New Year's, and he wouldn't consider leaving.

The library had asked for volunteers to work over the holidays, and it seemed like a great opportunity to earn some extra money, but I was torn between staying with Will and spending Christmas with my family. Deciding Mom would be able to put it all in perspective, I decided to call her to see what she thought. I knew she'd heard the excitement in my voice when I talked about Will, and that she would be sensitive to my feelings.

When I was halfway across campus, I heard something fly past my ear and saw a puff of snow as it hit the ground ahead of me. It all happened simultaneously, and I knew Gilbert must be close. Seeing the bottle cap lying in the snow bank, the memory of Gilbert's talent at shooting them by snapping his fingers came back to me. I turned to see him jogging up behind me.

"Hils, long time, no see. I'm still a pretty good shot," he said, as he nodded to the bottle cap.

"Isn't that considered littering? It's not exactly green to be leaving bottle caps everywhere," I answered, as I pulled the collar of my coat tight to keep in my body heat.

"Yeah, I suppose, technically it's littering," he agreed. He then moved to another subject. "Are you still hanging out with Will?"

"Changing the subject to my favorite one is clever, Gilbert. Yes, as a matter of fact I am hanging out with Will," I answered, smiling.

"Do you think you can hook me up with him for an evening after the first of the year? I'd really like to compare notes. It's not often you meet a person like him. You know, so advanced," Following my example, Gilbert pulled his coat tight.

"Sure, I'll hook you up, Gilbert. I'll see him tonight and ask him to book you into his schedule."

"Okay Hils, I'm going to hold you to it." He pulled his hands out of his pockets and gave me a hug. "I've got to get to class."

I gave him a hug and kissed his very cold, red cheek and watched him jog back toward campus.

It took another freezing ten minutes to walk home, so when I turned the key and opened the apartment door, the heat felt wonderful. I dropped my backpack from my shoulder and took off my gloves, heading toward my room as I pulled my cell out of my pocket and dialed the farm.

"Hi Hillary," Mom said when she heard my voice. "I've been meaning to call you, too."

"You can go first, Mom," I said, putting off the disappointment I'd cause her by suggesting I might not come home for Christmas.

"Your dad and I have been thinking about a few things. Kenny is planning a ski trip to Colorado with a few buddies over Christmas break. We hate for him to be away at Christmas, but how can we say no? It will be such an adventure for him and he's been saving all of his money. He's so excited about it. So …" she paused and took a breath. "Your dad and I were thinking of doing something a little different this year, too."

My heart sank. It was one thing for me to suggest not coming home, but for my parents to not be there was a different story altogether. I knew it was a double standard, but …

"Let me go on before you interrupt," Mom continued. "We think it would be fun to get away from the farm and come up to see you. Okay honey, you can say something now. If it's too much, just say no."

A few seconds passed, and a million things ran through my mind.

"We can get a hotel room. We promise not to be pests. I can still cook a Christmas dinner at your house. We won't worry about a tree this year." I could almost hear *please, please, please* in her voice. I think they were actually looking forward to visiting me.

"Mom, I would love for you and Dad to visit over Christmas. You know the library has asked me to work a few extra hours, and now I can let them know that I'm available. Should I tell Mr. Delaney you'll be in town?" I teased. "You know he'll want to see you," I said slowly just to rub it in. Even over the phone I could see her blushing.

"You know, I talked to your Uncle Paul the other day. Paul said he hasn't heard from Sam in years, but he got a call from him a few weeks ago. They took quite a trip down memory lane. I guess seeing you must have reminded Sam of his college days at Emporia State with your Uncle Paul … the two basketball stars. I think it would be nice to see Sam again. Yes, of course, tell him I'll be in town over Christmas, but be sure and let him know Terry will be with me, so he doesn't get any ideas."

"Okay Mom, I'll be sure to tell him how happily married you are. I'll take Dad up to my special room while you hang out with Saaaam," I said, drawing out the name for emphasis. "It'll be fun showing Dad the books I found." I could tell by her silence that Mom was feeling left out, but she could only be in one place at a time, so I let it go.

"Let me talk to Ruth," I said. "Maybe you can just stay at our apartment. She's going home for Christmas break and might not mind if we use her room. It would be nice to have you here."

We agreed to talk again in a couple of days and hung up. I heard Ruth outside cursing, once again desperately looking for her keys. There was no time like the present to find out her Christmas plans.

"Hold on Ruth," I yelled running to the door. Ruth carried the biggest purse I'd ever laid eyes on, and her keys were never in the same place twice. When I opened the door, she had half the contents of her bag dumped out on the landing.

"Are you sure you need to carry all that stuff?" I asked, bending over to help. It wasn't the first time I'd made this suggestion.

Ruth haphazardly piled all her stuff back into her purse. "I'd hate to be caught without something I need," she replied, heaving the bag up on her shoulder with a smile. "It may take me a while to find it, but at least I know I have it." She hurried inside to get warm, leaving snow in her wake as I closed the door behind her.

"Hey Ruth, I just talked to my mom on the phone. My parents want to come here for Christmas. What would you think about them staying here while you're gone? Would it bother you if I slept in your room and let them use mine?"

"No, I guess I'll let you use my room." She made deliberate eye contact. "Just don't have sex in my bed!"

I threw a sofa pillow at her as she walked away.

"I don't think I'll be having sex while my parents are in the next room!"

She picked up a pillow as she passed the chair, and not being fast enough, I got smacked in the head when she threw it.

"Okay, I give," I said, putting my hands up in the air declaring Ruth the undefeated Pillow Fighting Queen! "Thanks Ruth. No sex, I promise."

I thought about Christmas without a tree and decided it just wasn't going to happen, not at my house! I had seen a few small ones at the grocery store that were already decorated, and felt even a small tree was better than no tree at all. I could invite Will and George for Christmas supper, although I decided I should find out if they even "did" Christmas before I got too excited about including them.

Will insisted that I spend two hours studying before he came up, and at the end of that time I heard his muffled footsteps coming up the stairs. The knob turned and his face peeked around the door.

"Don't let the heat out. Get in here," I said anxiously. We had spent enough time together that I no longer felt the need to launch myself into his arms, so I actually walked over to where he stood and fell into his embrace.

"Did you have a nice day?" I asked.

"My day was great," he answered after kissing me. "I thought of this all day long."

"I need to ask you a few questions," I said, looking up at him. "Take off your coat and have a seat. I'll bring you some herbal tea." I picked up my cup as I walked into the kitchen and heard his heavy winter coat hit the couch.

When I returned, Will was seated at the table where I was studying, checking out my calculus book.

"Interesting stuff, Hillary. I like the way your mind works."

"Thanks, but that's not what I want to talk to you about." I reached across the table to take the book and set it aside. "My parents are coming for Christmas."

"And?"

"And I'd like to introduce you to them and invite you and George to Christmas dinner, if you believe in Christmas … I mean, I don't actually know!"

"I'd be honored to meet your parents." His words were so sincere they stole my heart. "And I do believe in Christmas; I believe in the celebration of everyone who has accomplished Christhood. But I'm not sure of my holiday schedule yet. It forms organically. For now, tell me more about your parents."

"I think you will really like them. Mom and I are nothing alike. She's beautiful, petite, and a wonderful cook." Before Will could give me an argument, I slid an envelope from under my computer. "Remember when I told you at the Fall Mixer that you sounded like my dad? Well, I wasn't kidding. Last year he wrote me a letter. I had invited him for Father's Weekend and added a P.S. to let him know I was disappointed in my grades. Nothing can tell you more about my dad than this letter can." I held it up for him to take.

"Are you sure?" he asked.

"Yes, I'm sure." He opened the envelope and unfolded the handwritten letter.

Dear Hillary,

Your letter made your old Dad very happy! What could be greater than to have your daughter say that she is proud of you and anxious to show you off? I'm sure my walk will be a little livelier and I will stand a little taller for quite some time.

Yes, I will be proud of you if you don't make it as a "big college girl." Whether you make a 3.0 or 0.3 makes absolutely no difference to me. I was proud of you, beyond words, the very first time I saw you through the glass at the hospital, and you couldn't do anything then but cry!

I can remember at the beginning of each semester feeling that it was far too difficult, I was in over my head and was sure to flunk out. It depends only upon how important it is to you because the only limitations we have are those we place upon ourselves.

I am not sure how really reliable an education is. Nothing new can come from a book. It's already old stuff or it couldn't be there. They can teach you the formula, but the inspiration, the vision, only you can furnish. The source of wisdom is within. You already have that. You need only to become aware of it.

School is kind of a game we play. The teacher's part is to impart to you certain information. You store that information away in the recesses of your brain, or on a crib sheet, and when he asks for it back, you give it to him in the form of an answer on a test. You learn to copy, mimic, parrot, and repeat what you have learned or read of others.

If you are particularly adept at the playing of this game, you are given all kinds of rewards — good grades, grants, scholarships, etc. When you are in a family gathering your Mom & Dad will brag on you, and you will feel very smug. Your ego will say, "Yes, look at how great and wonderful I am!" But what does it really mean to you?

No graduate, upon receiving a sheepskin can say, "Now I am fulfilled." On the contrary, most are confused as hell — and more paranoid than ever. Having little notion of what life is really all about.

As it is the nature of a honeybee to seek honey, it is the nature of man to seek beauty. That's what it is all about. The whole purpose of life is to reach that topmost pinnacle of human unfoldment. That topmost pinnacle beyond which no man can go is merely an awareness of beauty. Not just the beauty of those things around us, but that spiritual, mystical kind of beauty within.

We look for it in many ways; schools, a bottle, a pill, a smoke, T.V., a book, a movie, a lover, etc. You will not find it in any of those places. The best they can do is inspire you to make the search.

Beauty (beauty, peace, love, joy, strength, light, wisdom), although elusive, surrounds everything and everyone. It cannot be seen. It can only be hinted at. All who have known true beauty have found it within. Beauty originates in the soul and is expressed through creativity. That is why creativity is the only thing of an enduring nature.

Life is said to be "a perilous bridge between the physical and the spiritual." It is perilous indeed. There are many hurts involved. How do you transcend the physical and avoid the fears, disappointments, heartache and anguish that go with it?

It is very simple. Seek beauty always! Listen to your heart, not your Dad. Find a quiet place where you can be alone and just take the time to listen.

Much Love
Dad

When Will reached the end of the letter he carefully refolded it and placed it back into its envelope.

"Wow, thank you, Hillary. He is a profound thinker. I believe I will like him very much."

Finals week came, and I was more than prepared since Will had purposely stayed away so I could study without distraction. I felt great about all of my grades and posted them on the refrigerator door for my parents to see, just like they did when I was a kid.

There was a fresh dusting of snow on the ground the day Mom and Dad arrived. They had called me from the highway for final directions, so I knew it wouldn't be long before they turned onto my street.

Waiting for them in front of my apartment, I began waving wildly when I saw their truck. I had been looking forward to this for weeks. As they pulled to a stop, both doors flew open and Mom and Dad ran toward me. This was what family was all about. We hugged, and Dad twirled me around enough to make me dizzy.

Mom started unloading coolers of food onto the sidewalk. Of course she had been cooking for days and had every meal planned. Dad brought in the pies and lined them up on the kitchen counter: pumpkin, pecan, blueberry, and apple. I was going to love this holiday!

Mom prepared all my favorites for dinner—brisket, potatoes, string beans, and more potatoes. I loved all potatoes: sweet potatoes, mashed potatoes, baked, scalloped, French-fried, it didn't matter. When I was a kid, Mom told me that one day I would turn into a potato, and maybe I will. But for now, the meals would be wonderful, and made sweeter by my parents company.

I was pleasantly full and very sleepy as bedtime approached. We had talked about everything … twice. I promised to introduce them to Will the first chance I got. I figured I'd wait until they actually met Will before delving into the reasons he was spending his nights at a home instructing young boys in meditation. To tell the truth, I didn't really understand it all myself, although Will always made his path sound like music. I wanted my parents to hear that music, too.

I tucked my folks into my bed and went to Ruth's room to sleep. It wasn't long before I heard my dad snoring softly and everything felt like home.

My alarm went off early, and when I realized it was in the other bedroom, I felt a little pang of guilt for waking Mom and Dad on their first day of vacation. But listening to the soft footsteps and whispers that came from the living room, I could tell that my parents had probably been up for hours.

"Did you sleep well, Hillary?" Mom asked cheerfully as I opened Ruth's bedroom door.

"Like a baby. Did you guys sleep okay in my bed? I hope it wasn't too small."

"We slept just fine. I love any reason to snuggle a little closer to your father." Mom still had a way of teasing Dad that lit him up.

"Okay guys, that might be too much information," I said, waving my hands and changing the subject. "What time is your rendezvous with Sam today?"

"I talked to Sam on the phone while we were on the road yesterday. He said about 10:00 a.m. today would work fine for him, so we still have plenty of time. Maybe we can have lunch at the Student Union afterwards? I know the food won't compare to mine," she said, glowing, "but I haven't been in a student union for decades."

CHAPTER
TWENTY THREE

ARRIVING AT the library just before ten, we found it very quiet compared to when school was in session. We all walked to Mr. Delaney's office, and Mom made the proper introductions. Mr. Delaney's office was much cleaner than usual, and he was much better dressed. His crush on Mom still showed, even after all the years that had passed.

I could tell by the look on Dad's face he was a bit embarrassed to be watching it all. Dad was too much of a gentleman to gloat over being the winner. I'll even bet that in an odd way he found it charming.

Dad and I excused ourselves to begin the library tour. We started at Ann Marie's desk, and from there I showed him all the levels of the library, saving the best for last because I knew the glass-floor room would also be Dad's favorite place.

"You should tap your fingers on a shelf so you don't get a shock," I warned Dad before we got too far onto the glass. "Static electricity ..."

I heard Dad tap his fingers on the shelf behind me and as I continued talking and walking across the room, I got a funny feeling that I was the only one engaged in my conversation. I turned to look and sure enough, Dad was already thumbing through the books.

"Hillary, I've never been in a room like this! How can anyone in their right mind ever leave without reading every book in here?" He was mesmerized by the titles and started reading them out loud as his fingers floated by them: "*The Masters of the Far East, The Book of Early Whisperings, God Will Work with You but Not For You, Reincarnation and the Laws of Karma, Meditations of Maharishi*

Mahesh Yogi, The Bhagavad-Gita."

Dad was in heaven!

"That's why they call it a library, Dad," I said jokingly. "You don't have to stay in this room to read every book because you can actually take them home."

"Hillary, can you check out some of these books for me?" He was almost breathless as he pulled books off the shelf and lined them up on the reference table.

"Sure Dad, you pick out what you'd like and I'll check them out for you for as long as you like."

Dad sat down, pulling a stack toward him, and started opening each book in random places to see what treasures it had to offer.

"Kiddo, do you have a pen and paper? I need to take a few notes so I can keep my thoughts straight."

"Not on me, but I can run to Ann Marie's desk. I'll be back in about five minutes."

As I walked down the almost abandoned hallway, I thought about peeking in on Mom, but figured Dad was in more need of the pen and paper than Mom was of rescuing. I hurried back to the glass-floor room, and when I arrived, Dad had his books divided into three stacks.

The first were books he wanted to check out today, the second were the ones he wanted to read in the future, and the third were books he could do without, at least for now. I handed him the paper and pen and he began writing the titles and authors from stack two. He was as excited as a techie in a computer store.

After about ten minutes, Dad put the pen down to stretch and wiggle his fingers.

"Cramps," he said as he stood to work the kinks out of his back. Seeing his pen roll off the table, he walked over to pick it up, and when he didn't stand up again, I went around the table to see what he was doing.

Over the top of his head I saw him picking up pieces of a book that had been ripped from the binding.

"This book must have made someone very angry," he said, reaching for the last piece. "Hey, Kiddo, call your mom and see if she can come up here. I'm sure Mr. Delaney can show her the way."

I pulled my cell out of my pocket to call. "Hi, Mom, can you have Mr. Delaney show you to the glass-floor room? Dad needs you."

Mom didn't have a problem with the request, even though I thought disrupting her reunion because of a torn book was pretty lame. "Tell your dad that we'll be right there."

He tucked the pages from the torn book into his jacket pocket and then, from a kneeling position, he gently picked up the fragile life that had found its hiding place beneath the torn paper. He turned to me with his hands together, palms up.

"It's a bird!" I mused, wondering how long it had flown around the library.

"He's still warm, Hillary, and I can feel his heart beating." I looked into his gently cupped hands at the small body. "Your mom will know what to do. She's the one who's good with animals."

As we both gazed down at the tiny creature, I heard Mom behind us. She reached up, and Dad gently placed the little sparrow into her hands.

"He must have gotten tired and lost, flying around in here," she said. "Let's get him a drink of water." She looked up at Sam. "Where is the nearest water?"

"There's a men's room around the corner." Sam seemed very interested in helping, and was ready to do absolutely anything Mom asked.

"Can you bring me a wet paper towel? Just be sure to make it wet enough for me to wring out a few drops for our little friend." Mom held the sparrow and whispered softly, "It will be all right. We're here to help now. You are going to be just fine."

Sam rushed back into the room with a sopping wet paper towel and water running up his forearms into his rolled-up shirtsleeves. Mom took the towel from him and tilted it, so that a single drop was hanging from the corner.

"Okay Buddy, can you take a drink?" she coaxed. "Come on, it will help you get your strength back."

As we all looked down at the little thing, it raised its head and Mom squeezed the paper towel just hard enough for the drop to fall down his throat, followed by a second and a third. Dad had been right when he claimed Mom had a certa in magic when it came to animals.

"I think we need to be heading home now," Mom said, looking at Sam. "I'll give you a call when we know the status of our little friend." Mom handed the sparrow back to Dad to put in his coat pocket. Dad's body heat would keep him warm until the heater in the car kicked in.

Sam and Mom walked ahead of us to say their goodbyes while I carried Dad's books to the checkout desk so he wouldn't squish our new friend.

Dad had gone out ahead of us to warm up the car, so by the time Mom and I rushed out with our hands full of books, the car was already nice and toasty. Dad had the little sparrow out of his pocket and in Mom's hands within seconds of our arrival.

"I'm sure glad we decided to drive," I said. "Hope you aren't too upset about missing lunch at the Student Union." I turned to Mom and realized her full attention was on the little sparrow in her hands.

"I'm fine without the Student Union," Mom said. "Sam says almost everything is closed anyway because of Christmas break. I want to get this little guy home and fed." She cooed in a soft rhythmic voice so as not to upset the bird she had already named Buddy.

CHAPTER
TWENTY FOUR

WHEN WE pulled up to my apartment, I was surprised to see smoke coming from the chimney of the lower apartment. I hoped Will had been the one who started the fire. I was trying to not miss him, but looking at his apartment made me realize how empty I felt when he wasn't with me.

We put Buddy back into Dad's pocket while Mom and I each picked up an armload of books, and by the time we closed the car door, there he stood, smiling. Mom and Dad knew immediately who he was by the look on my face.

Will moved toward us, relieving Mom of her books as he introduced himself.

"Hi, I'm Will Emerald." He shifted the books so he could shake my dad's hand. "It's very nice to meet you sir, and you too, Mrs.—"

That was as far as he got before Mom interrupted.

"My name is Kate, and this is my husband Terry. It's very nice to meet you, too. We've been looking forward to this moment."

"I have some coffee on and a warm fire, if you'd like to come in." Will nodded toward his door.

"That sounds great, Will," Dad said, putting his arms around Mom and me to hurry us along. "It's damn cold out here, and we have an emergency patient on board." Noticing the puzzled look on Will's face, he added, "We'll explain once we get inside."

Will looked over the book titles as he set them down on his kitchen table.

"You also appear to be a *seeker*, Terry."

"Never found anything that interests me more in this lifetime," Dad said, warming his hands in front of the fire. When they were warm enough, he reached into his pocket and pulled out Buddy.

"Do you have some lukewarm water and some honey?" Mom asked, walking toward Dad to see if Buddy had regained any of his strength.

"Sure." Will smiled, watching Mom and Dad with the little creature gently held between them. "It will only take a few minutes to get it together for you."

"How are your classes going with the boys?" I asked, following him into the kitchen.

"Initiations," he corrected. "They're going great. Everyone is looking forward to the New Year's celebration. All the boys will be given a new mantra," he said, turning to finally look at me. "Is that what you really want to know, or are you really wondering when I'll be back?" He reached out for my hand and pulled me closer to him.

"I suppose both," I answered sheepishly, feeling like I'd been found out. "It would be nice to have you spend time with my parents."

"I'd like that, too, Hillary. I'll be around for the next few days." He stirred the honey into the water and looked at the color to judge its consistency. "Let's get this out to your parents and then we can talk."

As we walked back into the living room, there was a flutter of wings and a flash of brown, and Mom and Dad gasped with excitement.

"I guess he's all right!" Dad exclaimed, as we watched Buddy land on the fireplace mantel. "And by the looks of it, I think he's found a new home."

The lid on Will's antique wooden box stood open. It usually held a box of matches, but George had left them on the hearth when he lit the last fire. We all watched as Buddy hopped over to the box and into it.

"It must be warm in there," Mom laughed.

We added some fabric and cotton balls to make him more comfortable, and placed a bottle cap full of water in the box, along with a few sunflower and pumpkin seeds to one side. After he had a day or two to recover we would be able to set him loose.

Dad and Will took an instant liking to each other. They moved from one topic to the next with relative ease, and before I knew it, Dad had an invitation to visit Will's house for an introduction to McCollum.

I was impressed, and I thought that with any luck, Dad would be able to explain to me what went on over there. I don't mean to suggest that Will kept secrets from me; it was just hard to understand the terms he used.

Mom and I spent the next few days cooking, chatting, shopping, and looking in on Buddy. Will and Dad spent their time with his stash of library books spread across the table, constantly talking about states of consciousness, linear time being stacked, reincarnation, and the mind's ability to control … well, everything. They were inseparable until it was time to eat. They never missed a meal—because no one in their right mind would ever miss a meal Mom cooked.

The meeting with McCollum was set for the day after Christmas. Dad had been invited to participate in the *daily practices*, which began at sunrise, and he was ecstatic.

On one of our daily outings, I asked Mom if she were disappointed that Dad was going to meet McCollum without her.

"Absolutely not, sweetheart," she answered. "Your father has been looking for an opportunity like this for as long as I've known him, searching for someone who sees the world the way he does. Your dad views this world as a place of magic, not the doom and gloom they show on the ten o'clock news. He wants reassurance that he's not crazy. Your Will can give that to him, and I could not be more grateful." Tears were welling up in Mom's eyes. "I would have had Terry here a lot sooner if I'd known *the gift* Will had to offer him. I've never seen him so happy. He's like a Roman candle, just about ready to explode into a fountain of brilliant light."

"*The gift*," I thought of what Gilbert had said, and began to understand.

Christmas came, and it was very nice, but not the focal point of our holiday season. The most important day was now the one after Christmas. One evening, while Dad was taking a shower, Mom and I had asked Will what was needed for *morning practices*. We surprised Dad with these items on Christmas morning. He unwrapped each gift with surprise and an abundance of joy. Dad wouldn't have minded sitting on a ratty old towel, but was touched by the new items. There was a rug that would double as a yoga mat, and when folded it was just big enough to sit cross-legged on. There was also a beautiful meditation shawl whose lavender threads were intertwined with gold and indigo blue, and of course a pillow and an abundant supply of loose-fitting clothes.

"How did you find this stuff?"

"It was easy, Terry," Mom said. "The yoga store had almost everything we needed. We'll throw the clothes into the wash tonight, so they don't look brand new." Dad muffled her words with a big kiss.

"This has been a perfect Christmas," Dad said. He looked at us with such emotion in his eyes that I understood, without a shadow of a doubt, that my father was starting a *mystical* journey of enormous proportions.

December 27, 2010

Early Monday morning Dad and Will returned, with George bellowing behind them. They were acting like Super Bowl champs returning home after the big win, slapping each other on the back and reliving what had happened the day before, play by play.

We opened the front door and they piled in, along with Dad's yoga and meditation gear. All three of them were glowing, or should I say *humming*. The room was charged with their laughter.

"Breakfast?" Mom asked, as they turned and noticed us for the first time.

Dad took Mom in his arms and lifted her off the floor. Will grabbed me and swung me around in a circle. George was so overwhelmed that he picked up both Mom and Dad.

"So it was a good experience?" I asked, trying to keep my balance as Will put me down.

"Great. Just great!" Dad said with an ear-to-ear smile. And as I looked around, I realized all three of them had that same smile.

Mom went off into the kitchen to cook breakfast while I started to set the table. The three of them were out of control; maybe food would calm them down. As the smell of bacon filled the room, they started gathering around the table, and by the time breakfast was actually served, it was quite obvious they were famished.

Dad was looking more like a teenager than my father as he started to talk about the experience with a mouthful of eggs.

"I've never been so high! I was so expanded I had thoughts and understandings that I've never had before. I always believed that we were all connected—you know, ONE—but yesterday I was ONE with everything! It's the most amazing feeling I've ever had!"

Will smiled and explained, "Every kid in the house can give Shaktipat, so we just helped him along by letting him hitch a ride on our group consciousness."

"Man, what a ride!" Dad exclaimed, shaking his head in near disbelief.

"When he comes down, he'll probably want to sleep for a while," George said. "I've seen this before. That's why few people come to our house. If you're not ready for the experience, you can go over the edge." George spun his finger in a circle at his temple. "But this guy took everything we could unload on him." He slapped Dad on the back. "I think his crash will be hard."

"How did the meeting with McCollum go?" I asked Will.

"I think Terry should tell you himself; I was only there at the end. After you and your dad have a talk, we can all get together again. After all," he added mysteriously, some of the meeting was about you."

I looked at him, puzzled. "You can't just leave me hanging, Will."

"Oh, yes I can. I'm beat, and besides I need to go downstairs and check on Buddy," he smiled.

"We let Buddy go," Mom said. "He was spending a lot of time looking out the window and he was ready. We didn't want him to fly into the glass."

Will looked crestfallen.

"Maybe we can get you a dog," I added lamely.

"It's okay. It's better for Buddy to be free." Will bent to kiss my forehead. "He was good company, but I still have George."

George and Will picked up their coats and headed back downstairs, while Dad dragged his bags into the bedroom. All three were probably asleep before their heads hit the pillows.

CHAPTER
TWENTY FIVE

DAD WAS *not* up with the chickens or the sun. He slept well past 10:00 a.m. It was the sound of Mom and me talking that finally got him out of bed.

"See what happens when you stay up late partying with the boys!" I said as he walked into the living room. "I have sympathy for ya, Dad. Will wiped me out on our first couple of dates with that *hum* he has going on."

"You should be in a room that's full of 'em," he said, still out of it. "They give you quite the buzz!"

"Sit down, Terry, and after your first cup of coffee, Hillary and I want to know the whole story." Mom gave him her infamous one-raised-eyebrow look.

It was hard to wait patiently for Dad to start. He was drinking his coffee so incredibly slowly that I wanted to pour it down his throat. But finally he began.

"Before sunrise, everyone gathered silently in the main temple. It was a huge room with enormous windows that look to the east. The boys came in one by one and sat down to prepare their minds and bodies. Some had already been there for hours, sitting in *full lotus*, without moving a muscle. Will silently directed me to a place on the floor where George could sit on one side of me and him on the other. I thought they were being friendly at first, but as the energy in the room built, it became clear that they were sitting with me to make sure I was okay—and to tell you the truth, I was glad to have them there.

"We sat in silence for an hour or so—it was hard to tell; I wasn't wearing a watch. Earlier, Will had given me a short initiation, along with a new *mantra,* and I already knew enough about meditation to feel comfortable, so I sat on my rug and pillow with my legs crossed. No way could I sit like Will and those kids in full lotus. I'd have dislocated a hip." He shook his head and took another swig of coffee.

"I started to repeat my new mantra in my mind, just like Will had shown me. When a thought came into my mind, I would bless it and let it go. And eventually my mind began clearing, until there was nothing but me and the mantra." Dad spoke very slowly, struggling to put his experiences into words.

"Then there wasn't even me … or not as an individual. It's hard to explain," he said, with amazement glistening in his eyes while he relived the experience.

"First, I felt a warmth expand within me. Then, slowly, the feeling moved outside of me, until I became everything and everything was me. I loved and knew Will and George and everyone else in that room, the same way I know myself. We were ONE, but at the same time the experience was beyond that room and contained the whole world … maybe the universe.

"Then somewhere, miles away in the distance, I heard a bell softly ring. It meant that I had to bring my awareness back into my physical form. I had to try to fit *all of what I had become* back into my very small body. And you know something?" He shrugged with resignation. "It didn't all fit. I lost pieces along the way. I tried to gather them all up as I floated back, but when I opened my eyes I no longer could remember what I so desperately missed. Will had told me I had to do integration when I returned. It didn't make sense to me at the time, but after the journey I experienced, I can comprehend the importance. I repeated to myself, *I am so happy, I am so happy, my life is so simple,* and I was thankful that Will had taken the time to explain everything to me, because the feeling of oneness is so seductive that becoming an individual again is quite a shock.

"As I sat trying to settle all the pieces of me back into their proper places, I began hearing what sounded like a hundred bells ringing, all in different keys and at different speeds. It was beautiful, and the smell of incense and sandalwood filled my nostrils." Dad seemed content.

"I opened my eyes to find a procession of young men entering the temple with trays billowing with fragrant smoke. Seven formed a line at the front of the temple, each followed by a younger boy ringing a bell. They moved together rhythmically in a ceremony that overflowed my senses and nourished every part of me.

"Will placed a little book in my hands, already opened to a specific page. I began reading and chanting the Sanskrit words, and when I spaced out, losing my place in the book, Will or George would help. Those boys are something else. They were so kind to me. I never actually saw the sunrise like I thought I would. I think maybe I *was* the sunrise."

Mom and I sat silently with tears in our eyes. The man we both loved so much had found his heart's desire. It was just where he'd always told me it would be—inside. He just had to find the key.

"When the chanting was done, an older boy stepped forward and silently led us in yoga—slow stretches and deep breathing. It felt good to stretch after sitting cross-legged for so many hours. I was a little cramped up, but didn't even feel it because of the magic going on around me."

"At the end of yoga, we lay down on our backs for something called *Savasana*. Everyone was silent, and I wasn't sure what was going to happen, but I did what everyone else did. I was there one minute and the next I was gone again, just floating, disembodied.

"Once again, I heard a bell ring, reminding me to return. Will and George showed me to a room that had been set aside for us. We talked a little, but mostly we just relaxed until lunch. It's hard to find a lot to say after an experience like that." Dad looked into our teary eyes, "Don't you two make me cry. I haven't even gotten to the best part yet."

As the three of us sat in my living room, trying to regain our composure, I thought back to a conversation Dad and I had when I was still in high school. He told me late one night, after everyone else had gone to bed, that sometimes he felt lost in this life, that he had a yearning to go to live in an ashram in India, which he knew sounded foolish because he'd never been to India before. His confession was to me alone. *"I know I'm here with you, Mom, and Kenny for a very important reason, and I love you all more than I can say, but when you and Kenny grow up and Mom and I are finished farming, I'd like to go to India and spend my last years just meditating."* I couldn't imagine a time when Dad would ever leave Mom; they were two halves of a whole. But now, as I looked into Dad's eyes, I understood what he was talking about a little better.

"We ate fresh organic raw vegetables and rice for lunch," Dad continued. "Each taste was unique, and it was as if I was experiencing food for the first time. We sat together in silence, but nothing about it seemed silent.

"When I returned my tray to the kitchen, they asked me what job I'd like to do. They had a list to pick from, so I chose something relatively simple. I didn't think it was safe for me to do anything outside in my state of mind, so I signed up for dishes. Your mom has me trained up pretty good in that department." He smiled at Kate.

"The warm water felt good on my hands, and all I had to do was swish a brush around on the plates before I loaded them into a dishwasher. I was doing a satisfactory job, and I was into the swing of things when I felt a hand on my shoulder. A boy informed me that McCollum would like to see me in his private quarters and asked me to follow him. I was reluctant and excited at the same time to be meeting Mr. McCollum. Will and George had told me so many stories about him that I fully expected McCollum to have a halo and wings. I felt frantic when I didn't see Will or George nearby, but I gathered my courage and followed my guide up the stairs and into a private wing of the house, then waited for McCollum to answer the door.

"He has amazing eyes, you know. I couldn't stop looking at them. I felt his hand on my arm as he led me to a chair in front of the fireplace and placed a glass of water in my hands. We drank *to life,* and by the time I had finished my water, I was more coherent, although I found it difficult to stay attentive in his presence. I kept having the sensation of floating away, and then I'd find he had his hand lying softly on my arm again, bringing me back.

"He told me a story about a great band of brothers who had traveled through time together, from the very inception of time as we know it. They were all things, from fierce warriors to great spiritualists, and they were always held together by their mutual *dharma*. Moving through time, whether they fought on the same side or the opposite side, their balancing and growth became greater in each life they were born into together. He talked about their lives in Egypt, Mongolia, Tibet, and India, but the one place I remember him talking about the most vividly was in Great Britain, long before that was its name. That was when it dawned on me that I was part of it all, that he was speaking about me, my past lives—and his and Will's and George's—and all of the other young men I had spent the morning with in meditation!

"McCollum explained that the brothers had scattered to the winds after that last lifetime. Some incarnated immediately to retaliate against the army that had destroyed us. Others remained behind, merged with the *source,* to heal and rest, waiting for a time when we would all be together again. And *now is that time.*

"I think Will told you that he and George were sent out into the world to find the last few?" Dad said, looking at me questioningly.

"Well, yes, but I didn't know it was going to be you, Dad," I said in my own defense. "I swear I would have called you sooner!"

"It's not only me, but your mother and you too, Hillary."

"McCollum told me our planet is elevating and the vibration is increasing," Dad explained. "People will be leaving the planet in large numbers because the energy will be too much for their souls to handle at this time. It will look like war, murder, and even insanity as people become more agitated by the energy shift. Others will become ill, and there will be suicides. But in reality, it's a massive exit plan as the planet transmutes into a higher frequency.

"I know I'm sitting here talking like this makes perfect sense to me, but I'm trying to take it all in myself." Dad was silent for several minutes before reaching out to take our hands.

"McCollum also told me that we would reunite with our soulmates in this lifetime, if possible. It's a difficult task because so many things have to align. First of all, you both have to be here." He smiled. "Then you have to like yourself enough to be able to live with your perfect mirror." He shrugged. "It was planned in the heavens long before we took these bodies.

"Your mom and I actually went our separate ways many lifetimes ago. I learned to live a solitary life in my ashram in India, and would have continued incarnating there if my task in this lifetime weren't of such monumental importance. My soulmate and I needed to reunite to birth *you* into this world." Dad squeezed both of our hands. "It had to be *now*, because you had to be here to complete Will." His eyes never left mine. He needed to make sure that I understood what he was saying.

"I know Will and I belong together," I said, pressing on my temples. "I love him so much, but I'm having a hard time wrapping my brain around all of this. McCollum really told you this was all planned?"

"I know, Kiddo. It's a lot to absorb," he said, taking another breath. "But McCollum also wanted me to ask you a question. He wants to know if you remember being a female warrior … of legendary proportion." He looked at me expectantly.

"Me?" I said in disbelief. "You know me. I'm nothing special. For sure not legendary!" My head was splitting, and I wanted to talk to Will in the worst way, but I knew he wasn't home. "I'm sorry you guys, I need to lie down. With tears threatening to overflow due to my muddled mind, I went to Ruth's room. I took an aspirin and fought to get to sleep.

Vicki Renfro

CHAPTER
TWENTY SIX

AT THE Dark Moon, December 27, AD 37

Once again, I am in position at the forest edge, stroking my mare to keep her calm. I can feel the tension pulsate through her muscles as her skin twitches beneath me. Yet, she stands as quiet and motionless as a stone. The sun is dawning and we can do no more to prepare. Today is the day against which everything will be measured—our strength, our will, our training, our power. I hear the sound of Roman armor as they begin their advance. Closing my eyes and opening my hands, I begin to gather the power of the universe within me and pray to my deities, "Please provide me with the strength to defend my homeland—" and before I can open my eyes or finish my prayer, I hear the sickening sound of an arrow entering the body of my beloved, who stands beside me. I scream to the gods, begging that it not be so! My nostrils fill with the stench of blood. My mare bucks violently beneath me as a storm of extraordinary magnitude explodes within me. The wind blows with such a fury that I know the storm within is now manifesting around me. I lift my hands, and the skies darken and lightning flashes with a deafening crack. I bless the body that lies dead on the ground next to me, feeling the power of his soul join mine to fuel my rage. I am not alone as I begin the charge into battle. Liam is inside me, and together we are fury and revenge and bloodlust.

As I suck wind into my lungs, I find myself watching the battle from above rather than from within my body. I observe myself fighting a savage battle with grace and beauty, and I see the rawness of the brutality as I wield my sword, severing limbs and heads. Smelling the putrid scents of the dead and dying, I watch the bodies fall, screaming in agony, and the souls being released from the pain of their Earthly existence. I stand with one leg in both worlds, torn between the pain of humanity and the understanding that death is merely an exchange of energy. I want to leave my body behind to follow my beloved Liam into the light, knowing that if I return to Earth, I will find him dead ... run through by an arrow that was meant for me.

I can feel Liam's soul beginning to drift further and further away from me, and know I have no life without him. If it weren't for the thread that still binds me to my living body below, I would lower my sword and let myself be struck dead in battle. But I am the mystic warrior who commands our army, and today my destiny is to save my people to fight another day.

I feel the ripping of my soul as part of me leaves in search of Liam and part retakes control of my body below. I once again feel the weight of the sword in my hand and the warmth of blood running down my arms. I no longer feel the bliss; only the pain as a part of me drifts away into the ethers.

The annihilation is complete, but on this day it is my army that still stands! As I raise my eyes to the horizon, I see the sole survivor of this great Roman cohort as General Flavius turns and gallops away.

December 28, 2010

I woke up enraged, wet with sweat and fighting with my covers. Mom opened the door to check on the ruckus and noticed me sitting up, hair a mess, tears running down my face. "Who is still alive?" I asked, not knowing which world I was in.

"Dad and I are the only ones here, sweetheart." She hurried to my bedside to look into my eyes. "Are you okay?"

"I think so," I said, running my fingers through my wet hair.

"Do you have a fever?" Mom asked, reaching to feel my forehead.

I slapped at her hand, trying desperately to stay in the other world long enough to count the bodies. I needed to know who had survived, but Mom's hand was of this world and it caused the dream to quickly dissolve.

"Is Will here?" I asked.

"Will and George are at McCollum's. He called, but he didn't want to wake you and said he'll see you when we arrive for New Year's."

Nervous energy forced me to get up. I walked into the living room, again trying to remember what I had forgotten.

"So much for getting answers," I said mindlessly, realizing the remnants of the dream were gone. I looked up to see Dad sitting alone and working intently on something by the window, and for a split second I saw an image of someone else's face overlay his. The name *Terrance* flashed into my mind with a vivid feeling of déjà vu, and I found myself wondering if two worlds could overlap at times.

Dad was working to repair the book he'd found in the library. I had completely forgotten about it, and I found that concentrating on it helped me calm my frazzled mind.

"Have you figured out why someone was angry enough to tear it up?" I asked as I walked over to him.

"Well Kiddo, this book really tested someone's faith; so much so that they thought by destroying it they would destroy the ideas written within it." He placed the last piece of tape on the binding. "Unfortunately for whoever did this, *truth* can't be destroyed, even if you don't believe it.

"See, this book talks about what would have happened if The Gospel of Thomas had been put in the Bible. It would have dramatically changed history because Thomas stated that the divinity of Jesus was shared by humanity, and that Jesus repudiated the idea of finding God *through* him." Dad flipped through the pages of the book and inspected his tape job.

"The manuscript this book talks about was discovered in 1945 in upper Egypt, and even though experts acknowledge it as a first-century text, written at the time of Jesus, most treat the Gnostic Gospels as if they don't exist. The Mary Magdalene Gospels were discovered in 1896, and wouldn't it be interesting to know the truth about her." Satisfied with the job he had done, Dad closed the book. "This book can *open* a mind or *close* it just as fast. It depends on the person doing the reading.

"I think I'll take a walk over to the library to return this book to its rightful place on the shelf. I need some fresh air and a good walk. Since meeting your Will, I have a lot to think about." He looked at me with a slow smile. I couldn't help but give him a big hug.

"Can you pick me up in about an hour?" he said. "I'll wait for you

162

in front of the library. We can take Kate out for lunch somewhere nice," Dad put the book in his pocket. "You two can pick a place," I said. "I'm up for anything."

We arrived in front of the library at eleven sharp, and Dad was nowhere in sight. "Mom, I think he's been mesmerized by the books again. I can already see him with another stack to check out. Let me park the car and we'll go in and rescue him."

Mom laughed, knowing I was probably right.

The library was so dark and quiet that it was spooky. As Mom and I walked, the motion detectors turned on lights, which faded to darkness behind us. We soon heard voices talking softly and knew they were coming from the glass-floor room.

"The Thomas Gospel states that all of us come forth from divine light."

"I recognize that voice," I said to Mom as we turned the corner. Dr. Edwards, now holding the repaired book, was so deep in conversation with Dad that neither of them noticed we had entered the room. I cleared my throat to let them know that they were no longer alone.

"Hi Kiddo, Kate," Dad said sheepishly, realizing that he had stood us up for our lunch date. With a warm smile that could have melted ice, he added, "Let me introduce you to my new friend, Lee Edwards. This is my wife Kate and my daughter—"

"Hillary," Dr. Edwards finished. "Hillary and I are old friends," he said, cheerfully acknowledging me. Turning to Mom, he reached out to take her hand. "It's very nice to meet you, Kate. I've enjoyed talking with your husband. It's always nice to meet another of like mind."

Dad chuckled and said, "It's interesting, isn't it, that the more you learn, the less you know. The universe just keeps opening." He took Mom's arm and wrapped it through his. "We have a lunch date that it appears I'm late for. Would you like to join us?"

I blushed at just the suggestion of spending time with handsome Dr. Edwards. He had become quite a popular figure on campus. The females were absolutely enamored with him. I supposed hanging with him might ease that larger-than-life image I had of him and help me stop blushing every time I saw him. We all walked down to the parking lot together, and Dr. Edwards followed us to the restaurant in his own car.

It was a typical Italian restaurant, dimly lit with a scent of fresh garlic that made your nostrils flare with pleasure. Dad requested the four-top in the back corner to allow us more privacy. It seemed like the back corner of any establishment was fast becoming my usual place. When we began to talk, Dr. Edwards insisted that I call him Lee, making me blush all over again. I was interested in hearing more about Dr. Edwards' … Lee's life, so I hoped that he wouldn't hold back.

"For the last twenty-some years I've been doing research, or at least that's what I like to call it," Lee began to explain. "In the late eighties I found myself at a Hindu ashram with the opportunity to study with a great master. I arrived with the misconception that their teaching techniques would be similar to those used in college, and I would graduate with some kind of enlightenment degree." Laughing, he said, "There was a lot I didn't understand about the spiritual journey back then. My largest misconception being that you can be *taught* the Way to self-awakening. I soon discovered each person's journey is uniquely their own because "I" *was the Way* for me and me alone. You can learn technique, but how you apply it within your consciousness is very individualized. I began to spend hours going into the silent space deep within me, surrendering, allowing my mind to rest, until one day I couldn't remember the last time I had spoken. Silence is a profound teacher.

"I discovered I wanted nothing more than to spend the rest of my life going deeper and deeper into that silence, that space between the breaths. Of course, we all know that is when things *must* change. The universe never wants us to be too comfortable; it wants us to continue our journey. So one day, after spending time in a particularly insightful meditation, one in which I found myself almost levitating rather than walking out of the temple, someone handed me a note. The slip of paper merely said to 'report to the office.'

"When I reached the office, the ashram secretary handed me a letter. I didn't recognize the name or phone number that I was to call, but as I read on, I found out they belonged to the director of Menninger Clinic. Reluctant to call immediately, I spent a few days meditating with the letter in my hands, and I came to the realization that I must replace my worry with faith. If I accepted what had found me and opened myself to the new experience, even more blessings would come into my life. So I called and accepted a fellowship that was offered to me with great gratitude, because gratitude should always follow opportunity.

"It wasn't what I had planned for my future. I had imagined I would do something much loftier, but it did give me the facilities I needed to continue my research. Eventually, I was allowed to invite a group of gurus from India who had agreed to become my research subjects. Now those results would blow your mind." He seemed to want to take that tangent and tell us about the gurus, but instead he pulled himself back to the subject at hand. "It also helped me with a more personal project of mine, what I have always been interested in. I have been researching past life experiences."

Dad had ordered a bottle of wine and thought it was a good time to fill our glasses. He had a grin on his face the size of Texas, and I could tell he was bursting at the seams. He couldn't wait to tell his new friend about the boys!

We were all quiet as the waiter brought our lunch and refilled our water glasses. When he left, the conversation picked up where it had left off.

"My hope now is to unearth the answers to the questions that have preoccupied me for years, some since childhood," Dr. Edwards continued as he looked around the table. I suppose he was trying to gauge our receptiveness before he spilled his guts to three virtual strangers. "Maybe a more accurate explanation would be dreams and visions of *my* past lives. I get glimpses of memories and faraway places that I feel may be as real as the life I'm now living." He looked around the table for some sort of confirmation.

Dad was the first to speak after taking a big drink of wine. He first looked at me for approval, and then at Lee.

"I hope I'm not overstepping my bounds here, but I think I know someone who would like to meet you."

We planned to introduce Lee to Will as soon as an introduction could be arranged, and then the conversation moved onto less serious subjects. Lee told Dad how he'd met me and how he loved the glass-floor room, and Dad told Lee about the farm and how it was his ashram.

CHAPTER
TWENTY SEVEN

WHEN WE pulled up to my apartment, the chimney was smoking. A smile erupted across my face that needed no explanation.

"Go ahead, Hillary. Dad and I will make ourselves at home in your apartment. I'll have dinner ready about five o'clock if you'd like to invite Will up ... and George too, if he's here," Mom said.

"Thanks, Mom," I said, kissing her on the top of her head and turning to leave. "I'll let you know either way." I knocked on the door at the same time Will opened it. He kissed me hello and led me into the living room, where George was on the couch with Buddy perched on his finger!

"Buddy's back!" I hurried over to sit by George, knowing my parents would be happy to see him again.

"Will and I hadn't been here more than ten minutes before we heard tapping on the window," George explained. "When we went to check it out, we found the little guy asking if he could come in. I think he's grown accustomed to his warm bed above the fireplace."

"What are you going to do now, just keep him inside?" I asked.

"Go look at what Will's building on the kitchen table. He's going to make a birdie door," George said, pointing with his free hand.

I walked over to where Will had returned to work with an array of items on the table. He seemed to have fabricated a piece of wood the width of the window with a very small, lightweight plastic flap.

"Let's try it out," Will said, picking it up and walking to the window to see if it would work. He placed the piece snuggly along the sill and lowered the window down on its top. It sealed beautifully.

"Now the question is, how do we teach Buddy to use this door?"

Will said, turning to George.

George got up with Buddy still on his finger and walked over to the window. Lowering Buddy onto the windowsill, he pushed him through the little flap. We all put our faces against the glass to see what Buddy was doing on the other side.

Buddy took one hop, then two. On the third, he flew back through the flap. Jumping out of his way, we watched Buddy fly to his box on the mantel and snuggle in.

"I guess we don't have to teach him anything. He seems to know," George snorted.

Smiling, we all shook our heads and sat back down on the couch.

The computer Will and George had found in the trash was sitting on the coffee table. They were able to use our Wi-Fi from upstairs, and it was obvious they had been online.

"How's Ruth?" I asked. For a moment George seemed amazed by my psychic abilities.

"She's doing well, but she misses us," he answered.

"Yeah, yeah, George. She misses *you*," I teased.

George smiled and turned a beautiful shade of pink. Even though he was a full-grown specimen of a man, he always looked like a boy when the subject of Ruth was brought up. It made me wonder if Ruth might be George's first girlfriend. He seemed very innocent in the ways of romance, and it made them such an adorable couple.

Around four o'clock I remembered to call Mom to tell her that there would be two more for dinner. George and Will were becoming accustomed to Mom's good old farm cooking and would probably be very sorry to see her go.

We could smell dinner wafting into the apartment from above, and we were starving by the time we arrived upstairs. Mom had cooked fried chicken with mashed potatoes and gravy. It was a far cry from the vegan ashram food that Will and George were used to, but they loved it. All talking immediately ceased when the food was placed on the table.

Once Mom began serving after-dinner coffee, conversation started again.

"Hey, Will," Dad began, "I hope I haven't let the cat out of the bag by telling a new friend about you and the boys." Will looked at him, eyebrow raised, and Dad continued. "In regard to people that you and McCollum are looking for, I met a fellow who may be of great interest to you."

Dad had piqued Will's interest, and before long they were dialing Lee Edwards' phone number.

The conversation with Dr. Edwards was short. They set up a time and place to meet the following morning and returned to the conversation George had struck up with Mom. George wanted Mom to teach him how to dance.

"I want to be prepared when Ruth invites me to one of her high society Kansas City parties," George explained.

"You'll leave all those society girls stupefied when they come in contact with your Shakti," I said, and had a good laugh just picturing it. "I know Ruth's family will love you, George."

Everyone talked until well after midnight, and I knew I wouldn't have any alone time with Will. I was getting annoyed that I hadn't had a chance to talk to him about the mystical warrior and soulmate stuff Dad had told me about. As though he had picked up on my frustration, Will assured me just before he said goodnight that McCollum would answer all my questions. He said that until then I should find joy in the life I was living right now.

So when I closed my eyes to go to sleep, I thanked God for each one of the incredible people I had in my life, and drifted off into a deep sleep.

December 29, AD 37

I lie on the ground wrapped in a blanket against the chill of winter. It is but seven days since the Earth tilted away from the sun, and it is a time of rebirth. But I feel immense emptiness, and I am looking forward to sleep overtaking me. The part of my soul that remains in my physical form no longer dances, and the part that left to find Liam I can no longer feel. There will be no peace for me in this lifetime, for I am only half alive.

December 29, 2010

Dad insisted on giving Will some alone time with Lee to decide whether he might be one of the souls McCollum was looking for.

"You don't have to leave, Terry," Will said as he sat down in the coffee shop. "I will know within a few minutes if indeed Lee is one of us, and then we will adjourn within the hour for a more lengthy conversation in the privacy of my apartment."

Mom and I had walked with them as far as the coffee shop and then headed around the corner to the grocery store. We mostly talked while placing a few items in our cart.

"I always knew there was something very special about you," Mom said, looking up at me. "I'm not saying that Kenny isn't also special—because he is—but not the way you are. Dad always talked about the way you understood deeper, more philosophical things. Kenny could care less about mysticism. I'm not judging one to be better than the other, but you two kids are very different."

I knew what Mom meant. Give Kenny a sunny day and a ball to play with and he was in heaven. He didn't need to *know*. It just didn't matter in his world, and to be totally honest, he was the happiest person I'd ever known. And that was huge. As for me, I'd always believed there had to be more to life than the *American Dream,* and I knew I had to find *it* to be truly happy.

We finished shopping and rounded the corner by the coffee shop. Dad and Will were still inside sitting at our usual table against the back wall, and to my amazement there was one more person in the group than I had expected.

Will and Dad were facing the front window and waved us in when they saw us. Obvious by his ponytail, Lee was sitting across from Will, and next to Dr. Edwards was another very familiar backside. Gilbert turned, and his smile was the biggest of them all.

Dr. Edwards motioned to the barista to bring two more lattes, and two more chairs were quickly pulled up to the table.

As I sat down next to Will and eyed Gilbert curiously, I could literally feel the energy in the air. This was one heck of an electric group, and Will was grinning as broadly as everyone else.

"We may be complete, Hillary," Will said in a low tone while squeezing my hand. "We need to meet with McCollum, but I think this is our group. Well, plus George and Ruth. If all goes as planned, George will talk Ruth into coming back from Kansas City early, and then we can join the New Year's initiation as a group ... or should I say as ONE." I had never seen him so animated.

Mom passed me my latte and whispered, "Drink up, Hillary. We need to get these boys home before they cause a scene."

As I looked at each face around our table, I wondered how many people thought we were just having a cup of coffee. I was even more amazed that the people sitting near us couldn't feel it. The energy in the coffee shop was so high that my coffee was vibrating in its cup.

Will leaned in and the rest of us were all ears.

"It's a good thing that the customers in this coffee shop are oblivious to how auspicious this moment is," he whispered. "They will continue about their business as if this is just another ordinary day, but I'm here to tell you that today is anything but ordinary, because all of us have not sat at the same table for centuries."

Dad threw a big tip on the table before we became unruly, and he asked Mom if we had enough leftovers for the whole group. That was an absolutely ridiculous question; Mom could whip up a banquet if she had but five minutes.

As we all stood to leave, I noticed a few people looking at us, and wondered what they saw.

CHAPTER
TWENTY EIGHT

"DID YOU talk her into coming back?" I asked George as he walked into the kitchen. He had set the table in the lower apartment for seven, even though the old rescued computer was sitting out on the coffee table.

"I e-mailed her two hours ago, and all I have to say is that we'll need another table setting. By my calculation, she will be here before the food is!" I could see his heart was jumping for joy.

He was right about the timing. Mom barely had the food on the table when there was a knock at the door. George threw it open. Ruth jumped into his arms and he spun around twice before remembering they had an audience.

"Hi, Ruth, welcome home," I said as George set her down on the floor. Then she flung herself at the rest of us, in her dramatic Ruth fashion, until we all had been thoroughly hugged. I was impressed that she only hesitated momentarily before throwing herself into Dr. Edward's open arms.

The high level of excitement continued throughout dinner while the food was passed from hand to hand, and talking never slowed. Speaking nonstop as we ate, and laughing like we were half liquored-up, the room felt like magic. Even Buddy was chirping from the edge of his box, clearly home for the occasion.

Finally, when the food was all but gone and the utensils were laid across plates, George passed around glasses of Scottish port. We all leaned back in our chairs and Will stood to propose a toast. A sweet silence settled over the room, and Will held his glass high.

"I remember each one of you and have loved you for thousands of years. I can now see the many faces you have worn in past lifetimes, and I'm humbled to stand before you."

Looking toward my parents, he continued, "I've only known two Dreamers who could open so completely in meditation that they could feel the movement of each soul their consciousness touched." He smiled as he moved around the table, placing a hand on Gilbert's shoulders. "Gillian was the last of a bloodline that had the ability to interpret nature in such an intimate way that it was his to control. Dr. Eduardo was an Alchemist who traveled from a distant land, and together, he and McCollum became Shape Shifters, the likes of which the world had never seen before and has not seen since." He moved past Dr. Edwards to George.

"Then there's my most trusted friend, who stood guard over the bodies of my Druid students while we meditated in faraway places. Although our affection has always been mutual, Georog only had eyes for Rutiah."

Ruth blushed as she realized Will was speaking of her. "Ruth the one who found Hillary, lifetime after lifetime, to push her forward on her evolutionary path while offering her the comfort of a true friend."

Ruth placed her hand protectively over mine as Will moved to stand by me. "Hilsbeth led our army masterfully as the rumors of her mystical abilities grew. And she defended us until her death." He placed his hand over his heart, "And me, I am Liam, the one who will always love her.

"I feel all of your hearts as they rise to the forefront, defined by the essence of your divinity. Yes, we have been all things, but when we stand together we create greatness.

"Ancient stories tell of the many great souls in the heavens who have been searching though the Akashic records of the universe. These records contain all knowledge of the human experience and the history of the cosmos. They've been looking for a precise point in time, which is pivotal for the advancement of mankind." He paused, connecting with each of us with a glance. "That time is now, and we are together again. The heavenly souls are dancing tonight in celebration with us as we complete the circle we began so long ago."

"Here, here" George said, as he raised his glass and we toasted what the future held for us.

Vicki Renfro

CHAPTER
TWENTY NINE

December 31, AD 38

Pure adrenaline is all we have left. We ride night and day, but are not able to outrun the destiny that follows us. But even the strongest must rest, so last night we made camp and slept.

As the sun slowly rises, I hear the wings of geese as they take flight to greet another day. Terrance and Kathryn still sleep atop a rock outcropping, finding security in the high ground as they stand guard in protective meditation, tethered to their bodies by a thin, golden thread. Gillian finds his comfort slumbering in the fork of an ancient tree, spending his dreamtime gathering strength and secrets from nature. Rutiah is still asleep in her bedroll, while Eduardo is bringing last night's fire back to life. Soon all will rouse, seeking the fire's heat and a warm drink. I see Georog's face looking up the hillside to where I sleep alone, offering me his silent reassurance and understanding.

I hear the sound of hooves on rock, and I turn to see the silhouette of McCollum against the morning sun. Hobbling his horse nearby, he motions for me to approach.

I walk to where he stands, and there is no need for greetings between us, so I begin.

"My soul dances in sorrow," I say, my head hung low. "I went to Marcus Flavius last night in my dreams and found him waiting for me." I have never spoken in detail to McCollum of my relationship with the Roman general, but I suspect he knows the lengths I must go to in order to be in Marcus Flavius's confidence, even in his dreams. The general

allows his fantasies about me to come alive after dark, which causes him to feel a twisted affection toward me in the light of day.

"The General has a directive from Rome to kill us all and then destroy the memory of us," I state bluntly, raising my face to look into McCollum's eyes.

He looks back sympathetically, knowing that the great general must by now be in love with me, and that he and I could not be doing this nightly travel without becoming somewhat entwined.

Gathering my thoughts, I begin my report. "We must raise an army. We, alone, will not be able to defend this land. Roman ships with reinforcements will be landing at Dover at winter's end. Then their march westward will begin in earnest, and they will hunt us down no matter where we hide."

We move down the hill toward the fire, meeting Rutiah, who pulls me close, stroking me as I try desperately to hold back the guilt I feel over my nights with Flavius, and the overwhelming loneliness in my world without Liam.

"Gather round," McCollum commands. "We must determine our future! Each of you is an essential part, without which the whole cannot exist. We have honed our powers, using one another's energy to make this possible. I am a shape shifter, made invincible by my alchemist friend who shares my talent. Our Dreamers' power is multiplied by their merging in meditation. The magic of the River of Knowledge runs deep in our veins, and we are powerful when we stand together. Even the one smallest in stature," McCollum looks into Gillian's eyes, "is a giant among the mystical beings who have the power to control nature.

"Each of you is respected by all Chieftains of this great land, and you will now be sent forth to raise the army we must have to resist the onslaught sent from far shores." McCollum dispatches us, two by two, to the great tribes of Britannica, Eceni, Coritani, Brigantes, and Cornovil, with orders to return within the month. Only then, when we know the size of our army, will we be able to put together our final battle plan.

December 31, 2010

The sun slowly flooded the room, and the fluttering of Buddy's wings could be heard as he flew to his birdie door to greet the sunrise. Pure adrenaline had kept us going through the night, but now sleep was going to happen whether we wanted it or not. Dad, Mom, and Lee left to fill the beds upstairs, and the four of us retired to the downstairs bedrooms, leaving Gilbert content on the couch in front of the fireplace. We were all so completely joined that we didn't want to break the atmosphere by moving too far from each other.

My worry about what Mom and Dad might think about me spending the night with Will was a thing of the past. By now, everyone knew beyond a shadow of a doubt that we would all be together for the rest of our human lives. We were on a journey together, each one of us needing the others.

We joined the New Year's Celebration as a group of ONE, with eight souls united in one purpose. Will told us nothing about what to expect, except that each of our journeys would be unique, and that we needed to be open to the joy it would bring. We all were in great anticipation of what was in store for us.

McCollum smiled as he opened the door, bowing his head to Will in approval. We entered the temple with our new meditation pillows and shawls, and were intoxicated by the smell of incense. Will motioned us to the front of the room, where space had been set aside so all of us could sit together. Dad, Mom, Gilbert, and Lee took their places on the floor in the front row, and Ruth, George, Will, and I sat behind them.

Will told us before entering the temple that the chanting had been going on twenty-four hours a day to raise the energies in the house to a feverish pitch. Under those circumstances, even the densest person would be lifted to the heights of the group around them. The chanting was a repetitive verse in Sanskrit. Before long we were all able to chant along with the group—*Om Nama Shiva, Om Nama Shivaya …*

I found myself floating in and out of consciousness. Sometimes I was in the room chanting, and at other moments I wasn't aware of anything at all. Soon a line of boys entered the room with trays of smoking sandalwood and bells ringing. It pushed me even further into an unfamiliar place in my being, but I wasn't frightened. I felt safe, and oddly at peace.

Feeling a tap on my shoulder, I found myself looking directly into the innocent eyes of a boy of about ten. He handed me a well-worn book opened to a page entitled *Arati*. After shaking my mind into focus, I took the book and managed to mouth *thank you* to him. Looking around, I noticed that everyone had the same book, and as the chant began my voice joined theirs.

Om namah, parvati-pataye Hara hara hara mahadev …

A moment before I would have sworn I'd never heard these words before, but as they rolled off my tongue, I had that déjà vu feeling once again.

Letting myself go with the sensation of being adrift, I closed my eyes just to see what might happen next. I instinctively knew not to get too intellectual about what was happening because my rational mind would not have any logical place to put any of it.

The chanting around me got softer as I floated farther away, and I was intrigued to find a different group who were chanting a slightly different version. As I moved closer to that group and farther from my own, this new chant gradually replaced the old one. It was beautiful, as if the two groups were singing in *rounds* like we did in grade school. Remaining very still, I was tempted to open my eyes, but found my lids were too heavy, as were my arms and legs. The only option left to me was to just *be* and let myself bathe in the beauty of it all.

In my blissful state, I eventually heard the chanting voices reverse, and I knew that I was returning to the temple in which my body sat. My initial emotion was disappointment, but I continued to just let it *be*. I listened until the other voices faded completely to silence, and that mystical moment was over.

I remember very little about the ceremony that happened at midnight. I floated and merged with my thoughts, and at times had absolutely no thoughts at all. Will eventually laid me down on the soft temple carpet and placed my pillow under my head. I felt him drape my shawl over me, tucking it in at the corners with loving care. I wanted to say thank you, but couldn't really manage it.

I felt the heat of Will's body next to me, and his hum as he took my hand in his. That was the last thing I remembered before everyone fell asleep on the temple floor.

The soft shuffling of feet brought me partially to my senses. Will gently helped me to my feet. Apparently the sun was rising, and everyone was moving from the temple to their personal quarters.

We entered a hallway, and the six of us followed Will and George in silence. We climbed the stairs, and as Will opened doors, we dropped out of line two by two. Mom and Dad took the first room, then Gilbert and Dr. Edwards. Ruth and George disappeared into George's room, and Will took me to his. We all needed a little more sleep before breakfast was served.

Will's bed was a twin, but as we climbed into it and wrapped ourselves around each other, I realized we both would have fit even if it were nothing more than a cot. Engulfed in Will's arms, I slipped into a deep, deep sleep.

The soft tone of a bell moving along the hallway brought me to consciousness, alerting us that it was time for breakfast. The atmosphere in the house was very gentle, nothing like the hard-edged world that existed beyond its walls.

I tried to move, but Will's arms held me tight.

"Not so quick," he whispered in my ear. "This is the first time I've ever had a girl in my bed … or in my room, for that matter. I'd like to enjoy it for just a moment longer."

I felt his breath on my neck, followed by his warm lips on my ear. I moved to face him and felt some serious heat as he wrapped his leg around my hip to pull me closer.

"Going without breakfast would be fine with me if I thought we wouldn't be missed," he said, and chuckled. "But there's no chance of that. McCollum will want to meet with us after we've eaten."

I knew he was right. After all, McCollum was the leader of our little band of spiritualists. Will pulled himself up and sat on the edge of the bed. Running his fingers over his face, he turned to me.

"I'll go and find out the plans for the day," he said, as he put on loose fitting clothes. "You shower and I'll meet you in the dining hall for breakfast." Clothing in this house was worn for comfort, not fashion.

Will smiled and kissed me goodbye before leaving the room. I stretched while rummaging in my overnight bag for my robe. I made the bed by pulling the sheets tight with perfect military corners before grabbing my bag and heading to the shower room across the hall. It had been kindly set aside for Mom, Ruth, and me to use during this weekend. All the boys were using the facilities in another wing.

The showers were six stalls divided by plastic curtains. Leaving my robe on a hook in the main room, I closed a curtain and let the warm water wash over me. It wasn't long before the sound of other showers and the billowing of the curtains told me Mom and Ruth were nearby.

"Hey girls, how did we all survive last night?" It was Ruth's voice, and she was in high spirits. "Come on girls. Speak to me!"

Mom giggled. "I could have slept for another hour, but Terry couldn't sleep at all. I decided to get up to give him a break. I thought if he had to spend another minute trying to be silent and still, he might explode. He's in the shower now, and I'm sure he's talking to whoever will listen."

"Will and I slept like logs. I don't think my sleep has ever been so devoid of dreams." For Mom's benefit, I left out the part about how good it felt to sleep next to him.

"Does anyone know what the schedule is today?" Mom chimed, already turning off the water, ever the environmentalist. Mom always took short showers, not wanting to waste *Mother Earth's bounty*. Her daughter, on the other hand, always lounged as long as possible, with the hot water on high. I'm sure over the years I've wasted all the water that she has saved.

"Will told me we should meet in the dining area for breakfast," I answered. "I bet there's a table set aside for us."

"I'll see you girls downstairs," Mom said enthusiastically as she left the room. She was clearly enjoying her new adventure.

"Are we alone now?" Ruth asked from the next stall.

"I think so, why?" I answered, turning to let the hot water run down my back.

"I'm having such a good time." The swoon in her voice told me I was listening to a girl falling in love. "George and I talked about 'us' last night. Did you hear me, Hillary? I said us! There is an US! He loves

179

me!"

I reluctantly turned off the water, put on my robe, and stepped out of the shower. Ruth joined me, rosy red from the hot water.

"Come here, girl." I said, opening my arms. "I'm so happy for you, Ruth."

"This is my first time," Ruth said when we released each other from our sisterly hug. "I mean, I've loved guys before, but not guys who loved me back, and I've had guys who were wild over me, but I couldn't get away from them fast enough. But this time, George and I love each other equally, at the same time. It's what I've always wanted!" Ruth was smiling through tears.

"Has George told you much about what went on while you were in Kansas City?" I asked, wondering if George and Ruth were also soulmates. I figured George would tell her if it were important, and knowing Ruth, she would tell me even if she weren't supposed to.

She said nothing, so I kept my mouth shut. We hurried to our rooms to get dressed and walked to the dining hall together.

Breakfast was a mixture of raw and simple foods, along with some cooked rice from the evening before and a pot of hot water for tea. I worked my way down the line, taking a little of everything. Just the sight of food proved to me that I was starving.

The seating was in a room just around the corner, and as we made the turn, Will and George waved us over. All meals were supposed to be eaten in silence, but our table was not following the rule. Between Dad, Gilbert, and Dr. Edwards, the silence had absolutely been broken. The boys at the surrounding tables were having a good giggle, probably finding the excitement contagious. Having six strangers in their midst, three of them females, was highly unusual.

Will announced that after we finished our breakfast and washed our dishes, we were expected in McCollum's quarters.

Remembering McCollum from the Spring Fling party night, I was both frightened and fascinated by the thought of him. He had not been pleased with us that night, and I had shriveled a bit under his gaze. I wondered if I would feel any different now.

George led the procession with dishes in hand, back to the kitchen. We scraped the remaining food from our plates into a bucket, which would become mulch for spring vegetables. We then rinsed the dishes and placed them in a tray that would later pass through a dishwashing system, the grey water nourishing the gardens. It was all very efficient.

"You'll have a few minutes in your rooms before your meeting with McCollum," Will told us on the way upstairs. "Someone will be around to gather you up, so when you hear a bell, that will be the signal to follow your guide to McCollum's quarters. Don't be frightened." That last part was clearly directed toward me, because everyone else was giddy with anticipation.

My disappointment was tangible as Will told me he would be going up ahead of time. All my insecurities surfaced with a vengeance. I couldn't imagine entering that room without Will by my side, only to face McCollum eye to eye.

Vicki Renfro

CHAPTER
THIRTY

HEARING THE bell, I left Will's room to take my place in line behind our young guide. After knocking softly on a large door, the boy stepped aside and motioned for us to enter.

The room was elegantly furnished with old world charm. The walls were dark wood paneling, which gave the room a commanding feel, but the beautiful antique tapestries kept it warm and inviting. McCollum was watching the flames in a large stone fireplace, but he turned as we entered the room.

There were four chairs arranged in a semicircle and four plush pillows on the floor in front of them. Will was already seated on one of the pillows, and to my enormous relief, he stood to guide me to the place next to him. Ruth and George took the other two cushions on the floor, and Dr. Edwards, Gilbert, Dad, and Mom took the four chairs behind us. The room remained dead silent.

As McCollum took the massive chair at the front, he welcomed us warmly. Don't ask me what he said; I watched his mouth moving, but I was so enchanted by his face that I didn't hear a word he said. It was the first chance I'd had to truly study him.

He wasn't all that old—probably around sixty—but at the same time he looked as if he'd been alive forever. He had a full head of thick, grey hair, combed back and gathered at his neck with a finely engraved silver barrette. His face was lined, but not by age alone. His face was expressive; every wrinkle seemed to convey his emotions.

His build was strong, as was everyone's who lived in the house. Even though he wore robes that were a little medieval and outdated for my taste, he moved with grace and intention. His eyes were a piercing slate blue, which made me marvel at the fact that everyone in this house seemed to have blue eyes.

I looked over at Will. His dark hair was now tumbling over his collar, and a few strands had escaped from behind his ears. Although his eyes were a shade darker than McCollum's, they had the same piercing effect. His perfect nose and beautiful complexion flickered in the light of the fire.

Suddenly, I returned to the reality of where I was, and I tried to refocus on what was going on. McCollum was finishing up his welcome and had started the introductions.

Thank God, we didn't have to say anything about ourselves. McCollum was only interested in knowing what he should call us.

When it was my turn to speak, I merely said, "Hillary." It kind of squeaked out, and Will immediately placed his hand over mine. I felt Will's familiar hum, but there was something else in the room that was combined with it. There was an unusual kind of energy in this chamber, and I felt a new sensation inside me. I remembered Gilbert talking about it, but until I actually felt the tug on my soul, I hadn't believed it was truly possible. He had called it *Shaktipat*, the power of a *true master* to elevate your life force, and it was emanating from McCollum. I could actually feel a soft electric current circling through my body.

Trying harder to concentrate on what was being said, I looked up into McCollum's face. Blinking to focus my eyes, I could swear there was a slight glow around his body. Never having seen an aura before, I decided that must be what I was seeing. The colors were muted, but the golden glow around his head looked like a halo.

"Let me tell you a few stories," McCollum began. He arranged himself comfortably in his chair, as if this was going to take a while. "Once upon a time there was a group of beings. They were what I call *Companions in Time*, always incarnating into their new lives at the same place, at the same time.

"In the time of Ramses the Great Pharaoh, these souls filled the temples of Egypt. They were the highest of spiritual advisors, priests and priestesses who kept the energies perfectly balanced. The result of this manifestation was immense prosperity, and Egypt flourished. But just as moths are drawn to the light, so the dark side of humanity is also drawn to beings of light. The thing you must remember is that darkness always lies at the edge of light, and if the light goes out, darkness will take its place."

I felt goose bumps rise on my arms, but I could hardly keep my eyes open, so I let them close and tried to concentrate on what McCollum was saying.

"Unfortunately, that was the case in the story I now tell you. Darkness found its foothold in the weakest of the priests and eventually infiltrated the temples, and the balance shifted. The rains came, the Nile flooded, and the land flourished for another season. But sadly, when the water receded, the Great Pharaoh was dead and the light beings that served him had once again melted into the ethers. As the light was extinguished, so was the peace and abundance. Happiness and wealth slowly deteriorated into poverty, drought, and sadness, as invaders from the north found passage into the once impenetrable kingdom. The cycle of life continued until one day the paradigm swung in the opposite direction and a new light appeared. But the light was never again as bright."

Will gently laid his hand on mine and I opened my eyes to meet his gaze.

"This group of companions incarnated in Pompeii, once again bringing endless consciousness and compassion. They studied at the great Temple of Isis, which sat on a sea that was so blue it was like heaven mirrored here on Earth. The Dark Ages had not yet overtaken mankind, and there were many who were still aware of their divinity. Don't misunderstand me; there were also the denser aspects of mankind who lived in Pompeii. They have always been among us to mirror the light and the dark, the yin and yang that exist around us and also inside us. Do not ever be so foolish as to think it is your job to destroy all darkness. Your job is to be such a great light that the darkness is encompassed in your brilliance.

"The level of civilization in Pompeii far exceeded any other of its time." McCollum leaned forward in his chair, drawing us deeper into the story by the intensity of his face. "When the volcano blew and the ashes rained down, there were no survivors. But it's a very narrow view, don't you think, to believe that light can be extinguished by death. Light can no more be stopped by death than evil can. You see, the evolutionary path of a soul can only be changed here on Earth while in a human form, on this plane of Demonstration ... but I get ahead of myself.

"This group of companions last stood together during a time I feared I might lose my most precious Time Travelers forever," McCollum said, looking kindly at the group sitting before him. "I feared the damage caused to their spirits might be so great that they would elect to remain merged with the light, rather than choosing to incarnate during this most important window.

"The life I speak of is the one we lived as Druids, when we lived in a remote area of a land now known as the United Kingdom. I had believed we would be innocuous enough to live our lives unnoticed. We had incarnated to try to lift humanity out of the Dark Ages. During this time the Roman Empire had gained immense power. Julius Caesar had appointed himself Emperor for life and was destroying all people who resisted his authority. The lines between politics and clergy were so blurred that it was difficult to distinguish between the lambs and the lions."

Enthralled by McCollum's tale, everyone in our group sat motionless. Even Gilbert stopped his constant fidgeting.

"Living on a tiny island in a primitive country, no one in our small enclave of mystics could have guessed that we'd be seen as a threat to Rome."

A piercing chill shuddered through me from head to toe, and I became ice cold. I pulled my shawl tightly around my shoulders as I felt a creeping numbness inside me. Emotions began to rock me with such violence that it was hard to hear McCollum's account of the Druids. I felt a pain in my chest as my heart broke from the memories of that lifetime. The screaming in my mind soon poured from my lips.

Instantly, Will's arms were around me, but my body was already convulsing and I didn't know how to make it stop. Sweat ran down my face, and the beating of my heart was pounding through every inch of my body, pulsing, striking with such force that I feared my vessels might rupture! I heard the rushing of blood in my ears, and the vile taste of metal filled my mouth.

"What is happening?" I yelled inside my battered mind, but I knew no one could hear me.

I was becoming less aware of Will's arms holding me, and I could barely hear Mom and Dad pleading for me to stay with them. I needed

185

to escape from the pain, to find a place to rest. I wanted to float back to the peaceful hands of the universe from which I had come. I could not bear the retelling of the Druid story, knowing it was a bloody massacre of everyone I'd loved. My soul, overwhelmed by sorrow, refused to relive it again.

My body was swelling. No, this was the feel of my life force moving back into the ethers. As I watched from above, my body went limp, and I could tell by the unnatural bow in my back that Will was holding a lifeless shell.

Suddenly, the loud ringing of bells pierced my deep longing for peace. The bells were screaming in dissonant tones as McCollum barked instructions. The room became thick with incense, and I watched all the people I loved most in this lifetime gather around me. I felt like Dorothy as she lay unconscious in her farmhouse bed surrounded by the Tin Man, the Scarecrow, and the Cowardly Lion. And then 'there was the Wizard' and McCollum's eyes looked up to where my spirit was adrift.

Gazing down at the people surrounding me, I knew they were my Druids. Their faces were overlaid with many from other incarnations, and I recognized each of them from lifetimes gone by. I was undone by the intense love I had for each of them. Emotion filled my heart until it ached, and within moments I was not sure if I was being pulled to stay or leave.

"Let's get her to your room, Will, and gather the boys in the temple to chant for her soul," a voice said softly.

I knew the voice was McCollum's, and my mind let go of all consciousness.

CHAPTER
THIRTY ONE

FLOATING SOMEWHERE between here and there, I heard deep powerful chanting, mixed with soft muffled prayers and countless seductive voices calling to me to join them in the beyond. It became clear that what happened to me next would be my *choice*, a decision I would make alone.

I felt a hum as Will took my limp hand in his, but the essence had altered. It was weaker and filled with tangible sorrow. *Will*, I thought, my heart breaking while I drifted farther away. I was becoming free, pulled by a heavenly light.

My past lives drifted lazily by and for the first time I could see the brilliance of the Druids' plan. One by one the Druids took lives that would advance the plan to reunite in this lifetime closer to reality, each soul always remaining attached to McCollum by a thin golden thread, always being pulled toward him as if he were magnetic.

A thread of light was also pulling me, but in the opposite direction. I was dissolving into oneness with all that exists beyond the physical world. No longer confined by linear time, I let myself drift between one vision and another until I caught sight of a familiar young boy standing at McCollum's front door —and when I looked into his eyes, I realized that they were Will's blue eyes. He was small, but fierce in his determination that he had found his place in the world. I watched him grow from a child into an amazing man who never questioned his path. He knew his purpose in life, and I felt my heart soften. Drawn to his bottomless blue eyes, I was once again in the carriage house, mesmerized by his laughter, and I, too, knew where I belonged. *I belonged with Will.*

Overcome by the most basic of human needs—to love and to be

loved—I was infused with an intense desire to live. But how would I find my way back after I had traveled so far away?

I heard Dad's answer come to me as a whisper: "Ask the universe and then listen closely for the answer."

"It is really that simple," Gilbert said, his voice softly penetrating the ethers. "Take a few minutes to figure out what you'd really like to create ... *consciously*, with deep and intentional thought."

I moved within, drawing the memories of this life back to me, seeing the faces of those I loved. And as they came, the pull on my *being* reversed and the movement toward the physical world began. My ability to see the future and past vanished, leaving only the present. Will's face appeared, my heart opened and my soul took flight as if I were attached to a zip line.

I woke against Will's chest as he rocked slowly. I felt his cheek against the top of my head and his breath chanting softly into my hair. I shrugged to move my tight muscles, and squeezed my fingers into fists, releasing them before trying to wiggle my toes.

"Will," I said, with vocal cords that weren't quite ready to work again. "My mouth is so dry. Can I have a drink of water?"

"You bet you can," Will said, emotion caught in his voice. Lifting me off his lap, he placed a pillow beneath my head. When he moved away from me, I became aware that he wasn't the only one in the room. A young boy sat just inside the door, and I heard Will whisper to him, "Tell them she has made her decision and her soul has come back to us!" The boy stood and ran from the room, and I listened to his footfalls all the way down the hall.

Will came back with a glass of water. "Here, let me help you," he said, lifting me to a sitting position.

I slowly began to drink, and life seemed to fill me with every sip.

"Come in," Will said, in reply to a soft knocking at the door.

It was Mom and Dad, eyes rimmed with tears. They knelt at my bedside, and no words were necessary.

Ruth, George, Gilbert, and Lee took turns at my side. All had been desperately chanting for my safe return, lighting the path so I could find my way back to them.

I left the New Year's celebration in the company of my family and friends. Actually, it wasn't quite that dignified. I was held up between Will and Dad, with everyone else lugging my bags along with their own.

We drove in a caravan back to our apartments. McCollum had given us firm instructions to remain together until we got word from him. No one was given any further information, so we spent the afternoon gathered around Will's fireplace, watching Buddy fly in and out of the window. Mom found comfort in returning to her routine, cooking a wide assortment of food until the kitchen overflowed. No one talked with me about what had happened, nor did anyone recount any of the stories McCollum told.

Shortly before sunset, Ruth set my computer on the kitchen table in front of me. I wanted to ask what she was doing, but before I had a chance to get the words out, McCollum appeared on the screen.

"Good evening, Dear One. Are you recovering?" he asked, with profound concern on his face. "You should feel much more grounded since you've left the presence of my boys. The energies here can sometimes disconnect the body and soul."

I nodded and tried to smile, still finding it hard to talk to him. I was in awe of his powers, but still a little confused by some of my feelings. I flashed back to the first time I met him a year and a half ago, when he'd asked Ruth and me to leave his house. I hoped that he didn't want me to leave again!

Will laid his hands softly on my shoulders as I watched his reflection in my computer screen. I knew he had moved closer to give me support.

"Your friend Ruth was kind enough to loan me her computer, so we can communicate face to face," he continued. "She is a wise woman and a true friend to realize what was necessary, and to have the courage to introduce me to this technology. I had no idea this was possible until she showed me."

McCollum's face filled the whole screen, and I found myself looking only at his eyes. The blue of his iris looked almost grey, but the interesting part was the way the other colors mixed in. There were darker bits of blue and gold that created a beautiful random pattern. An iridologist would say each was a scar within the body, but I wondered if the scars were from this lifetime or if he carried them forward from life to life.

Everyone grabbed a chair from the kitchen table and moved into place behind me. Will also sat down, but without letting go of me. It felt like he was trying with all his might to make sure I didn't leave him again.

"The time of Earth's imminent destruction, foretold by many, has passed," McCollum gently began. "Many people across this great planet have worked tirelessly for centuries to elevate the *light* to a point where love is manifesting in the mind of man more often than hatred. The yearning for peace in humanity's heart is tipping the balance for the first time in history.

"The men sitting with you today, my dear Hillary, spent lifetimes high in the Himalayas in constant prayer and meditation, awaiting this day when the tipping toward the light would begin and the reunion of the Druids would come to be.

"The other women in this group took a different path. Since *that* lifetime, they have incarnated as mothers and homemakers, simply because they have an innate need to nurture.

"For me, I have lived incarnation after incarnation, wandering this planet in search of elevated souls who would enter an agreement with me. Those souls are my boys and each of you. Now that you have fulfilled your previous promise to me by finding me in this lifetime, we wait at the gate of the Twilight of Kali Yuga for the next moment to unfold."

McCollum looked at the faces behind me. I watched his expression at each encounter and saw each nod with an acknowledgment of their understanding. Then he looked at me and saw my *deer in the headlights* response. He smiled slightly and continued with a more in-depth explanation.

"The *Kali Yuga* brought about the spiritual degeneration of human civilization—truly the dark age of mankind. It began in 3102 BC and was to last 432,000 years." McCollum's eyes twinkled when he saw my devastation, as it dawned on me that only a fraction of that time had passed.

"Don't let this upset you, Hillary, because this is precisely the reason for our gathering tonight. It is now believed that the Kali Yuga has ended, and we are now transitioning into a period called the

Twilight of the Kali Yuga. If all goes as planned, the coming age will correspond with a global shift in consciousness.

"The end of the Mayan calendar is not a coincidence. It is the end of the thirteenth Baktun, which has spiritual implications in the Mayan culture. We are right on schedule." McCollum's eyes looked past me to Will, and I felt Will nod for him to continue.

"The veils that came with you into this lifetime are many, and they exist for your protection," McCollum tenderly continued. "They protect you against self-judgment for past deeds, and against harm from reliving difficult memories of previous lifetimes. You also came to this incarnation blinded to your great power, but I promise you this power still exists within you."

When I realized that McCollum was now speaking directly to me, the panic returned. I heard Will's gentle, soothing voice in my ear, telling me that I would be okay. As the hum in my body intensified, I knew it was Will sending me his strength, so I might have the willpower to hear what he knew I must.

"The feelings you are having are similar to post traumatic stress, or battle fatigue. Some warriors suffer wounds such as missing limbs or eyes; things that can be seen. Others are left psychologically shattered, broken within. The wounds of the heart and soul are harder to heal, but dear Hillary, I must ask you to face what frightens you most and know that we are here to support you."

Immediately, my mind takes me low above the stench of bodies left in the heat of the sun to decay on the battlefield. A flock of crows peck eyes from their sockets as I search for the faces of my fallen comrades. I hear the tear of rotting flesh from bone and try to erase it from my mind. Haunted by the sight, I pause to view the entirety of it, and with a rush of realization, I see that no one is here. All the souls have moved on and found peace ... all but mine.

Then the veil suddenly dropped back into place, leaving my emotions raw. But for the first time, I could feel the essence of who I had been in that lifetime, and the strength and immense power that once was mine.

"In that lifetime you watched Will die, and at that moment you lost not only your mate, but also part of your soul," McCollum continued. "In your case there was actually a physical rip. It's very rare, but you are a rare being.

"Part of you was drawn toward Will as he made his death journey into the light, while the other half of your soul rejoined your body to fight the raging battle you had left here on Earth. It was then that something was broken inside you, divided. And this division persisted even after the Romans terminated that lifetime. For centuries I looked for the pieces of you, but only heard rumors of a ghost trying to reunite with the beloved she had lost.

"That was when I set our ancient plan into motion, knowing you would not consciously remember the promise you had made two thousand years ago. My hope and expectation was that you would be drawn to this lifetime by the ones destined to be your parents. Terry and Kate honored their agreement by returning when the *Twilight* was imminent. They incarnated totally veiled, in the hope that you would follow. You see, Hillary," McCollum paused to think and then explained, "almost no one can make the journey back into this third dimension without the veils to protect the mind. At the moment of birth you are totally aware, and an instant later you are left with only your karma to lead you to what has been destined. Some make it, and others are led astray. I think our plan has gone quite smoothly, considering!" He said this with satisfaction.

"This brief history brings us to why we have once again been reunited." McCollum looked both tired and exhilarated. Everyone's chair was shifting behind me, almost as if they were bracing themselves for the impact of McCollum's next words.

Looking at the people around me, I wondered if this was really happening. I was just a farm girl who had no real accomplishments in life besides going away to college. I could see a glimpse of brilliant light in each of the people surrounding me. How could I possibly fit into this picture? When I reached the height of my self-doubt, I heard McCollum clear his voice and softly begin to speak again.

"Hillary, when I saw you in our Carriage House last year, I was speechless—although I imagine neither you nor Ruth remember it that way." He smiled. "I never knew if you would actually incarnate as planned. I had hoped ... dreamed ... prayed that you would join us in this lifetime, but praying for something does not always make it so.

"I can see the doubt and questions in your eyes, and you can rest assured that everything will be answered in time. Give it time my dear one, give it time. Your veils will begin to fall away as you become ready for them to. Don't worry, everything is perfect and unfolding exactly as it should," he consoled gently.

McCollum once again met Will's eyes.

"Dear boy, your search is over," he said with a sigh. "At times I worried that your beloved would choose not to incarnate again, or if she did, her energy would be too weak for us to find. I should not have doubted the power of love. Nothing in this universe could stand between you and the one you've loved through eternity."

Tears welled up in my eyes, and I concentrated on the computer screen for fear that I would fall apart if I didn't.

"Now, all I can say is, thank you for coming. We have much work to do!" Pure joy washed over McCollum's face and made him look young again. "It's been an eventful weekend and a good start. Now it is time for rest and camaraderie. Don't worry about tomorrow; it will come no matter what we do. Enjoy your time together and revel in your love for one another; talk, learn, remember, sleep, and dream. Our work will start soon enough."

He bowed his head and placed his hands together in front of him. We did the same as he whispered, "Namaste," and the screen went blank.

Vicki Renfro

CHAPTER
THIRTY TWO

WILL MUST have carried me to my bed that night, because as the sun came up, I woke curled in his arms. Lying quietly, I heard familiar voices in the living room and was amused that everyone was still together. I listened to their conversations while being careful not to wake Will.

George's voice was easiest to pick out because his was always the loudest. I knew Ruth was there because she was laughing, and I smiled when I heard Dr. Edwards and Gilbert in deep discussion about their past lives together.

Mom was having a private conversation with Buddy. She had recognized that he was on a path too, and a member of our group.

"And who are you?" she asked.

I could clearly imagine Buddy perched on her finger as they gazed directly into each other's eyes. Of all of the conversations going on, that was the one that captured my interest.

"I surmise we have known each other many times before," Mom said softly. "I can see the power of a falcon in you. Have you been the huntress for a great man, or were you the companion of a powerful woman?"

Then I heard Dad's voice, low and musical. I listened with great care to hear the words he spoke to my mother, and was surprised when the entire room went silent. It was apparent that he was speaking to everyone.

"I've always had a deep, unexplainable desire to travel to India. I know I've never told you this, Kate," he said apologetically. "Now I

194

know I should say *return* to India."

I slid out of bed, and although I was careful not to disturb Will, I felt him follow me as I walked to the door to listen.

"I've always been confused by the nagging emptiness inside me, because in this life I've been blessed with everything. When I woke this morning that feeling was gone, and this, the culmination of my life's purpose, well … I want you to know I am honored to be sharing this adventure with all of you."

Will and I emerged from the bedroom to make the reunion complete.

My folks called Kenny to let him know that it would be a few more days before they returned home. Of course Kenny didn't mind. He was quite independent, and very capable of handling anything that might come up around the farm.

"I'll eat at Gram and Gramp's house," he reassured Mom. "I promise I won't go hungry."

I quietly walked away in an effort to get Ruth alone.

"Ruth," I said, motioning her away from the group. "Thanks for leaving your computer behind for McCollum. That was incredibly courageous." I met her eyes with a solemn look on my face, and she started laughing.

"Come here, Hillary," she said, motioning for me to sit down in the chair while she sat on its over-stuffed arm. "You've got to lighten up! No pun intended. I think we've learned that you definitely outrank me in this Druid organization, so I should be the one boo-hooing." My mood lifted the more she teased me. "I'll be your guardian and take care of you forever, but you'll have to remind me what the job requirement is for that guardian position. It's been over two thousand years and I've forgotten!" She laughed.

"I don't remember either, but someday I will, and when that day comes, I'll thank you properly."

Ruth pushed aside my sentiment with a flurry of hand waving.

"I'm looking forward to a very eventful year," Ruth said, with the joy I had grown to expect. "I think things will really start happening when we're *swimming in the River of Knowledge*. I think I'll start with the backstroke and go back to check out our past lives together. Just think how fun it will be to talk about that stuff like it just happened yesterday."

"Do you really think it will happen that way?" I asked.

Ruth didn't seem to have a single worry in the world about what the future held. "I'm not sure what's going to happen. I just know I'm not afraid of it. The worst that can happen is that I die and find you again on the rebound. I figure it's going to be better than the best thing that's happened to me so far."

And with that, I realized she was right. This was going to be a much better ride than any job I might have found after graduation. This was going to be an adventure!

CHAPTER
THIRTY THREE

WE HAD one more gathering with McCollum via computer before Mom and Dad went home and Dr. Edwards took his position at Menninger Clinic. McCollum gave us very specific instructions on how to begin the journey to awaken our dormant powers. Our days were to begin with yoga to connect our minds and bodies, chanting to awaken our souls, and meditation to merge with the Universal Mind. We were not to compare notes with each other because each of our journeys was unique. McCollum gave no specific instructions on what to keep in our journals, beyond that we were to write for one hour each day.

It was amazing how perfect things were turning out. Even though on the surface it appeared that our New Year's weekend had fallen apart, we had received all the initiations required to begin our training. We had even received our mantras.

Will was given permission to teach us a new technique at the next full moon. So on January 11th, Ruth, George, Gilbert, and I gathered downstairs in front of the fireplace, bubbling with anticipation—especially George, who was barely able to contain himself.

According to Will's instructions, we were sitting cross-legged in a circle. When he arrived, he took his place across from me, but for some reason he seemed very uneasy. He brushed back his hair and locked his beautiful baby-blues on mine.

"Tonight McCollum has given me permission to be The Teacher," he began. "I have been The Teacher within the confines of McCollum's walls ever since the day I arrived at his home. He's helped me to understand that this is a great gift that I've been given, so tonight I am here as The Teacher." Sitting very still, Will softly inhaled as his head lolled forward.

"This is the really cool part," George said excitedly. "I've seen it a million times before, but it still blows me away."

With one huge inhalation, Will sat bolt upright and opened his eyes. I looked at him with sheer amazement; Will had grown! His clothes, which were typically loose, were now filled with a much larger physique, and the intimate hum that had always been Will's and mine alone now filled the room. He rolled his shoulders to get comfortable and spoke to us in a deep voice with an unfamiliar cadence as he placed a brass bowl at the center of our circle.

"This brass bowl was forged in a secret ceremony known only by the Buddhist Monks of Northern Tibet. It was created so long ago that some simply say it was forged before time began. It came to McCollum by mystical means, and now has been given into our hands for safekeeping. It is said to have the power to magnify many times over what is placed within it, so we must always bring our purest selves when we are in its presence."

Gilbert's eyes were as big as saucers, and he was as wound up as George.

"What do we put in this bowl?" Gilbert asked. "It's not big enough for much."

"It's big enough to hold an infinite number of thought, and that is what we will place into it—our intentions. We will reserve *saving the world* for a future gathering," The Teacher said with amusement.

"Tonight we will begin with a simple but not insignificant concept. We will release happiness into the world for all who are truly seeking it. Now, close your eyes and imagine happiness pouring from you into the bowl, and I will take you for a ride."

George was giggling like a little girl, and it wasn't long before Gilbert joined him.

Suddenly, I found myself alone in a magnificent place where the colors were so vivid that they didn't seem real. Rainbows of light were streaming from my palms, and the vibration of this light was laughter.

At that moment I fully understood the meaning of *bliss*.

When I opened my eyes, The Teacher was gone and Will once again sat quietly on his pillow across from me. We all looked at him expectantly, so he responded with love, and said, "Now we must not question our effectiveness. We must *know* that our thoughts and our light were sent forth. This light is rippling around the world, and those people who are receptive will feel it."

"I know we're not supposed to compare our personal experiences, but I'm about ready to burst," Gilbert blurted out. With a nod from Will, he went on. "We weren't alone. This room was packed!"

I spotted a twinkle in Will's eye as he explained, "The Buddhist Monks who forged this vessel, along with all who have ever participated in this ritual, were with us tonight. The bowl is very powerful."

"I wasn't in this room at all," Ruth interjected. "I was chanting with them, at the monk's place on a mountain top."

"Each person's journey is always an individual one," Will offered. "Very seldom does any person find their path to be exactly the same as another's."

"Time to eat," George said, clapping his hands loudly. "Hard work always makes me hungry!"

Will returned the bowl to its worn leather pouch and placed it next to Buddy's box on the mantel, and we all headed for the kitchen. When I looked at the clock, I was amazed at how many hours had passed since we first sat down with the brass bowl.

As things progressed, we grew more accustomed to sitting down every evening at seven o'clock with our brass bowl. Mom and Dad were always with us, sending their intentions long distance from their living room. Dr. Edwards joined us every evening from Menninger's Clinic or wherever he was traveling. On the nights that Gilbert couldn't make it physically, we knew he was with us in spirit. The Teacher had only joined us for that first meditation, but honestly, I didn't miss him. I did better with Will.

Sometimes Will and I would lie in bed talking late into the night about The Teacher and the role he had played in *all* of Will's lives. Will explained that it was his connection to his higher self, his expanded part from the River of Knowledge, but it remained hard for me to understand. The one thing that I could clearly perceive was that having The Teacher inside him as a child would have made him feel crazy. I also flashed back to the night Ruth's cards had said he was a teacher, and in my naiveté I failed to grasp the importance of this revelation.

Without The Teacher joining us around the brass bowl, it took a little longer to shut the chatter down in my mind, but eventually I arrived at that deeper, mystical part within. I guess the point was for us to get *there* on our own, and even though our dedication was still based on faith alone, I felt something growing stronger within me.

Gilbert never let me forget how right he was about everything. During physics class I often wondered, as I watched him behind the podium, just who the hell Gilbert really was. Over all the lives we'd spent together, was he the intellect or the student, the warrior or the scientist? I always reached the same conclusion. He was probably all of those things, including my friend, repeatedly telling me about karma, positive thinking, and reincarnation, reminding me of everything until I was able to remember it for myself.

I continued to collect research material for Dr. Edwards, keeping track of what he was researching by reading some of the material. I always attached a note about what the group had been up to, and every couple of months or so, I discovered him thumbing through the books in the glass-floored room. There was such joy in finding him that way. We would sit together for hours, just talking. Working late on those evenings to make up for the time I spent visiting was worth every minute. I always invited him for dinner, and sometimes he agreed, but most often he spent his time with McCollum.

Ruth had been able to get me back into our "giggly girlfriend" mode. It broke up the intensity of the whole Spiritual Journey thing. We even planned a trip to Kansas City for spring break, and I was really looking forward to pool time and pedicures. Will and George were planning their annual camping trip with the boys,

CHAPTER
THIRTY FOUR

WITH THE warmth of spring, we were no longer able to tell if Will and George were home by chimney smoke, and actually had to walk all the way to their door. So, after Ruth and I had finished stuffing the last bag into the trunk for our big K.C. trip, we trotted over and rang the doorbell. George answered, followed by Will. They had also been packing, and their backpacks sat just inside the front door.

Will put his arm around my shoulder, and as he walked me out to the curb, he continued to give George instructions over his shoulder.

"I want you to be careful in Kansas City," he said, giving me his most serious look. "I'm not going to be there to take care of you, so I need you to pay special attention to what you're feeling. If something doesn't *feel* right to you, even if things seem okay when you are looking around with your eyes, I want you to tell Ruth."

I guess I gave him a look that said *I'm not going to bug Ruth*, because he gently turned my chin so I couldn't look away.

"I'm not kidding, Hillary," he insisted. "Don't make me worry about you when I'm with the boys. This is my time to spend with them, and I need you to promise me that you will do that for me."

He kissed me on my forehead and pulled me into an embrace. I rested my head against his chest and knew that he wasn't being bossy. He just wanted me to be safe.

I gave in, unable to keep up the tough girl act. "Okay, okay. If anything feels funny, I'll let Ruth know."

"Good, because George is having this same talk with Ruth. We'll be back in ten days. If you need anything, you'll have to call Gilbert,

Lee, or your dad. McCollum will be with us, along with the brass bowl." Turning to walk me to the car, he continued, "I'm sure everything will be fine. After all, you will be in the upscale parts of Kansas City." He laughed at this reference to Ruth's wealth. "She sure manifested a luxurious incarnation this go-around!"

We all kissed and hugged one another good-bye. The guys opened and closed the car doors for us and kissed us again through the windows. Will made me repeat my promise one more time as Ruth put the car in drive and pulled away from the curb.

Remembering my bad habit of letting the cell battery go dead, I immediately plugged my phone into the charger. After all, part of my promise to Will probably included being able to access Gilbert and Lee's phone numbers if I needed to call them.

"What do you think all of that stuff about staying safe was about?" I asked Ruth.

"They just love us and can't stand being away from us," Ruth replied, in keeping with her way of blowing everything off. "I mean really, when was the last time we needed rescuing when McCollum wasn't around?"

I flashed back to New Year's, when I'd completely lost it. "Yeah, that was weird," I had to admit, "but, this will just be a regular weekend, without having to deal with the energy of our men."

Time flies when you're laughing your ass off with your best friend. Before we knew it we were pulling up to the gate of the Witherspoon estate.

"Hi Mom! Open up," Ruth said into the intercom. Her mom had changed the code and forgotten to tell her.

As we pulled through the gate and it slowly closed behind us, I looked around at the familiar manicured landscape. It was actually a lot like our fields at the farm. Everything was green and excited about growing. The smell of fresh-cut grass reminded me of the smell of the barley at harvest, which brought with it a pang of guilt that reminded me to call Mom. This was the time of year when Dad disappeared into the fields from sunrise to sunset. My guilt was only slightly relieved by the fact that Kenny was there to keep her company.

We still had a few minutes before we'd reach the house, and Ruth was still gabbing away. "Do you feel like going right to the pool, and if you say yes, which pool, the one at the club or ours?" I could tell Ruth was excited to be home and was easily slipping back into her *rich girl* identity.

"Which would you like?" I asked, knowing that I had my own swimsuit this time and wouldn't need to borrow Ruth's sister's very skimpy one. Also, Ruth and I had been tanning on our apartment deck for a while because neither of us wanted to show up at the club with a farmer's tan. Overall, I felt okay about being in public.

Of course Ruth chose the club, and this time I was actually excited to see Ruth's friends again—not to mention more emotionally prepared! We stopped in just long enough to unpack the car and say hello to Ruth's parents. We didn't want to miss the best part of the day, so Ruth told her mom not to worry about lunch.

"We'll have something at the club," Ruth yelled on our way out.

I'm sure Ruth's mom was completely used to Ruth's social life, because it was quite apparent the girl had been on the go since she was old enough to drive.

"Give me a call to let us know if you'll be home for dinner," Mrs. Witherspoon shouted from the steps as we pulled away in her convertible, which was a better fit for the club.

The sun felt like heaven as I spread my towel out on the warm surface of the poolside lounge chair. I placed my cell phone on the side table and set an alarm to remind myself when to flip. I turned to Ruth to ask if she would rub sunscreen on my back, but she had her usual greeting line forming to welcome her home.

"Can I help you with that?" I heard from behind. Blocking the sun with my hand, I turned and looked up into the face of Bennett Taylor.

A rush of emotions overcame me. First a flush of embarrassment, then the heat of lust, followed by irritation that he'd dropped me, and finally finishing with contentment and a smile as Will came to the forefront of my mind. All of this took a matter of seconds. I looked to Ruth for help, but her line was only getting longer, so I lifted my hair off of my shoulders and handed Bennett the sunscreen.

"I thought you would be in the Keys or somewhere on the Gulf Coast for spring break," I managed to say without a bit of sarcasm.

"I was thinking more of St. Thomas," Bennett answered, "but I'm glad I decided on K.C. now that you're here."

Turning around to retrieve my sunscreen I thanked him, pleased with myself for not having heart flutters. Oh, this was going to be so much easier this time around, I was *so* over this guy.

"What happened to bring you home?" I smiled, sitting up.

"My father set up a couple of interviews for me," he answered. "I hadn't thought much about coming back to K.C. after graduation, but Dad, you know, would love to have me here, and if he can get me a job in a good firm, I'll consider it."

I felt like saying something snide about taking the easy way out by letting his daddy plan his life, but I let it drop.

"It's nice to see you, Bennett. I'm sure you'll do great at your interviews," I said, putting my sunglasses on to shield my eyes against the blinding sun.

A crowd was now lying on towels around my social-magnet best friend, but not surprisingly, most of the females were sitting on the side closer to Bennett.

I rolled over and listened to the conversations going on around me. Everyone seemed to be making summer plans, but only a scant few seemed to be looking for jobs. This crowd was stress free, not yet out from under their parents' wealthy wings. They all seemed to be from families that had enough money to cushion their fall if things didn't go well on their first flight from the nest.

My mind drifted back to Dr. Edwards' lecture as I listened for bits of conscious thought among the conversations going on around me. His theory was proving accurate. The majority of people weren't looking for a path. They were just letting things happen. It's kind of funny because I too would have lived an *unconscious* life if I hadn't made myself attend that Spring Fling party. Even with all the guidance and the stories Dad told me growing up, it took Will to open my eyes.

Suddenly, there was a tap on my shoulder.

"You'd better move to the shade; you're getting burned." I opened my eyes and Bennett was already gathering up my things.

"What do you say, Ruth, want to move to the shade?" I asked, after noticing she was also a little crisp around the edges.

She poked a finger into her arm to check her color. "Yep, I think I'm well done. Let's move to the patio."

Bennett, not giving up, picked up Ruth's stuff, too. Deciding on a table near the bar, he dropped our things into a chair.

"What can I get you ladies to drink?" he asked cheerfully.

I decided to have a Dr. Pepper, I hadn't had one for months, and after all, this was a vacation! We weren't twenty-one yet, but Ruth was closer than me and it was her club, so she ordered a white wine spritzer.

The other sunbathers stayed at bay, so for the first time we found ourselves alone.

"Is it fun seeing all your friends again?" I asked her.

"It's more fun thinking about George," she said with a mischievous smile. "I've told a few people that I have a boyfriend, but where do I go from there? They want to know his major! What do I say, 'Elevated Spiritual Studies?' They just wouldn't understand." She laughed and turned to take her drink from Bennett.

"Understand what?" he asked, and that only made Ruth laugh harder.

"About my big hottie of a boyfriend," she chuckled.

To Bennett's credit, he didn't ask any stupid questions. In fact, he was such a gentleman that he sat and talked to us for hours, not glancing once at any of the scantily clad female sunbathers. I started to think I might have misjudged him.

"Would you ladies honor me with the pleasure of your company tonight? I know you've spent all day in your suits, but if you can put up with this summer scene for a few more hours, the Johnsons are having a pool party this evening." Bennett looked at Ruth first. Apparently the Johnsons were old family friends.

"We'd love to!" Ruth exclaimed. "I haven't seen Jen since we graduated from high school, and it will be great to catch up."

"Well then, what time should I pick you up?" he asked, blown over by Ruth's enthusiastic answer.

"How about eight? We're having dinner with my parents, but can be ready by then."

Once our plans were finalized, we picked up our belongings and Ruth started the long process of saying good-bye to everyone. I lagged behind, wanting to give Ruth some space, and then noticed Bennett hanging back with me.

"I've often wondered how you've been doing," he said, moving up to walk beside me.

Happy that all my animosity was gone, I answered, "I've had a great year. Ruth and I have become really close friends, and it's a wonderful thing to have someone you can always count on." I looked up to see his reaction.

"I have a friend like that back at school," Bennett agreed, nodding. "Sometimes we even talk about going into practice together. Our relationship is a lot like yours and Ruth's. I'd like him to be the best man at my wedding someday, and godfather to my kids. Most of the guys at school are pretty unmemorable, but for some reason Jake and I just hit it off."

In my mind, I heard Gilbert launching into one of his *previous lives together* lectures. I could finally actually relate to all those concepts, but I didn't think Bennett would, so I just said, "Funny how that happens, isn't it?"

I strolled along quietly, daydreaming and waiting as Ruth wrapped up her good-byes. It was a kick watching her; she had so many more friends in K.C. than at college, and I liked the idea that I didn't have to share her with such a large crowd at school.

Ruth caught sight of me standing with Bennett and waved us over to where she stood at the curb. "Come on kids! If we're going to make that party tonight, we have to move it along." Bennett had the valet bring Ruth's car around, and he waved good-bye as we sped away.

During dinner, Ruth caught her parents up on her college life by telling them absolutely nothing. She mentioned George in passing, leading her folks to think it wasn't serious. I decided it was best to keep my mouth shut and not blow Ruth's cover, because the little information she was dishing out seemed to completely satisfy her parents.

After dessert, we ran upstairs to don our swimsuits once more. We had sundress cover-ups, summer sandals, and newly pedicured toes, complete with purple polish. Bennett arrived at eight sharp and once again charmed Mrs. Witherspoon.

We got into the car, and minutes after we left the Witherspoon estate, we entered another gated residence with an equally long driveway. Bennett parked at the end of a long line of luxury automobiles and offered me his arm as I marveled at the amazing architecture.

The sidewalk wound lazily around to the back of the house. Following Bennett and Ruth to a bar at the far end of the pool, I waved at Ruth's sister, the only other person I knew. Bennett handed me a glass of wine, unaware that I seldom drank. I figured one wouldn't put me over the edge, so I accepted it.

Before long, Ruth wandered away to find Jen, leaving Bennett and me to do a slow stroll around the pool in search of a table. It was nice to have someone to hang with while Ruth got reacquainted with old friends. George would have been amazed at the sheer number of people she knew, and I was looking forward to seeing the expression on his face.

Bennett and I kept it light, visiting with people as they passed by. I adored not being in love with him. All the pressure was off and I could enjoy his company. He always introduced me and politely carried on a conversation, leaving me baffled by the fact that he never left my side.

We eventually spotted Ruth sitting in a very large hot tub adorned with a beautiful cascading waterfall.

"Do you want to join her?" Bennett asked, gesturing to the billowing steam. Evidently, Bennett had no idea about my affinity for warm water; I absolutely wanted to go for a soak, and gave an audible sigh of pleasure as I slipped in next to Ruth.

"Boy, what I would give to have that effect on women," Bennett laughed.

"Oh, don't give us that," Ruth snapped. "Your reputation precedes you." She smirked, and invited him to join us.

"Ouch!" he said, acting a little hurt. He looked at me as if he wished I hadn't heard that remark, and I got the idea he might be trying to impress me.

It wasn't long before a half dozen of Ruth's friends joined us in the hot tub. I scooted around so that the last person could fit. She was a cute little thing, clearly dying to cozy up with Bennett, but as I moved he moved with me, preventing her from sitting between us.

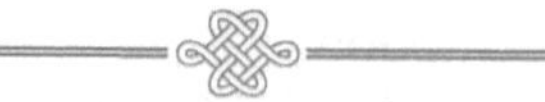

Beginning to overheat, I lifted myself out of the water to sit on the side of the hot tub. Romantically, I looked up at the stars and thought of Will and the possibility that he was gazing up at them, too, thinking of me. Leaning back even further to take full advantage of a cool breeze, I put my hands behind me for more support. A searing pain instantly shot through my palm as if I had just been cut. I pulled it tight to my chest, gasping and trying not to be sick.

Bennett's arm was around me in an instant and Ruth quickly moved to my side. Slowly, Bennett pulled my hand free to see what had happened. Turning it palm up, we saw that there were a thousand small, cylindrical, brown stickers covering my palm. I must have put my hand on a plant, and my immediate instinct was to swipe at the small thorns to relieve the pain, but Ruth stopped me.

"We need to get you inside and pull those out without breaking them off," she said.

Holding my wrist, Bennett pulled me to my feet while Ruth cleared a path to the kitchen.

"What can I do to help?" Mrs. Johnson moaned, looking at my hand. "Take her upstairs to my bedroom, the light is better and I have a nice set of tweezers in the bathroom drawer!"

"They are awfully small to hurt so badly," I mumbled, feeling dizzy. I sat down on the closed toilet in the master bath and wondered if I were having an allergic reaction. I leaned my head against the edge of the cool sink, hoping to stem the beads of sweat forming on my forehead. Ruth held my swollen hand while Bennett began the long process of pulling the stickers out, one-by-one. She finished doctoring me up by rubbing in an antihistamine before Bennett moved me to the bed and I felt my eyes close.

CHAPTER
THIRTY FIVE

APRIL 23, AD 38

I'm startled to find myself standing beside a river with a rope in hand and the familiar smell of horse sweat in my nostrils. I instinctively turn to stroke my mare's neck. She's been running, and we are here on the riverbank for a drink of cool water. Hearing a branch snap, her ears perk up and I feel my skin prickle.

"I demand you stand down," an authoritative voice orders, as I hear the sound of approaching Roman armor. It's General Marcus Flavius in the flesh, standing across the river looking directly at me. My heart stops. I see the men under his command back away as he motions for them to lower their weapons and to give him room. "You are alone now, Hilsbeth," he yells loudly enough for all to hear.

"No, you're mistaken General. I am never alone!"

"Let me detail what I speak of," Flavius's booming voice replies. "The army you are raising has already been defeated. To the east on the road to Coritani, you will find bodies who have relinquished their heads to give a clear warning to others who may be foolish enough to think of coming to your aid. The heads now find themselves atop spikes, which line the road. The first head is one of a beautiful young lady; her long hair is loose and blows in the wind. She was a masterful fighter, but no match for my army ... and all this time I thought she was merely your handmaid.

The second head is that of her man, who was a mighty warrior, indeed. The heavens darkened when he was unable to come to terms with the pleasures the soldiers took with his woman before her slow and tortuous death. He was driven to the edge of madness when my men used his female for such entertainment."

I feel myself falter as I realize he is speaking of Rutiah and Georog.

He seems pleased with himself as he continues, walking closer to the water's edge. "If you go to the road that heads west you will find a similar feature. Only this road is decorated with the head of a small creature with a tuft of white hair. His dark-skinned companion seemed to have some remarkable talents, but once subdued, he was sent to Rome to entertain Emperor Nero. He's not destined for a long life, but he will be memorable"

I fall to my knees, unable to draw a full breath as I realize he is speaking of Gillian and Eduardo.

"I also have to inform you that we have found your stronghold, and there was nary a survivor." Kneeling, he scoops up a drink of water. His eyes lock on mine, and his voice softens to a whisper that only I can hear. "My men are crossing the river two miles to the north. You must ride south, now, with great speed."

I'm consumed by grief when I hear him say, "Please Hilsbeth, you only have minutes to escape."

In one movement I swing my leg over the back of my mare, and I am in the wind before the foot soldiers have time to draw their bows.

With nothing to live for beyond honoring my friends, I spend three cycles of the moon searching until I find all of them. Placing each of their bodies on a pyre, I fall to my knees and pray to the gods for their safe passage home.

The wind whips the stench of decay around me and ignites the wrath within me, and for the rest of my life this will drive me to find the monsters responsible for the horrific deaths of the ones I love.

April 23, 2011

"Hillary, you're mumbling things I can't understand. Please, wake up."

Two sets of hands lifted me to a sitting position as I opened my eyes. Bennett had a washcloth on my forehead, and he and Ruth were searching my face for reassurance that I was okay.

"What do you think?" Bennett asked with concern. "Should I pull the car around so I can get you home to your own beds?"

"Yes, please Bennett," I answered, trying to look absolutely fine. I needed Ruth alone and fast! I tried hard to hold on to every detail of my experience because I knew that it was more than just a dream. As gruesome as it was, I knew it was a conscious glimpse into our Druid lifetime.

My mind was racing, but I remained still all the way home, replaying every terrifying moment of my alternate reality. My sweat soaked Bennett's leather seats as I fought to keep my grief at bay, and to remember. As we pulled up to Ruth's front door I told him I would be okay, and I promised to call him as Ruth and I climbed the front steps and finally closed Ruth's bedroom door behind us.

I tried purposefully to keep myself drowsy so the vision wouldn't fade away. I didn't want my mind to start racing until I'd told Ruth the whole horrible tale. I sat down on her bed, and before she could say anything, I started telling the story, memory by horrific memory. I closed my eyes to breathe the damp forest air and recalled every detail from my horse's color to the clothing the soldiers were wearing. I felt massive grief, and I understood why McCollum had feared to tell me this story. I cried while describing each funeral fire I'd lit.

With my eyes still closed, I felt Ruth's weight readjust on the bed beside me, and I was surprised to hear her scratching notes on a pad of paper.

"Doesn't this totally freak you out, Ruth?"

"Well, yes. But we need to get the details down now, while they are fresh in your mind. I can be freaked out later when I have time to think about it."

"You know, Bennett and Marcus Flavius are the same person."

I looked at Ruth for a reaction.

"It's not just a feeling I have; it's a fact. All the other Roman soldiers were just faces. I didn't recognize any of them except Bennett." Closing my eyes, I tilted my head, feeling that my last statement might not be totally true. I recalled my experience and searched the background for any others I might recognize.

"There was someone I know behind the General." The thought made me shudder. "But I can't bring the face into focus." I gave up.

My words faded as Ruth put her hand on my leg. "Let me get you a drink of water."

I nodded yes and I lay back on the bed, trying to see the soldier's faces until Ruth re-entered the room.

I drank while listening to Ruth's perspective. "Bennett is a good guy now, and even *then*, in a way. And he did save your life at the risk of his own!" As we talked, Ruth lightened the mood enough so it was possible for me to sleep, but no way was I sleeping in a different room than her. I knew Ruth felt the same, so I pulled up the covers and hoped that when I closed my eyes I would only see darkness.

Bennett called Ruth's cell at 7:00 a.m. to see how I was feeling, and she assured him I was back to normal, all swelling and stickers gone. He was going to have to be satisfied with Ruth's explanation because there was just no way that I could face him.

"It's funny, Ruth. I know he took a big risk to save me, that none of the rest of you actually died at his hand, and I shouldn't hold what happened two thousand years ago against him, but I really want to know why he didn't throw his military career to the wind and die for us?"

"I think he should have," Ruth chuckled. "We're worth it."

"In reality there was no way he could have saved us. We were doomed the minute Caesar gave the order to exterminate our kind from the Earth."

A visible chill went through Ruth. "Don't know; don't want to think about it."

Knowing we needed a change of subject, I asked, "Do you think that Will and George missed us last night when we didn't put our energy into the bowl?"

Ruth and I stayed away from the subject of Bennett for a couple of days. It was too mind boggling to continually think about.

"Let's go to the Plaza and have a cappuccino," Ruth suggested. "It's a beautiful day."

"Sounds great to me. I have a bit of a sweet tooth." Within thirty minutes we were looking for a parking spot.

We found a nice seat on the deck of a coffee shop, and I ordered the biggest cookie on the menu.

"How's your hand, Hillary?" a familiar voice asked from behind.

"Yeah, I was in the hot tub, and that looked painful," another voice added.

I watched Ruth put on a smile. "Hi Clint. Hi Bennett. Fancy seeing you here."

I closed my eyes for a second, took a deep breath, and turned with a smile. "Hi guys."

"You okay?" Bennett asked with total sincerity.

"I'm okay, thanks. You want to sit down?" It wasn't as uncomfortable as I imagined it would be to see him again. It's hard not to enjoy being around a guy like Bennett because he's really genuine. Clint pulled up a chair next to Ruth and we fell into easy conversation.

When the sun began to hide behind the nearby buildings and the temperature started to drop, we decided to call it an afternoon. Bennett stood and helped me up.

"Let us at least walk you to your car. It will probably be months before we see each other again." Accepting the invitation, Clint and Ruth walked a short distance behind us.

We strolled the long way back to our car, not saying a lot. Suddenly, Bennett's head jerked to attention.

"What's going on?" I asked casually.

"I'm not quite sure," he said, visibly bothered. "I thought I saw something, and I have a funny déjà vu feeling. It's probably nothing." Taking my arm, he pulled me closer to him.

"Who are the guys?" a voice sneered from an alcove, and Jackson Black stepped out to block our path.

Bennett's reaction was fast and protective—he slid in front of me and confronted Black.

"I'm not here to mess with you, kid. I'm here to talk to my friend, Hillary."

"She's with me, and believe me when I tell you, I'm not a kid. Just be on your way before we have to make more of this than it needs to be." Clint stepped forward to stand by Bennett, and together they made a formidable wall. Ruth placed her hand over mine, making me feel safe, if somewhat foolish.

"Okay, okay," Black said, holding his hands up to indicate

surrender. He leaned forward to peer around my barricade and snarled, "I'll catch up with you at school," and gave a little salute.

Clint was the first to say something. "What was that about 'my friend'?"

Bennett replied, "Like I just told Hillary, déjà vu come to life, and I have to admit that man scares me. He's evil. I feel it in my gut." Turning to me, he asked, "Is he really a friend of yours?"

"No, Ruth and I call him Creepy Guy. Guess you felt it, too."

CHAPTER
THIRTY SIX

RUTH AND I both waited by the window for Will and George to come home because it had been a very long ten days. Spotting their car as it turned the corner, we ran out to meet them, overjoyed that they apparently had missed us just as much.

The boys who rode back with them unloaded the camping gear as they regaled Ruth and me with stories about their camping trip. Eager for a few minutes alone with our men, Ruth ingeniously mentioned the cookies she had left on the kitchen counter, and the room was instantly emptied of everyone but Will and George. I sneaked a kiss to make myself less nervous about confessing we'd missed a few meditations. Will intuitively knew something was up, so to ease his worry I gave him and George the *Reader's Digest* version of my injury at the party, the past life experience that ensued, and lastly, our meeting with Jackson Black.

While Will was pleased with Ruth's response to the situation, he seemed way too concerned and totally miffed about Bennett's involvement. Will's reaction took me by surprise because it was so out of character.

"Well, the short answer is, we'll never leave you two on your own again," George said lightheartedly. "Hope you don't mind your own personal bodyguards, because that's what we'll be."

Ruth snuggled in and gave George a kiss on his check.

Will tried to laugh, but couldn't make it look natural. Still obviously bothered by something, he took my hand and led me outside to our usual spot.

I leaned against the tree as I turned to face him. Will rested his forearm on the trunk just above my head and moved in close. "Do you remember a year ago when I told you on this very spot that you were immortal?"

"How could I forget? You walked away with my heart that night." I knew he loved hearing that. The corners of his lips held back his smile, but he didn't forget why we were here.

"I meant it when I said you are immortal. We all return to take another life, but I'd really like to keep you safe and living this lifetime. It's taken me two thousand very long years to find you again. I'd like you to stay with me for a while."

I smiled up at him. This guy knew how to melt me.

"I need you to know what the bowl meditation is *really* for," he said in a very serious tone.

I stopped flirting, knowing this must be important.

"Everything you know about it is true, but for you and me the bowl is so much more." He took my hand again and we walked over to sit on the curb. "McCollum and I need to see more from you," he said as he pulled me closer. "When you send your energy into the bowl, we also need your *energetic body to move forward*, that part of you that doesn't exist physically in this world. It will be like your soul talking to me on your cell phone without the phone." He raised his hand before I could interrupt. "Okay, not a very good analogy, but McCollum believes your soul will come to me and the brass bowl will become a mode of communication between us."

He saw the uneasy look in my eyes. "Don't worry so much, Hillary. We've done this before. All you're going to do is learn to do it again. That's why McCollum always has me keep the bowl in my possession, so you can find me. The bowl is a beacon, and it holds an energy that will draw you to me." Will reached up to rub the lines from my forehead. "Don't worry. It will happen easily. You'll just need to change your focus a little. You're already halfway there."

"If you're willing, so am I," I said, hiding my fear of failure. "Could you feel me in the bowl while you were away camping?"

"I can always feel you with me. Not only because of the bowl, but also because you're a part of me. We are two halves of the original flame, and yes, I can feel you when your life force is projected into the bowl. It is like music to my ears." He raised my chin to kiss me lightly.

216

"Now I need you to take another step toward me."

"I know it's possible Will, because my soul wants to jump out of me and into you right here and now. The pull is amazingly strong."

Will lifted me to my feet, and as we walked, hand in hand, he explained the second part of his statement, *McCollum and I need to see more from you.*

"What do you remember about the first night we met?" Will asked.

"Are you fishing for compliments again? Because I've told you a million times how glad I was that you were the one standing across from me when the big door opened and—"

"No," Will said, amused. "Not that. I want you to explain how you felt when I touched you, and I need you to be serious."

"That hum! At first I thought I would vomit. Is that what you mean?"

"Yes, the hum … my *chi*, the life force that circulates within my body." Will took my hands between his, placing my palms together. "Close your eyes and tell me what you feel."

I did as he said and discovered that I could actually feel the energy circulating in my body. He repositioned my hands back-to-back. "What do you feel now?"

"The energy has reversed its flow," I said, surprised. When I opened my eyes, he seemed satisfied. "What?"

"The energy you are feeling is your own chi, not mine," he said, putting his hands behind his back so I understood. "This is the second lesson McCollum wants you to master—the control of your life force. Eventually, with practice, you will be able to extend it beyond your physical body."

I just smiled and figured in time I'd either learn or not learn, but for right now, I wouldn't worry about it. If Will and McCollum had confidence in me, I wouldn't doubt myself before I had given it a serious try.

We smelled something wonderful as we approached Will's front steps. Ruth and George had delivered the boys safely back into McCollum's care and cooked dinner for us. Seeing Ruth's smiling face, I said a silent prayer of thanks that she was also in my life.

George stood to give me a big bear hug, lifting me off my feet. "Ruth gave me the details about your weekend. Great stuff, that memory you had. I remember that lifetime myself, some parts fondly and some parts not so much."

Will leaned against the doorframe, still as miffed as he was the first time the subject came up. This made George howl with laughter. "You were the one that didn't see the arrow coming. I expected you to be faster than that!" George teased.

"I was a little preoccupied by the Roman army's impending advance, and by the almost certain massacre of all that was dear to me!" Will retorted.

"Don't give me that bull. You know as well as I do that you were preoccupied with the general who was in love with your woman." Looking at me, George continued, "He comes by his attitude toward your friend Bennett honestly. That rivalry has been going on for a very long time." George just couldn't manage to stop laughing.

"You're the one who lost your head!" Will said, with anger I'd never seen before.

"Okay, let's cool down," Ruth said. She began to ask a question, but stopped short before the whole "headless bodies" conversation ruined her appetite.

CHAPTER
THIRTY SEVEN

OUR MEDITATION group had eagerly been waiting for Labor Day weekend, when we'd be together again. Our sleeping arrangements were the usual: Mom and Dad in my room, Dr. Edwards in Ruth's, and poor Gilbert took the couch without a complaint. I stayed with Will, Ruth, with George. Buddy was in his box, and the brass bowl was in its place on the mantel.

Once our group reunited we were inseparable, spending every waking moment together. McCollum had given Will and George new mantras for each of us, which was an auspicious occasion because it meant we had outgrown our old ones.

We gathered in Will and George's apartment for our first meditation. We sat on our pillows around the bowl and began using our new mantras to send light into the world. The room was totally silent except for the ticking clock. I positioned myself across from Will so I could look into his face after I returned from my travels. I always came out of meditation before him, so I had lots of time just to stare and wonder a thousand things about him.

I was trying my new technique, to move my energetic body out of my physical one, but despite my personal training with McCollum via computer, I wasn't finding it any easier to accomplish. My hope had been that the power of the group might give me a boost.

Beginning calmly, I cleared my mind and focused on my third eye. Breathing, I pulled my soul upward and focused on moving to a point just a few inches outside of my body.

Soon the chatter in my mind won, and I moved from McCollum's technique to my own. Silently, I spoke to Will. Then in frustration I began to silently yell at him, "Please, help me!" Then I moved on to focusing on my insecurities, and started telling the universe that they had the wrong person. I was definitely not who they thought I was. If they were truly serious about saving the planet, they needed to locate the correct person, pronto!

When I opened my eyes, it felt like I had run a marathon. I did my re-integration—*I am so happy, I am so happy*—but in reality I was so pissed and disappointed in myself that I just wanted to cry. But as I looked across the circle at Will, there was no doubt how very happy I was to have found him. I looked into that beautiful, serene face, so peaceful that he looked like an angel, and knew he hadn't heard one word of what I'd been yelling at him. *Oh well, there's always next time,* I thought. *And if Will believed in me, I can, too.*

We talked non-stop during dinner. It turned out that Mom and Dad had started a meditation group of their own. They had placed an ad in the local paper and an ex-priest they fondly called Father John had answered, and they'd been having a ball.

Gilbert had been practicing living consciously, but found he forgot more often than he remembered. We howled with laughter as he told his stories. "I wake each morning intending to live my life totally in the moment. I usually make it until the first good looking chick walks by. Then my mind takes off to places I can't talk about in mixed company, but definitely not in the moment."

Dr. Edwards had been using CDs to reunite with Yogi Shanti, and was finding it just as relevant today as he had in the eighties.

Ruth and I told our story about the past life experience in K.C., catching everyone by surprise, and when we'd finished, everyone looked at Will for confirmation.

"Hillary's story is accurate, but I was powerless to help her. I had been dead for years!" Will said in his own defense. "I learned my lesson, and I will never leave her unprotected again." I knew his proclamation was true.

Our long weekend was over far too soon, and we were all teary-eyed as we said good-bye. It had become painful to leave one another.

"We need a name for our group," Gilbert blurted to lighten the mood. "We can't use *The Order of the Phoenix*; although it's cool, Harry Potter's already taken it. But maybe something like that. What do ya think?"

With all in agreement, we made a solemn promise to each other that at our next reunion we would each have at least one potential name.

"I got a call from McCollum last night," Will announced. "He'd like us to join him and the boys at their Summer Solstice Celebration on the twenty-first of June. How about it? Can everyone make it back in June?"

Vicki Renfro

CHAPTER
THIRTY EIGHT

JUNE 21, AD 38
I'm the last Druid, and I'm on the run to save a life I no longer care about—mine. The tribes' chieftains willingly feed me and give me companionship, but I never stay long enough for the rumor of my location to spread. There are stories of Romans setting villagers on fire for information, and I will not let myself be responsible for that. My last respite was a small encampment not far from the river that now lies before me. My mare is still my constant friend, nuzzling me when I feel I can't go on and standing guard when I rest my weary bones.

I only drop my guard for a moment to let my mind drift back to better days, but even that moment is too long. My mare whinnies, and when I open my tired eyes, there he stands, one lone foot-soldier looking at me as if I am the prize that will make him a legend.

He licks his lips as he shifts his position, and I know he has made a fatal mistake. Once his mind moves from capture to rape and he sheathes his heavy sword, I have the time I need to mount my mare and ride into the river.

I feel the water on my back as she kicks up a wall of mud and water, and I hear my determined hunter enter the river behind us. My prayers are answered as my horse leaps into the deeper current of the river and begins to swim because I am aware of the weight a Roman horse carries. When we reach the far bank I lean forward to help my mare lift herself out of the water, for she is getting old and I dare not think of my life without her.

I turn to give a sarcastic wave to my pursuer for having the audacity to interrupt my daydream. I was sure he would have the intelligence to stop his mount before they entered the deeper water. But

222

no, his horse is floundering and is not able to win the fight. The armor is dragging it under. I look into the soldier's face as he struggles to disarm himself, fighting to shed his boots and clothing before the current devours him. I see a pleading in his eyes that is from one human being to another. He's so young, barely into puberty.

I damn my decision as we reenter the water, for the current is swift and my mare is tired. We reach him as he goes down for the last time. I stretch my arm into the water and drag him up by his black Roman hair, and to my shock the eyes are not those of a helpless boy, but the dead, black eyes of an enemy. He fights to pull me into the water and my mare goes under from our combined weight. I dismount to save my horse's life and am pulled into the darkness by hands gripping my tangled hair. Twisting my body, my feet find the belt that holds his remaining armor. With all the strength my exhausted limbs can muster, I thrust my heels into his gut and jerk myself free. I watch him sink as his burden takes him deeper, an expression of horror frozen on his face. Unencumbered, my body floats to the surface. Too exhausted to pull myself from the river, I lay half in, half out of the water, letting my mind drift back to a time when I wasn't so totally alone.

June 21, 2011

Will and George were at the campground by dawn to put up the volleyball nets and claim our picnic tables and camping spots. Ruth and I arrived at 7:30 a.m. to begin setting up the tent, but we found that Will and George already had the area looking like a little city.

Jumping out of the car and running toward the volleyball area, I kicked off my flip-flops and buried my feet in the sand. It was damp from the morning dew and felt great. Will and George had organized the kitchen under one central tent, with a dozen smaller ones set up along the perimeter for the boys. The whole park seemed to belong to us.

"Where will we be sleeping?' Ruth asked, throwing her arms around George's neck and nearly dragging him to the ground.

"We're going to set up the tents for our soon-to-be-named meditation group over there," he said, and pointed to a grassy area on the other side of the volleyball court. "Far, far away from impressionable children," George said, with mischief in his eyes.

The boys arrived in four vans, and when the doors opened, they all ran full speed toward Will. By now I knew all of them by name and loved each individual personality, but no one held a place in their hearts quite like Will did. They had all missed him enormously since he moved out, and each of them wanted to be the first in line to receive a hug.

I was amazed when they enthusiastically hugged me, too. My heart sprang into my throat as the smallest boy, Jimmy, jumped up into my arms and clung to my neck affectionately. I had wanted to become a part of their family, but until that moment I had never known if it was a possibility.

Ruth and I helped unpack the camping supplies from the vans while George and Will assigned the boys to their tents. Lee and Gilbert had set up our campsite, and without asking had pitched the tents in a circle rather than a line. When we walked over to see if we could help, I saw the brass bowl in the center. Lord, this was going to be a great weekend!

Dad's truck pulled into the parking lot around 10:00 a.m., making our group complete. I ran to meet them with uncontrolled enthusiasm. Dad slid out of the driver's seat to give me a big hug and walked to the tailgate to start unloading. They had brought everything but the kitchen sink, and when I saw that he had a few rocking chairs, I thought, *of course!*

Leaving the farm this time of year was a big thing for them, so I was surprised to see Mom's face looking so worry free through the back windshield. A tall man, grey hair shorn close and wearing a diamond stud, slid out of the truck first, offering Mom his hand. Now this was a real surprise.

I slowed down as I approached, still looking at the guy on Mom's arm. "Don't worry, Kiddo, McCollum called and asked us to bring John."

Picking up Mom's pack, I turned to get a better look as they both rounded the back of the truck. He already had his hand extended toward me.

"Hello Hillary, I'm Father John," he said. He had lived some very hard years by the looks of his face, but his blue eyes were crystal clear. "I think I have the advantage, since your mom and dad never stop talking about you and your group of mystics. I think I'll be able to put a name to each one of your faces."

By the time I shook his hand, everyone else was on their way over, and as Father John introduced himself, he called each by name without making a mistake.

Once the boys had settled in, McCollum came over to join us. "Greetings, and welcome to our celebration." He took time to have a few private words with each of us, and as he worked his way toward me, I wondered what I should say. I had not seen him in person since the great New Year's Eve debacle. I watched him as he talked to our newest member, Father John, and I saw McCollum actually lean in to embrace him.

I stood back, waiting for my time with him. I was still in awe of him, and a little afraid. When I was the only one left, he took four long strides and arrived directly in front of me. I bowed my head, brought my hands together in front of me, and said "Namaste." He placed his hands on the outside of mine, and when I looked up, I was looking directly into those infinite pools of blue.

"I also see the God in you, Hillary," he replied to my greeting, "and I am becoming more aware of it every day. Your light is becoming brighter."

I found myself speechless, and I stumbled over my words as I said, "Thank you."

"I know how far you still have to go, but I want you to be aware of how very far you have come," he said, still holding my hands. "I'm proud of you, dear one." He inclined his head toward me, giving my hands one last squeeze, and turned toward the kitchen tent. "Come on boys," he said in a playful voice, clapping his hands. "Who wants to play volleyball?"

The volleyball games raged on until we broke for lunch, and all of us were ready for some water and sandwiches. Of course, Mom had put herself in charge of the food tent, and everyone was secretly pleased.

Will and I found a place to sit in the shade of a huge elm on the edge of our campsite. The tree must have been a couple hundred years old, judging by the way its roots bulged out of the ground. With a feeling of déjà vu, I spotted Gilbert tucked amongst a tangle of roots where his body fit perfectly. He was in his element.

Dad ate his lunch in one of his rocking chairs, with McCollum in the rocker next to him. They both looked incredibly peaceful and happy, and with iced tea in hand they exuded contentment.

The boys seldom had this kind of free time, so they made the most of every minute. They were calling for everyone to line up again to pick new volleyball teams as Will and George finished up in the lunch tent, eager to get back into the game. I, on the other hand, looked around the park at the green, open space and decided that taking a walk might just be the ticket.

I told Ruth where I was going and asked her to please let Will know so he wouldn't worry. I found my tennis shoes in my backpack and sat down to put them on as I eyed the road, which turned into more of a path as it wound around the little lake. I paused as a large shadow fell over me, but when I looked up I found it belonged to the smallest of my friends, Jimmy.

"What are you doing, Hillary?"

"Going for a walk around the lake," I said. "I figure it can't be more than a couple of miles."

"I can walk that far. May I go with you?" Jimmy asked.

"Sure, you can come, but you have to get permission first." And before I finished tying my shoelaces, he was running toward McCollum. I watched, amused, as Jimmy waved his hands excitedly, trying to convince the master that he should accompany me.

McCollum looked up from where he sat in his rocker to meet my eyes. As I nodded yes, he patted young Jimmy on the shoulder and sent him back in my direction.

CHAPTER
THIRTY NINE

I WALKED with the warm sun on my shoulders and Jimmy by my side, relishing the wonderful day. I had to slow down my regular pace so Jimmy could keep up without breaking into a trot.

"How long have you lived with McCollum?" I asked, trying to begin a conversation.

"Always, I guess. McCollum's my great uncle. I was just a baby when my parents had their accident."

A lump formed in my throat. "McCollum must love you very much," I said, watching a smile light Jimmy's face, his cherub features only made more adorable by his missing front tooth. "Does the tooth fairy come to your house?"

"Of course he does," Jimmy stated emphatically, and the image of George sliding his big hand under Jimmy's pillow popped into my mind.

We found ourselves walking along the tree-lined road, chatting like a couple of old friends. I told him about growing up on a farm, and he talked about his life.

"Yeah, McCollum tries to treat me like the other boys, but sometimes when I'm lonely I sneak into his room. He makes me a bed in front of his fireplace and rocks me to sleep. No one knows," he added quickly.

"Don't worry, Jimmy. I can keep a secret. Besides, I think you deserve a little extra attention because you're so darn cute." I reached down to tickle him and his giggle was delightful. "Have you started to meditate yet?"

"Yes, ma'am! I'm learning how to swim!"

He beamed, and I told him how very proud I was of him. Somehow, all things felt possible on that beautiful day, even the idea that someday I would become as brilliant as my small companion.

We paused to look back across the lake as we made our next turn. I saw the volleyball game in the distance and heard the boys raising a ruckus when I felt Jimmy slip his little hand into mine.

Laughing as we turned another corner, I had to squint against the sun, and we paused to see what was ahead of us. It was an old abandoned concrete structure that looked as though it might have been used for boat rentals in the past, and we had to walk straight through it to stay on the path. It was covered with a layer of neglect, and I could smell the mold that had grown from the dampness. We were definitely on the path less taken.

I heard Will's voice in my head, "Pay attention to how things *feel*, Hillary."

"But what could happen?" my voice argued back. It only appeared to be about twenty feet to the sunshine on the other side. The scenario only took about three seconds to run through my mind, but I should have thought longer. As we entered the decrepit structure and my eyes adjusted to the dim light, it became quite apparent that we were not alone.

A low growl sliced the air, evoking an image of just how large the animal making it might be. My instinct was to run, but I only had time to shift Jimmy behind me. My ears picked up a low command, *kill,* and I felt more than saw the animal spring from the shadows. In desperation I instinctively spread my hands in front of me and braced for the impact. Heat rushed through my body as a stirring in my heart erupted into the full-blown instinct of a mother bear protecting her cub. I took my stance, feet shoulder-width apart, and felt a burst of energy rush down my arms into my hands. The heat burst from my fingertips, my chi visible as a stream of light. I watched it slam into the animal in midair, causing it to fly backwards. The animal crashed into the block wall with a solid *thud.*

"Not my dog," an agonized voice cried as the owner of the dog lunged toward me out of his dark hiding place. "Witch!" he yelled, and I watched the indigent man's face with amazement as it changed to that of a Roman foot soldier, scarcely old enough to shave. "Mystic Warrior, my ass! You're a fraction of who you used to be," and then the face was only that of a disheveled madman.

It took a precious moment to gather my thoughts; I was not exactly sure what I was fighting. I felt Jimmy's small hands still tightly wrapped around my leg, and my only impulse was to ensure his safety.

Making myself ready, I squared my shoulders and gave the order, "Run Jimmy, now." I felt his little fists release my jeans and heard his footsteps fade away behind me. I kept my eyes locked on my enemy, who burned with hatred for me.

"You'll pay for what you did to my dog!" he shouted, and I saw a flash of metal slice through the air.

Lunging to my right to avoid being cut, I saw the dead eyes of the Roman once more. "They may call you a warrior, but you're nothing but a murdering bitch. I hope you rot in hell for what you did to me in the river."

Memories from my Druid life came flooding back and terror consumed me. This madman was the soldier who once tried to drown me. Bile caught in my throat as I remembered the look on the boys face when the river's current sucked him under. I was consumed by guilt, when I felt the full force of the man's body hit me, the impact brought me back to the present and I knew I had to find a way out.

An open window caught my eye as I landed a blow that knocked my attacker to the ground. I ran for my life, leaping through the opening.

My feet hit the ground, but I couldn't gain traction. I scanned the length of the building for dry land only to discover the path had been devoured by the lake. I sunk deeper into the muck with every step I took. My only choice was to head toward the lake and swim. My muscles strained as the suction of the mud fought to hold me in place. With one fleeting look toward the volleyball game across the lake, I pulled myself free and dove into the dirty brown water as the dazed dog cleared the window followed by its crazy owner.

I swam as far as I could under water to hide myself from my pursuers, but my forward motion was slow. The mud stuck to my shoes was weighing me down. As I was forced to break the water's surface for air, I saw both man and dog had entered the water after me.

I took one last breath and sank in a struggle to pry off the shoes, as my sodden clothes pulled me down. The double knot I always tied only tightened as I desperately pulled at it. My chest hurt from lack of oxygen and I prayed I hadn't misjudged how long I could hold my breath. Sinking ever deeper, I grasped the futility of my situation, and I began to become confused about which way was up.

I moved my consciousness to my third eye as my lungs burned, and then I gave one last frantic pull at my shoes. I felt them release. There was an explosion of color behind my eyelids as I pleaded for a miracle. "Will, please hear me, I need you!"

Finding myself in total darkness, my hand brushed the silt-covered bottom of the lake. I fought to calm my mind as I rotated my body so that my feet were beneath me, and I prayed to whatever Gods could hear me that I had enough air to make it to the surface. I bent my knees and pushed upward with every scrap of strength left in my body.

I felt the rush of air into my lungs as I broke the surface and shook the water violently from my face. I could tell by the screaming of profanities that the madman was close behind me, and I swam with all the fight left in me to the nearest shore.

As I felt the bottom of the lake rising underneath me, I pulled myself from the water and sprinted barefoot toward our camp. Adrenaline was all I had left to fuel my cramping muscles.

I would have run past the car if Will hadn't jumped out to catch me, wrapping his arms tightly around me.

"Shhhhh," he said, holding me tight against him, "I've got you. You're safe now."

"Where's Jimmy, where's Jimmy?" I wildly scanned the area.

"He's safe. We found him running along the road and sent him to find McCollum."

As my body gave up the struggle and my mind calmed, I finally understood what Will had said to me. Jimmy hadn't made it back to camp to get help; Will had come because he *heard* me call him. And without restraint, I began to cry.

CHAPTER FOURTY

DAD HAD called the police, and I could already hear the sirens in the distance. Gilbert, Dr. Edwards, Dad, and Father John had followed Will on foot, and now stood like sentinels around Will and me. It wasn't until the police pulled up that I realized no one actually knew what had happened to me. My friends had all responded to protect me no matter what the danger was.

When the door opened on the patrol car, I could tell by the expression on Officer Hall's face that he recognized me, too.

"Ms. Rubner," he said, checking out my bodyguards. "What's happened here?" He noticed Gilbert and reached out to shake his hand.

For the most part, the sun had dried me, and while I wasn't cold, I was reluctant to leave Will's arms. A second patrol car pulled up across the lake, and I saw the madman trying to hold back his vicious dog as the police attempted to figure out what to do.

Eventually I joined Officer Hall in his patrol car and gave him my statement. I remembered everything vividly, but I was reluctant to give all of the details because I could still hear the screaming from across the lake: "Black magic, die you warrior bitch!"

Returning to Will's arms, I breathed in the scent of his skin and closed my eyes.

Will and I took our time driving back to the campsite. Everyone else had walked back, leaving us alone, knowing that I needed to tell

Will everything that had happened. He smiled when I told him about the dog's reaction to me putting up my hands to block his attack.

"You did great, Hillary! Whether it happened purely as an instinct to protect Jimmy or as divine intervention, it happened, and you've felt the power of your chi, your life force. Now you need to spend time refining your control."

"Is Jimmy *really* okay?"

"Besides being overly excited about his dangerous excursion and telling the story to anyone who will listen, he's fine but, Hillary—"

"Don't say it, Will. I already know. A voice told me the building wasn't safe, but I didn't listen. I had a chance to avoid all this misery and I chose to walk right into it. I won't do it again."

"Good! But that wasn't what I was going to say. I was going to thank you for turning to me when you were in trouble, for having confidence in me. Your light body came to me, asking me to follow. You are lovely as light."

Letting the terror of the day fall away from me, I said, "And I'm not lovely soaking wet and streaked with mud?"

"You're alive," he replied, "and nothing is more beautiful than that."

I could tell when we arrived at camp that the kids were totally unaware of what had just taken place, and I was relieved to see them playing. The only worried ones were gathered in the parking lot, waiting for our return. Dad and Mom's faces were both drawn. Ruth and George stood hand in hand next to Father John, Gilbert, and Dr. Edwards. Then there was McCollum with Jimmy in his arms. I got out of the car and everyone hugged me to reassure themselves that I was okay. Then, with head hung, it was time for me to face McCollum. But before I knew what was happening, Jimmy leaped out of his arms and into mine. All of the tension drained from my body as I held him tight.

"Are you all right, Hillary? I ran as fast as I could to get help."

"I know you did, sweetie. You're a very brave young man." I nuzzled his neck and he giggled that intoxicating laugh. Hopping from my arms, he raced off to play with the other boys.

McCollum motioned us toward our lawn chairs, and once we were settled, I delved back into my nightmare and told the story one last time.

When the full moon was at its most powerful position in the night sky, McCollum woke me from where I had fallen asleep in Will's arms and directed me to sit in the chair next to him. Standing to walk across the circle, I pulled myself to my full height, and for that moment, with the moonlight full on my face, I became the person everyone perceived me to be, the one I knew I was becoming.

"Hillary," McCollum began.

I turned to meet his gaze. "May I call you Hilsbeth?" he asked. "It's been an eternity since I've had that name on my lips." Looking at him, I noticed that there were more strands of grey in his hair than a month ago, and hoped he was better at controlling stress than me.

McCollum waved for the other eight to pull their chairs closer to listen to his confession. "I would have spoken sooner, but I thought we had more time … a few more days to enjoy each other's company and play in the sunlight with the boys. But it is now apparent that I have misjudged. You see, Hilsbeth …" McCollum took my hand. "Those who prefer the darkness never like the light to be turned on, for it sends them scurrying into the corners to hide in the shadows. Only the maddest amongst them stays to fight in the light, and we saw that today. Now there is no doubt left in my mind that the dark forces have detected our arrival." McCollum looked at me and smiled. "Our advantage is that they were not expecting *us* to return at all. I have often wondered myself if we would all be together again." McCollum sighed inwardly and continued the story.

"There are many beings who have come to witness, well … let's call it *'the uplifting of the planet.'* They came as ditch diggers and doctors, gurus and pastors, mothers and fathers. They are souls that turned in every karmic point and every bargaining chip they had in order to be on this planet at this particular time."

A golden aura began to glow around him.

He patted my hand kindly and released it. "Up until recently, my group has gone undetected because *they* have never considered my boys a threat. But now that you're here, Hilsbeth, they feel our power growing like a thunderstorm gathering on the horizon, and they fear the balance may be turning. We are each powerful individuals, but as 'One' we are remarkable!"

McCollum rose to walk among us. "For quite some time now, beings of light have been incarnating, one by one, under the radar, so to speak. And because of all the wonderful work they have done, our platform has already been built for us; we have only to complete our plan!

"I also believe the original 2012 date has been altered, and the window for planetary change has already opened. Another thing has happened in our favor. The universe has dealt us a wild card, and your father had the wisdom to recognize him." Turning to Father John, McCollum said, "He may look like a tattered book cover, but the pages he holds within will prove to be magical." Bending to touch Father John's third eye, McCollum continued in a voice so soft that listening to it felt like eavesdropping. "Don't worry that you do not know, Father John. You will know when it is time, and you will shine like a brilliant star."

McCollum stretched, gazing up at the stars and then at us. "As it has been since the beginning of time, dawn will come, and we will be given another chance to bring forth the light. We have within us the ability to manifest the destiny we desire. It is the reason we exist, the reason we have come."

"Now, my Druid warriors disguised as mere humans, you still need your sleep. I'll see you as when day breaks."

I found myself thinking of all the small things people do in life that give away their power to the dark side unknowingly—negative thinking, white lies, discrimination, lack of self love, holding grudges, guilt, the feeling of lack—when Gilbert interrupted my thoughts.

"Maybe he can sleep," Gilbert said as he watched McCollum walk away. "He's got all those mystical powers. But I think it's time for a name. What did everyone come up with? I mean, if we are going to fight together, I think we deserve a handle."

Gilbert fully expected to hear grumbling, but instead received only enthusiasm, and an exuberant exchange of ideas ensued. George's suggested *The Lightheaded,* which made Will laugh. When he had finished laughing, he said, "What do you think, Father John? We haven't heard from you yet."

Placing his hands on his knees to support his weight, Father John took a deep breath. "I first met Terry when I replied to his newspaper ad, and when Terry and Kate finally let the cat out of the bag about the brass bowl, I literally sat for hours seeing that bowl in my minds eye and sending my thought into that magical object. I imagined every detail of what it must look like, feel like, and sound like. I also imagined what each of you looked like based on Terry and Kate's descriptions of all of you. And just for your information, they were spot on. I could literally feel all of us together with that bowl sitting in the center." Father John rocked back in his chair, stretching his long legs out in front of him. "In my mind we have always had a name. Come on guys," he said. "We meditate with a mystical *brass* bowl and have come through time to reunite with a *band* of brothers. In my mind we've been 'The Brass Band' for a long time now.

The group erupted into laughter. But as the laughter subsided into smiles and heads began to nod, we all knew we had found our name.

"I'm on board with that!" Lee said. "I can take a tuba case to work and store it in an obvious location in my office. When I need time off work, I'll explain that I'm doing a part-time gig with a brass band. It's easier than explaining that I'm a shape shifter incarnate, sent to save the planet!"

After the final joke was told, Will looked at me and said, "You know, eventually you'll be the conductor!"

"No, not me, I'm a groupie," I joked. "You know, the girl standing in the front row at every gig, drooling over the good-looking lead singer with the dreamy blue eyes. That's you Will," I winked. "I'm absolutely infatuated with you and every other member of this band."

"Even me?" Gilbert asked. "The flute player with lightning fingers."

"Especially you, Gilbert, because you're the one who taught me to listen to the music in the first place."

We smiled at each other and knew that we were referring to our long talks about realities, seen and unseen, and the magic in life.

I began to sway slowly back and forth as I put my arm around Ruth on one side and Will on the other. "The lights will come up, and the band members will be called upon to play their parts," I stated, as everyone stood and linked their arms with ours. "And our souls will dance as The Brass Band."

CHAPTER
FOURTY ONE

July 17, 2011

The sun rises without its usual cloud cover, so I use it as an excuse to shake my cabin fever. I put my tennis shoes on and walk outside to meet the sunny day. I take the long way to the Student Union, wanting to soak in as much of the sun's warmth as possible. As usual, I'm daydreaming about Will. He's been spending most nights at McCollum's house, and I miss him.

I'm brought back to reality by the motion of a bike riding past, and look up to see none other than Jackson Black pulling up to the curb next to me.

He smiles as he lifts his bike onto the sidewalk to walk with me. My heart sinks.

"It works!" he says, as I calculate the shortest route to the Union. "I can close my eyes and wish for us to be together ... and like magic, here you are!"

"I've got to go," I say, changing directions to try to get around his bike.

"Don't tell me you're going to meet that boyfriend of yours," he says snidely, "because you're not. I know he spends his nights with little boys."

The look on his face is frightening. He matches every move I make with the front tire of his bike, and I find it impossible to escape. "Come on Hillary, be my friend."

"We're NOT friends and we never will be."

"Come on, Hillary. Take a closer look at me!" His hands reach for

me, and I feel myself falling back through time, to a place I dread—the road to Coritani. There in the mud beside the road, Rutiah lies in Georog's arms, battered and used beyond recognition by the Roman soldiers. George is unable to stand because his Achilles tendons have been severed, and he is slowly bleeding to death as he holds Ruth's lifeless body.

I hear the ax fall, and nauseated, I turn to find the answer to a question that has haunted me for two thousand years. The Roman butcher drops his ax and picks up another severed head, sticking it on the end of a spike. As he slowly turns his gaze toward me, he smiles ... and I'm looking into the bloody face of Jackson Black.

July 18, 2011

I jolted straight up in bed, waking from my dream and trying to gather my scattered thoughts. I was soaked with sweat, and my heart was beating at a dangerously fast pace. "What the hell?" I said, trying to get past my panic to remember the dream before it once again retreated into the void from whence it came. I felt a warm arm reach up and wrap around me. The room was filled with Will's sleepy scent, and he pulled me back toward my pillows. "What's wrong, Hillary? Did you have a bad dream?"

Book 2
Coming soon

Soul Searching with the Brass Band

CHAPTER ONE

AD 38

I am the final rider to abandon the battlefield, with no other choice but to leave our dead and dying behind. I feel as if I am suffocating, being dragged under by the screams of the fallen and the stench of blood that's held aloft by the unrelenting humidity. Gillian, the sole survivor of the untainted Druid bloodline sits precariously atop the rump of my mare, his heels digging into her hindquarters to stay astride. Mounted backwards to face the Roman soldiers who are in pursuit, the tiny, enchanted Gillian is my best hope. Our escape depends totally on him using his ancient Druid magic to weave a fog bank that we can hide within.

My mare's hooves hit solid rock as we slide down a sheer hillside toward the turbulent river below. I fear the enemy can hear our decent even over the racket of their own armor. We hit the waist-deep water with such force that I reach out behind me to grab Gillian by his shirt. It is the only thing that keeps my magical friend from disappearing into the swift current.

Emerging from the water on the opposite shore, my mare's hooves land upon the sodden leaves of the forest bed. At last our progress becomes silent, and I feel my heartbeat slow as the world changes around us. The fog thickens and wraps around us. We become invisible as we soundlessly disappear into the haze.

September 21, 2011

I woke with perspiration soaking my hair and knew without opening my eyes that the light of the full moon would be streaming through my bedroom window. I'd grown used to these midnight journeys out of my body, and used to the ghostly white moonlight that filled my apartment when I returned. Rolling on my side and opening my eyes slowly, I looked at the pillow next to me for reassurance. I needed to see Will still lying beside me, alive and unharmed.

A year ago, when I began having these dreams about my Druid incarnation, I would fight to remember every detail. Now I would give almost anything to not relive the deaths of my friends in vivid Technicolor at each full moon, when the pull of the lunar tide takes my soul back to the time of the standing stones.

I quietly slipped out of bed and into the living room to phone my best friend, Ruth, who lived below us with her boyfriend, George. She had learned to anticipate my calls when the full moon dominated the night sky.

"We're still here, Hillary. Everything is okay," Ruth assured me. Her voice was calm as she predicted each of my questions. "Go back to sleep now, sweetie."

I hung up and hit speed dial, waiting impatiently for Gilbert to answer. Frantically, I spun my new gold wedding band on my finger, watching it shimmer in the moonlight, the feel of it still unfamiliar to me.

When Gilbert answered I asked him, "Can you make fog?"

"Well, yes! The physics department has a machine and—"

"No, I mean can *you* make fog?"

"What was our dream about tonight, Hils? If McCollum wants me

240

to begin developing the capacity—"

"You were riding on the rear end of my mare and weaving a fog bank with your old Druid magic," I told him, willing his brain to conjure images as sharp and real as mine had been just moments ago in my dream.

"No Hils, I'm here in my bed and my toes are still not webbed, although I'm sure my hair will soon be totally white if I don't get my beauty rest. Go back to bed. Write everything down, if you need to. We'll talk in the morning, but for now go back to bed."

It was unlike me to stay caught between two worlds like I was on this night, not knowing for sure which details belonged in which lifetime. But it was the equinox, and at the instant the night and day became exactly equal, my consciousness had been released and I once again roamed the past.

Mindlessly, I stood at our front window, gazing half hypnotized at the dance between the breeze and the trees that lined the street outside. The shadows appeared to move independently from their hosts, but in reality they were just a reflection of the tree's physical form. It reminded me of the images I experienced from the past, and how they mirrored so much of my present life. Things were packaged differently in this life, but the people and the journey were very much a reflection of my past life.

I was surprised to feel Will's arms wrap around me in a gentle embrace. I hadn't heard him get out of bed or walk across the living room floor. I relaxed into him without turning.

"Come back to me, Hillary," he whispered softly into my sleep-tousled hair. "It's 2011. You are a student at Kansas State University, and we have found each other again."

When I turned to look into his bottomless blue eyes, I had no doubt about which life I preferred. He picked me up as if I were weightless. I rested my head on his shoulder, breathing in the scent of him as he carried me back to the comfort of our rumpled warm bed.

I had relived last night's bloody battle and many others during my nightly travels back to the time of my Druid warrior incarnation. They had begun a year, when I was a freshman in college. And still at each full moon, I was pulled back to my primitive existence, where food was sparse and the damp air cut through my tattered cloak, making me think I would never be warm again. I spent those nights sleepless and alone on the hard ground of a homeland I fiercely defended, returning at dawn to my comfortable apartment, a bed piled high with pillows, and the central heat maintaining a pleasant temperature. There in my bed, I would replay the details of that faraway lifetime, over and over again in my mind, trying to place my memories in chronological order.

During the past year I had spent innumerable hours fretting over how I was to fulfill my role in the enlightenment of planet Earth if I remained no more than plain old Hillary Rubner Emerald. If McCollum's insights into the future were accurate, and I believed that to be the case, I was to become the same mighty warrior I had been in my Druid life, when I lived as Hilsbeth.

McCollum was either blessed or cursed, depending on the way you looked at it, for he traveled through time with total recall of the ancient plan we had put into motion two thousand years ago. He had explained many times to me that I was to be a major player in the Earth's transition into a higher dimension. And believe me when I say, there is still plenty that I don't understand.

For the past year, I had thought of little else but how to regain my Druid powers. I came to the conclusion that I needed to return to that very first battle scene that I had experienced while asleep in my freshman dorm room a year ago. At that time, I had foolishly brushed it off as just another dream. At that point I didn't realize its significance, and couldn't have guessed that those same Druids would be so intricately woven into the pattern of this life.

Through the process of connecting all my nightly visions from two centuries ago, I was beginning to realize what had happened to Hilsbeth—to me—during that grim time that had diminished her power. I felt the crashing sorrow that had shattered her as she watched Liam, her heart, her lover, die when he took an arrow that had been meant for her. Finding her Druid soul torn between living or dying, utter despair had propelled half of Hilsbeth's soul on a futile journey to follow Liam into the light, leaving the remaining part earthbound, locked in a bloody struggle to save her people from annihilation. That split had weakened me in this incarnation, and I surmised that if I could consciously return to that place in time again and save Liam's life, that would correct everything and allow my abilities as that "Mystical Druid Warrior" to move forward with me into this life. Or at least I desperately prayed they would.

So now, each night as I closed my eyes to sleep, I hoped to find myself once again at the forest's edge, feeling my mare's skin twitch with nervous tension beneath me as I waited silently to led my militia into battle against the great Roman general, Marcus Flavius. That was when I would change my future by stopping the arrow that had taken my beloved Liam's life.

<hr>

September 21, 2011—the morning following the equinox

I woke feeling exhausted and looked over at the clock on my nightstand. It was long past the time my alarm should have gone off. I smiled to myself as it dawned on me that I had gotten a few extra hours of sleep thanks to my husband's thoughtfulness. I eased my legs over the edge of the bed, finding them to be stiff and sore. I furrowed my brow in an effort to figure out why. Then the memory of the previous night's events passed before my eyes, and I glimpsed the fierce battle that I had fought as Hilsbeth. I rotated my shoulders and lifted my right arm, knowing it was the one that had brandished my long sword. This type of weapon had an exceptionally long hilt, requiring two hands to maneuver the weight. But I'd had the silversmith balance mine in a fashion that allowed me to use it as I pleased. I moaned with pain and found myself eager to let the last night's journey fade back into the past from whence it had come.

Gaining my legs, I limped to the bedroom door. Upon opening it, I faced a small group of expectant faces. Will, George, Ruth, and Gilbert were sitting in our living room, while Mom, Dad, Dr. Edwards, and Father John appeared on a flat screen that Gilbert had kindly mounted on the largest wall of our small apartment. This modern technology allowed the far-flung members of the Brass Band, which was what our reincarnated group of Druids called ourselves, to interact together.

"Hi everyone," I groaned as I hobbled over to the well-worn corduroy wingchair that had become my place of honor.

My physical state after returning from a past life excursion, usually wobbly and stiff, was now such a regular occurrence that the emotions in the room ranged from humor to sympathy. Will, being his perfect self, placed a cup of strong, hot coffee in my hands.

"The equinox looks like it took a toll," Gilbert commented with a huge yawn, which reminded me that I had disrupted his sleep with my phone call the night before.

I shifted in my chair until I found the least painful position, and I gave a lame and embarrassed wave toward the large screen. "Hi all. Give me a minute here." I took a swig of coffee and closed my eyes, regretfully trying to dredge up the details of my night's adventure.

I took my time to play it all the way through in my mind, from beginning to end. I took myself back to a place where I could feel a breeze on my face and inhaled the scent of the damp forest, tinged with the smell of my own sour sweat. Then I began speaking.

"We were losing ground, being pushed from the open field into the trees. The Roman cohort advanced in heavy pursuit, trampling the bodies that lay in their path." I stopped to take a deep breath, trying to block out the screams and the putrid smell of the deceased and still dying. The crash of swords rang in my ears and I felt another thunderous reverberation run up my arm as my sword made contact with a Roman chest plate. "I only saw Dr. Edwards … Lee," I corrected, "above us on the ridge. I think McCollum had already been wounded, but not mortally."

The group let me abbreviate and expound on the story as needed. They listened closely, but for the most part they had heard about this particular battle before. Once I had determined the parts that I'd conveyed previously, I began to skip things, only filling them in on the newest details.

Gilbert was moving to the front edge of his chair, trying unsuccessfully to hide his goofy smile. He was waiting for me to tell of our escape, but I let my voice fade off from exhaustion, filling in the end of the account with *blah, blah, blah*.

Gilbert was incensed! "Wait just a minute!" he exclaimed. "You've left out the best part!"

"What's that?" Ruth asked, assuming that if the story had changed, I would have mentioned it to her during our midnight call.

"The part about me," Gilbert declared. "It's new! Hillary, tell them what you asked me last night!"

Closing my eyes, it came back to me. I saw the small figure of Gillian, backwards, legs straining to hold tight to my mare's hindquarters as we shot headlong into the undergrowth. And since Gilbert so very seldom got to be the hero, I took my time to embellish. I watched Gilbert's face light up as I explained that his ancient magic, garnered from his ability to draw his power directly from nature itself, had saved the lives of hundreds of Druids and enabled my army to hide in plain sight, shielded within Gillian's enchanted fog.

Like me on FB at Vicki Renfro Author to be notified of release date for
Soul Searching with the Brass Band

Quotations taken from:

Keep a True Lint by Charles Fillmore 1936
Prosperity by Charles Fillmore 1936
God Will Work with You but Not For You by Lao Russell 1955
The Secret of Light by Walter Russell 1947
Beyond Belief: The Secret Gospel of Thomas by Elaine Pagels

Soul Dancing with the Brass Band

247

Vicki Renfro